PLANTAT

SILVER MOON BOOKS LTD
PO Box CR 25 Leeds LS7 3TN

SILVER MOON BOOKS INCORPORATED
PO Box 1614 New York NY 10156.

New authors welcome

Printed and bound in Great Britain

**If you like one of our books you will probably like
them all!**
To order other titles see details and extracts on back
pages

**For free 20 page booklet of extracts from previous
books (and, if you wish to be on our confidential
mailing list, from forthcoming monthly titles as they
are published) please leave name and address on
our 24-hr message only telephone 0113 287 6255
or write to:-**

**Silver Moon Reader Services
PO Box CR 25 LEEDS LS7 3TN**
or
PO Box 1614 NEW YORK NY 10156

CONTENTS

Your usual full length novel:-

PLANTATION PUNISHMENT
Rick Adams

BONUS PAGES

PLANTATION PUNISHMENT by Rick Adams.

PART ONE: THE POORHOUSE

1

The mystical nectar that the young nurse had given me in the early hours of sleeplessness seemed to have incited Morpheus, the God of Dreams, to enter my mind, and I became tortured by white-robed virgins who caressed my body with their sweet breath, and hordes of inexhaustible nymphs and orgiastic wenches seemed to have their little heathen fingers round my John Thomas.

Hallucinations gradually gave way to a blurred cloudy realisation of a soft hand performing a lewd act under my bedclothes. A sudden spasm of the flesh woke me and as I opened my heavy eyes I found that the fingers were mine...

"Good morning sir."

It was the young nurse shaking my shoulder, waking me from my salacious dream. "Here is your tea." She placed the tray on the table beside my bed, walked over to the large window and opened it wide to allow in the refreshing sunny morning air.

"Are you new?"

"Yes sir," she said, coming to my side. "I started my training yesterday. My first job was to give you something to make you sleep, but it was dark and you probably don't remember me."

"I don't," I said. "But I see now that you are very pretty - do you have a calling for nursing?"

"Oh well sir I have no alternative. I had to get away from home, since my mother married again. But now I'm here, sir, yes I do think I have a calling, oh yes indeed."

As she prattled on about her noble ideals, I noticed how her blonde hair peeked out of her nurses's cap to harmonise with her lily-white cheeks. Her clear blue eyes sparkled innocently and her pert little nose moved in rhythm with her rosy lips.

"And what is your name?" I asked, to stop her silly prattle.

"Patsy sir."

"Very well, Patsy, I see that speaking of your home distresses you, and I am sorry about that, but I am sure you are an excellent nurse."

That had a strange effect on her, for she suddenly burst into tears. "Oh no sir," she sobbed, "oh I'm not, I'm not! Oh, it's terrible!" She looked at me strangely. "Are you alright this morning sir?"

"As a matter of fact," I said, "I feel rather strange."

"Oh dear oh dear it's my fault! The medicine I gave you last night! It was the wrong medicine!"

There was a long pause.

"I see," I said at last. "Well, it can't have been too bad or sister would have dismissed you!"

"Oh sir," she said, "she will if she finds out. You musn't tell her sir, oh please don't tell her!"

"You didn't tell anyone?"

"No sir."

"That was your worst mistake! I might have been severely ill. I might have died!"

"Oh sir!"

Her innocent distress and the nearness of her were rousing my John Thomas, giving me thoughts of having this gorgeous young creature in my power.

"Well, you must be punished for your carelessness, Patsy. You do seem to be a very careless girl."

"Yes sir."

"A nurse cannot afford to be careless."

"No sir," she said meekly.

"Shall we send for sister?"

"Oh no sir, couldn't you do it, you could spank me or something, better you do that than I am discharged and my whole future destroyed."

Another pause ensued, whilst my John Thomas rose stiffly to the occasion.

"Lock the door then," I said, "if you really want me to punish you. Come and kneel on the bed beside me and I shall see what can be done."

"Oh thank you sir."

"Lean over me."

She knelt on the bed by my side and bent submissively forward at my command. A hand to her back quickly collapsed her so that she lay across my lap. She was surprisingly warm and desirable, and she was trembling and taking quick little breaths. Fortunately the bed clothes hid my risen state as I slowly peeled back her long dress to discover that she had no knickers on!

I felt a lot better, recovered enough to enjoy beating her though not, regrettably, to taking her, not this morning anyway!

I gently eased her chubby thighs apart and caressed her trembling flesh higher and higher, until very softly I was able to slide a hand beneath her and hold her warm cunnie in the palm of my hand.

She suddenly realised what was happening. "Sir, what you are doing is indecent." She started to wriggle. "I am only seventeen."

"I would not dream of distressing you," I said, leaving my hand where it was. "Let us send for sister, then."

"No, no!" She started to cry. "I can't go home, I would be disgraced and my step-father would be furious, he would beat me sir, worse than ever."

Taking that as permission to proceed, I began to finger her all over. I spread her excellent legs further apart despite some resistance and ran my fingers up and down them, investigating all her secret places at leisure as she quivered and shrank from me.

I ran my fingers round and round her splendid white buttocks. They would redden nicely. "Get up and fetch one of my slippers," I said, "and then come back here, over me like this."

She came back reluctantly but obediently with the slipper and wriggled back over my lap.

"Pull your dress up," I said. "Continue to lie on your stomach and hold it up at the back with both hands."

"Oh sir this is so wrong -"

"Be quiet, you stupid girl!" I said. "I will punish you my way or not at all! Well?"

"Yes sir," she snivelled. "Whatever you wish, sir."

"You think your step-father is worse than me?" I asked, my John Thomas nearly bursting at the thought.

"Oh yes sir! Real nasty he is sir, he's taken a fancy to teasing me and tormenting me and and..."

"You are not a virgin, then?"

"No sir," she snivelled miserably.

She pulled up her dress as I had ordered, and I gazed upon her naked bottom with relish. Then I ran the slipper over it. Her soft plump flesh recoiled in dread, but when she started to cry and sob, my eagerness became all the greater. I was overwhelmed with an uncontrollable need to punish the wench severely. My practised hand descended viciously upon the shrinking flesh.

Thwack!

Thwack!

Thwack!

Patsy began to yelp with every stroke of the slipper, and after a few minutes her yelps turned into moans, then into screams so loud that I had to stuff a handkerchief into her mouth. At last I was satisfied and she fell off the bed onto the floor.

"That will do for now," I said. "But you will come to me for further punishment every day until I am discharged. I hope I shall be more fully recovered before that."

She ran off as fast as her feet would carry her, and I reached for my bottle of rum and hungrily drank a few glasses before slumping back on the pillow to reflect on a good beginning to my stay in England.

I intended to build upon it before sailing to take charge of my second plantation, where I expected the experience gained among the slave girls on my first one (which is a story I have already told) would allow my career as a debauchee finally to blossom.

2

A few days later I was ensconced in a carriage on the way to my appointment with the family solicitor.

The clip-clop of the horse's hooves and the freshness of the morning sun invigorated me and after my stay in the hospital I looked at the wenches that paraded down Oxford Street with some vigour.

After a few minutes the carriage turned left and stopped. I gave the driver an extra shilling to deposit my baggage into the basement storage, then went upstairs. My arrival must have been noted, for Charles himself opened the door to greet me with outstretched hand.

"Well well Percy my dear fellow, how are you?"

He invited me into his library and I sat on a red leather sofa, knowing my tastes, he poured me a large rum, and then, after some small talk, another.

"Let us get down to business, dear fellow. Time is money and especially at my age time becomes more precious than money." He chuckled, stroking his grey whiskers. "But first, here is a small gift to celebrate your recovery from the unfortunate ending to your first plantation venture."

He handed me a silver pocket watch which was inscribed with my initials and the date: 'P.A. 1802'. It was a good gesture and I thanked him profusely, hiding the unworthy thought that I was a very valuable client, about to sell one plantation and buy another, not to mention some specially chosen female slaves - I had already instructed him as to the kind of women I required this time.

"Now Percy," he continued, "I need to know what your immediate plans are, for this will take some time to arrange."

"I have no immediate plans," I said. "I will need to find somewhere to stay and something to occupy my mind until I hear from you."

"My dear fellow, I believe I may have the solution," he said. "Would you be interested in some charitable work?"

What the hell did he think I was? Some stupid middle-aged pack-horse?

"Yes indeed," I replied with enthusiasm. I could make my excuses later, after creating a favourable impression.

"Well, Percy, a friend of mine, a certain Lady Cordelia, who administers the Home Secretary's charitable Poor Houses, is seeking a curator to take charge of one on the South coast. It is a most noble institution that caters specifically for young ladies that have found themselves unfortunately penniless in society. Most of these young ladies, it seems, come from the upper class and through no fault of their own now find themselves totally destitute."

I almost choked on my rum as I listened to Charles. What a truly amazing proposition! My John Thomas came to life as my mind raced with the countless possibilities

10

such a position would give me and had trouble composing myself before I answered.

"Indeed, a most noble work. I would be glad to give something to my fellow creature who has fallen by the wayside."

"Very well, Percy. Lady Cordelia lives not far from here, and you shall go now with a letter of introduction."

He immediately set to writing it, and it was only a short time later that I found myself at the door of a most imposing house. An elderly butler answered and showed me into a large elegant drawing room and informed me that Her Ladyship would be with me shortly.

A stack of books on a corner table attracted my attention and I went over out of curiosity. Although I am a man of some education, I became spellbound by some of the abstruse titles. However there was one that I understood well enough: 'The Successful Domination of the Wilful Girl'. I opened the pages and was astounded to see drawings of naked girls bent over whilst a cruel looking Master applied the whip. I was becoming totally absorbed when...

"Mr Ashton, I presume?"

I turned in surprise and saw a tall severe looking woman of around fifty with greying hair pulled back into a bun and dressed plainly in a long black dress.

"May I offer you some refreshment?" she asked.

"Perhaps if you have rum...?"

"My favourite tipple!" she exclaimed. "Now, Mr Ashton..."

"Percy, please."

"Now, Percy, you must not take a too fanciful approach to the book you have just studied, for the ladies that will be in your charge are in need of a corrective disposition."

I nearly choked on my rum. I could hardly believe my good fortune as I listened to her, but of necessity I adopted a most serious demeanour as she went on to explain the

11

nature of the problem that she found herself in.

"The inmates come from the best families in England. Because the hand of fate has procured to them the scourge of unbearable poverty, many of the girls will not accept their change of fortune. They remain haughty, stubborn and tempestuous. The last three curators were all women and not severe enough, therefore I have decided to find a charitable man who will stand no nonsense from these insubordinate Jezebels. Most of all I seek a firm disciplinarian. Are you such a man, sir?"

I drew myself up. "Madam," I said, "I managed to control over two hundred unruly slaves on my plantation in the Caribbean. I doubt if a few volatile English fillies will give me much trouble."

"Excellent, my good man. I knew Charles would not let me down."

She poured me another rum - her own capacity also seemed excellent - before she continued.

"It is fortunate that I made your acquaintance today, Percy, because one of my kitchen maids will be punished shortly by myself. She is a most unruly girl and I pray that by observing the chastisement it may hold you in good stead in your new position. I must warn you, however, that although she is only a young girl she is not quite normal, for her buttocks are somewhat enlarged. Since she is small of stature and slim, the problem is so much more obvious."

As as I stood in delicious anticipation of this marvel of nature, Lady Cordelia rang the bell and after a few minutes there was a timid knock at the door and a girl walked in, dressed in a black and white maid's outfit, which was partly covered by a large apron.

She stood demurely on the carpet, hands clasped in front of her. I estimated that she was was about seventeen or eighteen, but her short brown hair and her pixie face gave her the appearance of one younger.

"Come forward child," said Cordelia. Don't dither, we haven't got all day! And take off that apron!"

The size of her bottom became apparent at once, very large indeed for her small size. It certainly made my John Thomas spring up in salute.

"Take all your clothes off!" demanded Cordelia.

Daisy started to unbutton her blouse, totally oblivious to my presence, until she stood half naked. From the head downward she had small shapely breasts and a pleasing bone structure, but it was her bottom that was outstanding.

"And the rest," instructed her Mistress.

"B-but Ma'am, there's a gentleman present."

"Very well, child," she said, "you may turn round if you must."

Daisy turned away from me gratefully and began to fumble with the waist buttons of her black skirt. I took the opportunity to admire her slender shoulders, her white marble skin and her slim waist that contrasted so wonderfully with her absolutely splendid haunches, haunches that were without doubt made to be beaten. Inch by inch Daisy's busy fingers pulled and pushed until finally the skirt was manoeuvred free and fell to the floor.

Cordelia stood up and took a few steps to Daisy's side. She grasped the waiting girl by the nape of the neck and bent her over completely, then began to smack that admirable bum.

I watched Daisy's punishment in a state of delirium. Unable to contain myself, I stood up to help. Instinctively Cordelia concentrated on the left globe whilst I began to smack the other. Daisy started to cry out with each alternating strike, and as Cordelia increased her blows, I increased the speed of mine also.

Suddenly Cordelia left off and stood red faced, huffing and puffing from her good work. Then she pushed the naked Daisy onto her knees against the sofa.

"Quick, Percy, give it to her!"

So saying, she frantically pulled at the buttons of my crotch and gasped when she eventually managed to free my monster.

"Kneel, Percy, kneel!"

I positioned myself in front of Daisy's renowned bottom and Cordelia bent forward, grasped my cock and began to massage it from the tip to the base. It did not need much encouragement! When she was satisfied that it had reached its full hardness, she gripped Daisy's inviting great cheeks, pulled them apart, and positioned me at the threshold of her open wet cunnie.

"Give it her now! Push! Push!"

I eased my helmet in and Cordelia began to push me onward in jerks. Daisy cried out at the intrusion, but after a few hefty thrusts relaxed and began to meet my long strokes with a slight jiggle of her bottom. Cordelia put her fingers round the base of my truncheon, squeezed tightly, and continued to push me forward after every deep lunge.

My head began to spin madly with orgiastic sensations as Cordelia gasped with total abandon.

"Fuck her, go on, quicker, deeper."

Eventually, unable to stand the explosive combustion in my head, I spent deep inside Patsy with one final lunge. Cordelia then sat with the whimpering girl on the sofa, grabbed my penis and forced Daisy's mouth onto it. She opened her lips reluctantly, and as my helmet entered, Cordelia grasped the back of her head and began to force it back and forth.

"Faster, you bitch!" she cried. "Faster, faster!"

After about five minutes of this, a sudden frenzy appeared to envelop Daisy. She instinctively grasped my buttocks and increased the speed of her mouth, forcing my helmet deeper and deeper into her throat with each movement.

14

Then she began to shake hysterically and with a final lunge withdrew her mouth. "Oh God oh God!" she mumbled, then started demonically to kiss the whole of my weapon from top to bottom like some creature possessed.

Lady Cordelia saw her opportunity and pushed Daisy aside. She then displayed her own scurrilous nature by instantly sucking my rampant cock deep into her mouth. After having watched Daisy's performance, she seemed intent on surpassing her and like a newly unleashed typhoon built up such a speed and turn of force that her head became a blur.

My mind felt as if it were about to explode and after a few minutes I allowed the lewd bitch her reward and threw deep inside her tight throat.

I buttoned up my trousers as she bustled Daisy out of the room. I expected some embarrassment, but she simply poured out two glasses of rum and drank hers in one go.

"Let me tell you something," she chuckled. "Each woman possesses three entrances. In your new position of Curator you would be wise to avoid one of these. We surely don't want a lot of little Percy's running around, do we?"

3

A sudden jolt of the carriage awoke me and I realised we had arrived at the Poorhouse. We had driven through an open gate and before me stood a large grim house that had seen better years. It was surrounded by a high wall that gave it a foreboding look.

As I dismounted, the large wooden door opened and a woman of about forty came out. She was attired somewhat severely in a long grey dress covered by a newly starched white apron and with hair neatly bundled up inside a fluffy white kitchen hat. Her features were neat and pleasant, but aggravated somewhat by half moon spectacles that sat on the tip of her nose.

She stepped forward to shake my hand. "Welcome, sir, it is most certainly a privilege to have a gentleman to take charge of this house. I am sure Lady Cordelia has mentioned the troubles we have had with our charges. Come, come, I'll show you round. It being Sunday, all twenty girls are at church in the village."

When James, the driver, had off loaded my luggage, I wished him a pleasant journey back and gave him a few shillings for his trouble, then followed the woman into the house.

"Forgive my rudeness!" She turned round, blushing. "I forgot to introduce myself: my name is Beatrice, but it would be proper in front of the girls if you would kindly refer to me as Madam and I will obviously, as is befitting, call you Sir."

"That is most agreeable, Beatrice, and I insist that in private you call me Percy," I answered. She blushed again and I detected a twinkle in her eye.

She took me down to the large basement kitchen, which spread the whole length of the house, and I noticed how meticulously clean everything was, from the scrubbed stone floors to the steel pans and the various utensils hanging on the walls. We then proceeded to the next floor, where a large recreational room was simply furnished with plain chairs and functional tables. Some of the chairs had unfinished articles of crochet carelessly strewn over them.

Beatrice brought my attention to this negligence. "You see, Percy, the laziness and indiscretion of some of these girls?" I muttered critically in agreement, scarcely believing my good fortune at these opportunities for proper chastisement.

We entered a door leading off from the recreation area

16

and Beatrice showed me the wash room. It had low circular steel containers, suitable only for a standing position.

Then we climbed the stairs at the far end and entered the sleeping quarters. On each side of the long central corridor were small individual bedrooms, each one containing a plain single bed and austere furniture.

"I would have thought the girls would have slept together in a dormitory?" I questioned.

"Our benefactor insisted that because the girls originated from the same background as his own he would afford them some privacy," Beatrice replied.

Finally we came to the top floor. Here Beatrice had her room at the far end. In the middle were various store rooms. Then she showed me my quarters.

I had expected a sombre arrangement, but I was very impressed by the luxurious standard of affairs. The large drawing room was enhanced by tall windows that opened onto a balcony. Half was in effect a library with a large selection of books, and the other half was furnished with magnificent leather sofas. Mahogany wall cabinets gave a final impression of a small gentleman's club and the oriental rugs that covered the wooden floor would have shamed many a good London house. The bedroom that led off was equally well furnished, and I was pleased to find a third room which was equipped in the latest French fashion for bathing.

"Sit down, Beatrice," I said. "Let's get down to business. I need to know the workings of the house."

"Can I get you some refreshment?" she asked.

"I doubt if we would have rum?"

"Oh yes indeed," she said. I had acquired a taste for the sweet nectar on the plantation I had recently left, and was very pleasantly surprised when she pulled out a bottle from the cabinet.

"Please help yourself," I said, but she insisted that when

17

she was on duty it was out of the question.

Once settled, she explained that the house catered for twenty young ladies, all now aged between sixteen and nineteen. Most of them had been there for at least five years, she said.

My John Thomas instantly stiffened with the sudden realisation that I was very likely in a coven of virgins.

"When is the last time that the girls had any contact with the opposite sex?" I asked.

"As I have just stated," she said, "in the case of the present inmates, not for at least five years. The nearest village is some three miles away and the girls are supervised by two older inmates who are in their mid twenties, who have been here most of their lives. The church is about half a mile from the village and the elderly priest, out of his charitable nature, opens the church exclusively for the girls. Therefore, I must admit, apart from the priest and the memories they have of their previous lives the girls have no contact with men whatsoever. You must remember, Percy," she continued, "that this is a charitable institution and the girls have no entitlement to any worldly pleasures."

My mind raced at the incredulous words that Beatrice uttered. The matter-of-fact way in which she stated them made it obvious that she was as institutionalised as her charges.

I stood to pour myself another rum, but the real reason was to allow my rock-hard John Thomas some movement from the tight restriction of my trousers. My head throbbed at the thought of the licentious boudoir I had the good fortune to find myself in. I drank the rum and saw that Beatrice's eyes were fixed upon my John Thomas. She blushed, then quickly averted her hungry eyes.

"Beatrice," I asked, "Have you ever had the good fortune of a husband?"

"Oh no sir," she replied softly.

18

"Have you ever had any dealings with a man?"

She blushed an even deeper red, and after a long silence replied shyly. "There was a time when I was only fifteen when the master of this house used to beat me. It - it made me feel like a woman!"

I took a deep breath. What an opportunity! "And now you are to be beaten again," I said. "For allowing things to get so slack here."

"Yes sir," she replied softly.

"Stand up," I ordered, "and turn round with your back to me. Right. Now pull up your dress. Right. Now pull down your petticoats and drawers."

"But sir," she sobbed, "the master always beat me on my drawers."

"I am your master now," I said sternly. "You will do as I say."

After a moment's hesitation she tied her dress round her waist, bent forward and pulled the garments to the floor, then rested her hands on the sofa.

The sight of the silky smooth alabaster that greeted me was truly intoxicating. The absence of the rigours of childbirth had enabled her to keep her youthful charms. Her sumptuous curvy legs and bottom would have done justice to any young flowering wench.

Smack!

Smack!

Smack!

After a few minutes her yelps became subdued and then slowly turned to moans. The cries had aroused in me monstrous imaginations. I pulled her virginal plump bottom apart and found her open pink arsehole, and soon had fingers within.

"Uuugh!" she spewed out.

I slowly began to move my fingers back and forth, gradually speeding up until eventually she began to grunt.

19

"Ugh!"

"Ugh!"

"Ugh!"

She was panting now. The deeper my fingers plunged, the faster she matched me. But it was obvious that the bitch still wasn't satisfied. because she abruptly began to move her whole arse backwards and forwards.

"Ugh!"

"Ugh!"

"Ugh!"

I pulled my hand out and felt for her dripping cunt, then immediately thrust my stiff penis all the way in.

"Aah!" she yelped as my solid helmet plundered. With renewed vigour I assaulted her until unexpectedly a triumphant scream joined us together in a tumultuous communion of insanity...

4

A knock on the door woke me from my reverie, and Beatrice walked in, looking her prim and proper self. She placed the supper tray on the table and asked if I required anything else.

"Just another bottle," I said.

I finished the supper of ham and eggs, then poured myself a large rum to christen the new bottle. I needed sustenance after the little afternoon's adventure.

After another glass, I glanced at the pocket watch Charles had given me. Six forty-five. It was already past the time I had stated, but I felt that it might be prudent to keep them waiting a little longer as a sign of my authority.

At seven I left my quarters and went downstairs in a state of some excitement. As I opened the door to the recreation room there was instant and gratifying silence.

20

I had instructed Beatrice to arrange the chairs in a semi-circular manner, with one out in front, from where I could speak. Beatrice sat at the side against the wall with two women whom I assumed where the supervisors.

I strode purposefully to the chair and sat down.

"Ladies, allow me to introduce myself. My name is Mr Ashton, but you will address me as Sir. As you are aware, I have been sent by Lady Cordelia to administer this house for the foreseeable future. It is my intention to instill order and correctiveness into this charitable institution and to allay the Home Secretary's fears of the possible future necessity of closing down the house in the interests of economy. If that was to be necessary, then all you ladies would be separated and sent to other institutions where your companions would be less, er, compatible. I therefore require your strict co-operation in a new set of rules and regulations that I will instigate tomorrow. Can I count on your strict compliance with these new rules?"

All the girls instantly voiced their agreement.

The unwitting wenches had given full agreement without realising what might be required of them. I consoled myself with the thought that they had no alternative. That is a woman's role in life if she has no means of support. She must belong to a father or a husband or she is nothing.

Whilst I spoke of the necessities of leading a humble and ordered life, I secretly admired them in turn. They all wore the regulation ankle length grey dress, tied loosely at the waist, with black boots peeping from under their hems. Their hair was tied in bands off their shoulders.

What struck me immediately, as my searching eye disgorged itself from one wench to the next, was the vast differences in beauty, demeanour and colour of hair. The whole of creation's spectrum was displayed before my eyes. Although the girls were seated, my learned gaze detected all manner of shapes and sizes. From the plump to the grace-

21

ful, tall and small, seductive and bewitching, alluring and captivating, all the girls had the beauty that only derived from good breeding and worthwhile stock. Their hair ranged from coal black to saintly white, with all the variations of complexion and hue in between.

I rose and instructed Beatrice to send the two supervisors to my room in half an hour.

I entered my quarters and poured a stiff rum before sitting down. Being in such close proximity to so many lustful wenches was unsettling my steadfast demeanour.

A knock on the door interrupted my thoughts, and a tall buxom lass walked in and stood before me.

"Where is the other supervisor?" I demanded.

"I'm sorry sir, but she had some work to do in the kitchen."

"Are you not the senior supervisor?"

"Yes sir, but -"

I immediately interrupted the disobedient wench.

"You are at fault," I said. "Go and stand in the corner with your back to me in silence until I decide what to do with you."

She immediately complied and stood with her head bowed.

The reason I had so swiftly despatched her to the other end of the room was not because of her disobedience. It was because when she had entered the room I was instantly attracted by her size and ruddiness. I needed a few minutes to savour the woman. She was easily a full twelve inches taller than myself, with sturdy arms, statuesque legs that pushed against her then grey dress, and blessed with a full voluptuous bosom and prominent arse. Her ruddy plump face harmonised perfectly with her bushy ginger hair.

Her name was Julie, and that is as far as I got in quizzing her.

I looked at her standing demurely in the corner with the

pangs of a man who had the unpremeditated realisation of the possibility of seeing his future wife. Indeed, I was so taken aback at finding myself becoming fond of her that instead of punishing her I merely wished her goodnight and watched her as she reluctantly left my quarters, doubtless extremely puzzled!

I poured myself another rum and set to work on the new set of rules and regulations.

The warm weather was now upon us and because of the isolation of the house I decided upon a new economy. I checked the ledgers that pertained to the costs of washing underwear and their replacement and decided forthwith to abandon their usage. Long dresses were another expensive luxury and because I had seen rolls of thin white material in the store rooms, I decided to set all the girls to work tomorrow on a new dress which they would make for themselves. I wrote down clear instructions that each dress must be supported by thin shoulder straps set low on the chest and back to encourage the passage of healthy fresh air over the flesh. I also stipulated that the length must be at least six inches above the knee. Finally I again reiterated the necessity of allowing fresh air to circulate round the naked body and strictly forbade the wearing of any type of stockings or underwear. I also gave instructions for the girls to change their heavy boots for the light brown sandals I had also discovered in the store rooms.

I spent the next hour drinking rum as I sat by the open window finishing the new regulations. The cool night air gently caressed my brow and the distant full moon winked magically with every passing cloud.

Eventually I finished the list, which now included the forfeit of Sunday privileges and for more severe indiscretions the use of the whip or the strap at my discretion.

As I walked towards Beatrice's room to hand it to her, I

heard a faint noise drifting up the staircase. I descended the stairs. Now I could just hear a strange chanting emanating from the last of the girl's bedrooms, the one nearest to me. It was an eerie chant, and the unearthly moonlight falling through the high window seemed to lift my senses into a devilish trance.

As I approached the bedroom I heard a faint girlish voice. 'Lions will be laid to rest with lambs and saints with sinners, shame and everlasting disgrace will be theirs...'

What hellish sort of girl is this, I wondered, as I pressed my ear to the door. The voice slowly rose in intensity and passion. 'The stench of sulphur around a lake of flames, where the unredeemed are tormented day and night, bodies writhing in agony, horned imps in their chamber of horrors...'

I couldn't stand any more of this madness and quickly ran down the stone stairs into the dark kitchen. I stood panting in the darkness and wished I had brought my rum.

A flicker of candle light by the distant window slowly unfurled itself, until I could just about make out a dark figure huddled over the light.

It was Beatrice!

"Thank God it's you," I said. "I thought for a moment that something abominable was about to appear!"

"Oh sir," she giggled, "I believe that you've been listening to Purity. Don't worry so, she's a strange one, but she means no harm."

Beatrice poured me some tea and examined the list and instructions I had given her.

"Yes sir, I'm in full agreement with the economies that must be made. I will assemble all the girls tomorrow, and by the evening we shall have the new attire ready. I suppose I should be frugal with the material?"

"Yes indeed," I said. But I told her that she could keep her normal dress, as well as Julie if she so wished. I also told her that we needed only one supervisor, so she should send the other girl back to work.

"And I will need a girl to clean my rooms in the mornings. Perhaps you will be good enough to arrange for Julie to do that."

I climbed the stairs to my apartment and after a last glass of rum retired to bed.

5

The early morning sun crept through the open window and gently eased me out of a turbulent sleep. I had dreamt of grey clothed witches that changed into dainty nymphs who prophesied my eventual downfall.

I jumped out of bed and was soon invigorated by a glass of rum and the sunny morning air as I looked out over the green fields towards a clear blue sea.

I dressed quickly and walked down the empty stairs into the cold kitchen, where I made myself some breakfast. Beatrice had thoroughly prepared me a carrier of food for the excursion I planned and had also slipped in two bottles of rum.

Within a few minutes I was on my way.

The trap was comfortable enough and the old horse demonstrated a steady temperament as she clip-clopped down the country lanes.

I spent the morning wandering about the countryside, stopping every hour or so for a tot of rum. The sleepy village turned out to be a jumble of only about eight houses, with one store, all served by the small distant chapel.

In the hot midday sun I settled on the edge of the cliff that overlooked the sea and drank more rum. The effect of the heat soon soothed me into a deep sleep...

... a strange hooting aroused me. An owl? Surely not! But I found myself in starry darkness. And a moon beyond the trees. I had slept away the whole afternoon and evening, and a glance at my prized pocket watch revealed that it was almost midnight!

I looked round for my horse and trap and found to my relief that they were still there. I picked up the two bottles, one apparently empty, and began the long journey back to the house. The eerie moonlit night and the strange nocturnal noises of the countryside forced me finish off the second bottle of rum.

The dark silent house soon appeared and by this time my demeanour was suitably fortified again. I had wanted to return in the early evening to see in what form my wishes had been carried out, but now I must wait for the following day.

After stabling the horse I entered the house, and some degenerate impulse persuaded me to walk through the long corridor from which the girls' bedrooms opened. I approached the last bedroom quietly. Silence. I was just about to walk away when the strange girlish chant began.

'... the mysteries of salvation will be revealed, finally and irrevocably, to those who had lived virtuous lives and those who had bathed in the sink of licentiousness. Revelations from the vineyard of angels, will soothe the brow and temper the spirit of the prophets of everlasting joy in salacious misdeeds. The sacrament of inquisition...'

I couldn't bear any more of this, and with head spinning I fell into my quarters and slumped into a chair. I opened a fresh bottle of rum and opened the windows. The unnatural creatures of the night that howled and screeched and committed lewd acts upon the stage of the large yellow moon, seemed to incarnate my spinning mind into incestuous loathsome thoughts. In some delirium, I forced myself up off the chair and with superhuman will, undressed for bed.

A thousand nights and days seemed to pass as I dreamt the unspeakable, explored every abomination, and suffered every blasphemy.

After an eternity a golden-haired angel, dressed in white, floated and danced as she serenaded the God of wind, who, much pleased, directed his most precious breeze over my brow.

I half opened my heavy eyes and expected to find myself either before the gates of Hell or in front of the protecting angel.

My head swam as I found an angel.

"Good morning sir."

"Uh, good morning - is that you, Julie?"

"Yes, sir. I've opened the windows. May I start to clean your rooms?"

"Yes, carry on - oh, Julie, bring me a bottle of rum."

I needed the morning nectar to drive out the night's demons, and after a couple of large glasses I felt sufficiently refreshed to open my eyes.

The incredulous sight that met me also fully awoke my John Thomas!

Julie silently and slowly moved about the room with a dust cloth. Her thick ginger hair, tied at the back, exposed her full naked shoulders and half her back. The skimpy new white dress was supported by two straps that rested loosely on her shoulders. I had not quite realised how thin the material was. A cloth belt slightly pulled in the dress round her waist. The constriction of the waistband emphasised the outward angle of the material in the way it fell off her splendid bottom without touching her equally splendid legs.

The most pleasurable part of this vision was that Julie had seen fit to cut the dress at about nine inches above the

27

knee. which exposed nearly the whole length of those shapely legs.

I watched her clean the room and marvelled at the way she could move around so daintily. She moved and turned as deftly as any pixie, yet she was so strong that if she were to kneel on all fours she could carry me on her back as easily as an labouring horse in the field.

She bent towards me to wipe one of the tables and the low cut of her dress exposed most of her breasts. As she cleaned the table, they swung from side to side and I was sure that the loose covering would soon give way. As I stared transfixed I realised that in that bent position her glorious naked bottom had to be fully exposed from behind.

I poured another rum to steady the unbearable ache in my John Thomas and hoped that with a little patience all would be revealed.

She continued to clean the room. With her back to me now, she came over to the window, then just a few feet from my bed, bent forward, instantly exposing her naked bottom to me. I began to shake like a man possessed as I gaped at the fleshy orbs separated by her open crevice that blatantly unmasked her pink cunnie and rosy open arsehole. Seeking something that was invisible to me, she bent completely down, which enabled me to see the anal opening as her arse opened as wide as it possibly could. I was in a total state of unbridled insanity when she stayed in that position for what seemed like minutes. Unable to contain my madness any more I reached out, but just before I touched her she must have heard the bed creak, for she abruptly straightened herself and walked towards the door.

As she left I called out "Tell Beatrice to come here AT ONCE."

After a minute the door burst open and Beatrice rushed in.

"Kneel down," I shouted.

She immediately complied. I threw the bedclothes off and grabbed her head, pulling it towards my hard cock.

"Oh no sir," she screamed out, "no sir!"

I was in no mood to listen and forced her resisting head onto my cock. Her lips had no choice but to open and having secured her mouth I jerked it in one move all the way down to my base, then lifted her by the hair and mercilessly began to use her like a toy. After a few seconds only I spent deep inside her virgin throat and let her go.

She burst into a flood of tears and ran out.

Comforted by my release, I poured a drink and relaxed, knowing full well that I could do what the hell I wanted with her or Julie or any of them. I decided to allow Julie to tease me if she wished, up to the point when I would show her where every future wife's duty lies.

After I had dressed, some strange instinct drove me towards one of the storage rooms instead of going downstairs. I entered the room and walked over to the window.

I looked down onto the small vegetable patch which was at the back of the house, and there at work were ten women and girls, all clad in short white dresses, just as I had ordered. Some knelt, others bent over, and the rest were sitting.

My John Thomas stirred at the incomparable view. I hurried down to the kitchen and composed myself before entering.

"I was about to bring the tray to your room, sir," said Beatrice.

"Don't trouble yourself," I replied, "I'll have my meal in the corner of the kitchen, out of your way."

Soon Julie entered the kitchen, followed by ten girls who carried fresh vegetables. I could hardly eat as I watched them scurrying around the central table. All wore the new regulation white dress. Some were loose enough to allow a glimpse of half a breast as they reached for a knife from the wall, others were tighter. All were thin enough to allow tantalising shapes to show through, especially if the light was behind them. Each girl had used the material allotted to them differently, and this showed in the length of dress - although all had obeyed the instruction of a minimum of six inches above the knee, some hems were considerably higher.

The prohibition of underwear had been obeyed, of course, and I nearly choked on a piece of bread as one black haired beauty reached high for a spoon on the wall and momentarily exposed at least half of her naked bottom. Another girl who stood before the table and scrubbed a metal pot vigorously was obviously unaware of how her unrestrained breasts shook from side to side.

Each girl's bottom was different, each seductive in its own way. Some were ample, others tight and firm, but none could touch Julie's for sheer shapeliness.

I stood up to relieve the pressure on my John Thomas and looked out of the window. To my amazement I saw one girl, a tiny slim creature with short black hair, kneeling against the wall of the vegetable patch deep in prayer.

I called Beatrice over.

"Oh, that is Purity," she said. "She prays every two hours."

So this was the little sorceress who weaved her odious spells in the dead of night!

I walked out of the kitchen and along the perimeter of the vegetable patch until I came upon her. She sensed my approach and silently rose to her feet, attired like the others in her new regulation white dress.

"May the Lord be with you!" she said softly.

"Are you happy in your work, my child?" I asked.

I was looking down at an imp of a girl who barely reached the height of my chest. If I had stood her beside

Julie she could easily have been taken for her pre-pubescent daughter. The short black hair and tiny pixie face emphasised her youthful appearance.

I could not help but notice that she had cut her dress high up her neck and back, covering as much as she could, but this had led to a shortage elsewhere and the hem was aggravatingly high even as she tried to smooth it down.

"Are you a believer, sir?" she asked me in a childish voice as she innocently gazed up at me.

"Oh yes my child," I replied. "If I were not, would I devote my life and work to this most charitable cause?"

She seemed placated and returned to her work. It was just as well, because the minx had excited my passions and I imagined as she stood before me what a spankable little bottom she had.

"Keep up the good work," I said, restraining myself with great difficulty as I turned away and sought the refuge of my quarters and the solace of a glass or two of rum.

I opened the window and sat looking out over the green fields. I knew that I should contain my more lascivious thoughts as I was not lord and master of a Caribbean plantation any more but protector and custodian of a charitable institution. But the more rum I drank and with the heat of the midday sun upon my brow, I wondered how long I could hold out against my darker nature.

To take my mind off Purity I thought of one particular girl I had noticed in the kitchen. She was a true classic beauty. She was tall, feminine, with a noble figure and deep auburn hair of such an intensity of rich golden brown as I had never seen before. It was plaited loosely and hung suggestively down her half naked back/. Her face was haughty and proud and I suspected that she originated from a particularly aristocratic family.

Whether it was the effect of the rum or the intensity of the midday heat I cared not any more. I went over to my drawer and pulled out my certificate: 'Professor of Gynaecology and Doctor of Medicine'. It was gold embossed and looked very impressive. It was of course totally bogus. I had studied medicine for a while, but an unfortunate mishap with the professor's wife meant that my studies were cut short.

I then summoned Beatrice.

"As you see," I said, "part of my task here is to see to the health of the inmates." She studied the certificate in awe, being particularly impressed by the signature of His Majesty. "When I was in the kitchen," I continued, "I noticed a girl with an auburn plait who appeared to be unwell. Be so good as to send her to my quarters for an examination, before her sickness spreads to the other girls."

"The Countess Diana, sir? Yes, yes, at once."

Beatrice departed in panic and I donned my white coat and displayed a number of medical instruments on a black cloth on the table before fortifying myself from the bottle. My John Thomas raged like a demented bull and I was determined to give the wench a thorough examination.

In walked the Countess Diana, closed the door behind her, and stood before me in all her glory.

For an instant I was paralysed as I gazed at the vision of Aphrodite, dressed in pure white. She had tanned golden brown skin topped with a rich auburn crown. Her heaving half naked breasts lifted the hem of her short white dress seductively up and down her sculptured thighs.

She sat on a stool before me. Her proud eyes were deep blue atop magnificent cheek bones and her patrician nose gradually gave way to wide soft lips.

"Why have you summoned me?" she asked arrogantly. "I have never in my life suffered any sickness."

"Have you never had any experience of a medical practitioner?"

"I come from healthy stock and wouldn't recognise one

if he sat on my dinner plate as the first course!" she exclaimed in a cavalier manner, while my John Thomas burnt endlessly as I realised the possibilities that a first examination could offer.

"How old are you, my child?" I asked, beginning to make notes.

"Sir, you dare to ask a lady her age... very well, since you are a doctor, I shall soon be seventeen."

"What mishap finds you in this house?"

"My father," she stuttered. "Through bad investments my father was bankrupted and is currently indisposed for a number of years."

"Ah well, we need not dwell on that. Here, medical attention is free. Show me your arm."

She lifted a curvy bare arm towards me and I examined the skin and pressed on her muscles from her elbow up to her naked shoulder.

"Hmmm," I said, in such a manner as to frighten her.

"What do you mean?" she asked, a little more timidly now.

"Oh nothing," I said doubtfully. "There may well be no problem. Open your mouth if you please, and we shall soon see."

She parted her mouth to its full extent and with one finger I pressed on her ruby red tongue and began an exploration with my other fingers. Her white teeth where magnificent to the touch and I prodded and pushed all round inside her mouth. When I reached her throat I was surprised to find that she didn't gag, so proceeded to push two fingers inside.

My John Thomas twitched uncontrollably at the thought of what I could do with this welcoming orifice.

"Thank you, my child," I said as I withdrew, sounding disturbed.

"Sir, this is so humiliating," she cried. "Please may I go

now?"

"It is better you steady your nerves with this drink, my child, for I'm afraid the news is not good."

"Wh-what's the matter, sir?" she stuttered, whilst accepting the glass.

"Well -" I said. "Unfortunately -" I shook my head and looked at her with grave concern. "The condition renders the woman incapable of bearing a child."

"Oh no!" she cried, bursting into a flood of tears..

"The evidence is not conclusive," I said. "I have not finished my examination. I may yet find a way to avert it."

"I beseech you sir," she said, "you must do so, then." She gulped down the rest of her rum. "My father will be out of - will be in a position to collect me in three years and after he has rebuilt his fortune I must be capable of bearing a grandchild."

"I hope I can help you," I replied. "Allow me first to finish my drink whilst you undress."

"Undress!" she exclaimed. "Oh no!"

"I fear it is necessary if I am to help you. A very thorough examination is required."

I thought my John Thomas would break through his severe confines as she bent to remove her dress.

"Come and stand by me," I said when she was naked, trying to keep the shaking out of my voice.

My John Thomas was fully rampant and my mind was in a whirl as I stroked the length of her peerless body. I caressed the round shoulders down to her slim waist and then gently separated her bottom cheeks to gaze at the little pink rosette.

"Relax my child," I said, for she was shivering uncontrollably. I took her by the hips and slowly lifted her docile body upwards until she rested on her elbows and knees. Her body was supported by the back of the sofa and she seemed to be quite comfortable. The heat in my loins was unbearable as I slowly inserted two fingers into her moist open cunnie.

"Oh!" she gasped.

She was sopping wet! She was enjoying this, though I knew she would never never admit to that.

She was in my power and I determined to teach the proud haughty bitch a severe lesson. I positioned two fingers at the pink entrance to her arsehole. Against her reluctance I slid them inside and she gasped out but remained still. I began to gently push them in and out and with every thrust she let out a muted groan. It was obvious that her lustfulness had been fully aroused.

I yanked out my fingers and began to spank the haughty smug bitch.

Smack!

Smack!

Smack!

From one shrinking cheek to the other I repaid her arrogance and superiority with increasingly hard blows.

After a few minutes I stopped and went over to a cabinet on the wall.

She was laughing! The hypocrisy of the scurrilous bitch was unbelievable. I had no doubt that she had seen through all my manoeuvring right from the start, and had enjoyed everything.

I determined to take full advantage of her scarlet depravity. I pulled out an instrument made out of wood which was covered tightly in pig skin and closely resembled a rampant cock. It was ten inches in length and three in diameter.

After a quick gulp of rum, I sat by her shameless upturned arse and pulled her cheeks apart. Slowly I inserted the large bulbous end of the instrument and as it slid in she gasped. I grabbed the end of the instrument in my fist, held her down, and plundered her, pushing in and out with the whole length of it, remembering the disdainful condescending way she had treated me.

Then I pulled out the weapon and picked up her leather sandal that had fallen on the floor. A fury overtook me at the feel of it and I began to inflict stinging blows on the haughty bitch's wriggling rump.

Thwack!

Thwack!

Thwack!

On and on like a man possessed, I covered the whole of her pulsating arse with every type of stroke in my armoury. The severity of the onslaught would have awoken the dead, but the degenerate whore's appetite seemed never ending. Her arse shook and quivered, whilst she stifled her groans and moans with difficulty as she tried to conceal her rising excitement.

I knelt up on the sofa behind her pulsating arse, pulled out my raging weapon and positioned the helmet at the entrance to her moist soft cunnie. Then I grabbed her flanks and with one brutal lunge speared her up to the hilt...

6

The howls and screams of the abominable night creatures roused me from an uneasy doze, full of sinister dreams. I glanced at my pocket watch. Twelve thirty. I poured a glass of rum and looked at the full moon. The flickering of the dancing bats and hooting of the owls and threat of ever waiting evil spirits assailed my fragile mind.

Eventually, after a few more rejuvenating glasses, I recovered my senses and made myself a solemn vow that I would beat the whores under my control into total submission. Only after they had gratified my every unspeakable sadistic whim would I relent.

I crept down the stairs and silently along the girls' bedroom corridor, somehow inextricably pulled towards the light of the moon at the end.

Girlish chants from Purity's room stopped me in my tracks.

'... the licentious, together with the harbingers of lustfulness, will feel the scourge of the bottomless pit of redeeming fire. Terrible will be the dark one's chamber of horror in its everlasting and excruciating final destruction of man's lascivious dark soul...'

I could not stand any more of the sorceress's vile lamentations. I would deal with her later, and then she would get the beating of a lifetime. I quickly went back to the sanctuary of my rooms. Suddenly I heard a girlish giggle from behind a tree below the balcony. I stood up and looked down.

Three dark figures sat huddled together.

My mind, twisted by the demonic sounds of the night and plagued by the avenging prophesies of the sorceress Purity, became convinced that divine retribution had arrived in the form of three witches sent from the depths of hell.

I drank deeply of the enticing red nectar that was now my only earthly refuge just as, suddenly, the moon reappeared from behind a dark cloud and I saw, to my intense relief, that it was only three girls drinking from a bottle of rum. Rum! They must have stolen it! Stolen it from me!

My John Thomas instantly reared up and, like a hungry lion within sight of easy prey, I ran quickly down the stairs, almost falling in my eagerness.

"What is the meaning of this?" I said sternly, as they stood up in dismay. "Where did you get that bottle?"

There was an uneasy silence as they stood shuffling their feet and hanging their heads.

"From the store room?" I asked grimly.

They could not deny it. One even had the effrontery to nod.

"Up to my quarters," I shouted. My voice was a little unsteady with lust. "You will all be punished immediately."

I followed the silent wenches up the steep stairs, catching intriguing glimpses of trembling naked bottoms.

Finally they all stood before me with guilt written all over their apprehensive faces.

"Well, thieves," I thundered, "How old are you all?"

"Seventeen sir."

"Sixteen sir."

"Nineteen sir."

"Then you are all old enough to know better. You have all been here long enough to know that only the most severe punishment can be given for this."

As I admonished them, I gazed at each one individually.

The seventeen year old was quite slender with long brown hair, a cutely pretty face and curvaceous limbs.

The sixteen year old was small and plump. Her lack of height emphasized her petite chubbiness. She had shoulder length blonde hair and her face was pert and cheeky.

The nineteen year old had a mass of fluffy red hair falling to her shoulders. She was as curvy as the sixteen year old but tall for a girl. Her face was healthy and her breasts thrust indecently against the confines of her thin dress.

After studying them as they stood guiltily before me, I said: "Because I am a charitable man I will allow you all to wear a blindfold over your eyes to cover your shame." I gave them all pieces of cloth which I had previously prepared upon my arrival at the house. Thus I could take full advantage of each wench without the others being able to protest.

I took the belt from my waist. My John Thomas was

almost bursting at the thought of applying it to their behinds.

"You will all bend forward in a row," I said, "with your hands touching the floor."

They immediately obeyed and instantly exposed the bottom halves of their already squirming bottoms. What a splendid sight! I poured a rum and sat down to gaze at the exhibition, my head pounding at the blatant display and my John Thomas was at full attention.

Unable to contain myself, I went down the line lifting each dress high above the waist to rest on their shoulders, administering a light slap to each bottom as I did so and eliciting small gasps at the unexpected warning of chastisement to come.

I sat down again for another sip or two and further contemplation of the differences between my three targets. All were superbly attractive in their own way, and it was a puzzle which to assault first.

The youngest had already started to whimper softly, so I was attracted to her first. I laid down the belt and gave her a quick succession of stinging smacks with my bare hand.

Thwack!
Thwack!
Thwack!

Her soft flesh easily absorbed the initial onslaught. Her whimpering increased a little, that was all, so I picked up the belt and swung it with a will.

Crack!
Crack!
Crack!

She began to howl as I increased the pace.

After a few minutes I paused for refreshment, leaving her bent over, sobbing and red bottomed.

I was tempted by the plumper bottom next to her. It was

already squirming delightfully, stimulated no doubt by the sounds next to her. This bottom, being well padded, could withstand more punishment and was a better target, so I started to belt it with even greater enthusiasm. I vowed to subdue the thieving whore and teach her the error in her lascivious ways, dressing like that, exposing her bottom, tempting any red blooded male. I struck like a man possessed and soon had her howling louder than the first, who was still sobbing beside her, because I spared her the occasional attention also, just to keep her in proper dread of the strap.

Now it was time to bring the nineteen year old into action also. She was the one who could presumably take the most punishment, and with that in mind I really let myself go as I belted her gorgeously squirming bottom as hard and as fast as I was able.

At the same time I gave the other two arses a crack or two from time to time to keep their owners howling, and when the third girl joined in I had a really good chorus going! I was soon going from one to the other like a circus man I had once seen who tried to keep an increasing number of plates spinning on top of sticks, always starting another before dashing back to renew the first. I had only three bottoms to play with, and was well able to keep all three on fire with my lashing belt!

I sat down to draw breath and refresh myself, and gaze upon those still heaving bottoms, and after a while my John Thomas demanded a change of plan!

"Stay down!" I said. "If any of you dare to move, your punishment will start at the beginning again! Remain bent over whatever happens or I assure you it will be the worse for you and prevent nothing in the end!"

Three virgins, and all at my disposal. It was merely a matter of where to start.

I drew my rampant weapon and soon had it thrust into

the youngest girl's tight wet cunnie. She squirmed and gasped, but did not dare to move, for she had received a pretty good thrashing already, and obviously did not relish more.

The girl yelped as I ripped open her virginity, then after receiving a few hefty thrusts she settled down and started to moan as I plundered her. Just when I began to suspect that the little minx was accepting her new found feelings of desire, and realising that my weapon was now fully lubricated, I pulled out to the first inch. My initial thrust had been simply to break her virginal wall and she was about to feel the full force of my whole length.

Without warning I jammed the whole ten inches into her. She screamed at the top of her voice and then I started to thrust deeply in and out and at the same time began to hit her arse with the belt.

After a few minutes I couldn't stand the warm tight milking sensations any more and I pulled out and thrashed her some more before proceeding to the tallest wench. I broke into her with one mighty thrust. She screeched as I pummelled her with a few strokes, then again I pulled out to the first inch and with a supreme thrust speared her to the limit. The sudden massive attack prompted a scorching scream from her lips and I began to belt her as I lunged in and out of her slippery tube. She grunted and squealed as my iron weapon pillaged and ransacked her depths.

Finally I fell upon the plump girl and in a state of unbearable dementia went for her arsehole. I was in with one sudden lunge, then started to smack her plump buttocks as I ravaged her. She screamed and wailed at the force and brutality of the intrusion and the stinging blows of the smacking. When I detected that the chubby little minx was getting into her stride with her sudden pushes towards my every thrust, I pulled out and positioned my John Thomas in front of her astonished face.

I opened up her hot little lips and gently but firmly eased my whole weapon into her gulping mouth. Once I was lodged well into her throat, I started in on her arse with the belt. With every stroke onto the plump shaking flesh her head was pushed forward until I was able to stand still and allow the stinging impact of the belt to move her head back and forth.

Then I changed my tactics, and instead of hitting the top of her rump, which drove her whole body forward, I began on the sides of her bottom. This had the effect of making her body and consequently her head and mouth sway from side to side, but incredibly the little whore continued with her deep sucking thrusts. I allowed her a few minutes of obscene pleasure then looked at the other two bitches who awaited my attention.

I withdrew from the hot sticky mouth of the plump girl and positioned my helmet at the open lips of the tall redhead. The scurrilous whore, without any prompting, seized on the fruit hungrily and immediately began a long sucking action. By the third push she had embedded my weapon deep in her greedy throat.

Her eagerness inflamed my already unbearable pulsating head and I started to belt her bewitching arse with demonic blows. The faster she sucked, the quicker I bludgeoned her rump. After about five minutes of this unrelenting excruciating pleasure I withdrew and staggered to the youngest girl, who was waiting patiently.

I again positioned my steaming helmet at the entrance to soft lips. She allowed it to tease and chaff her open mouth, then suddenly she began to tremble and shake like some tormented spirit. She lifted her head off the intruder and like some demented creature began desperately to tug at my trousers. After a few seconds she had them off completely.

Then she fell to her knees and lifted my right leg off the

42

floor and slid completely underneath me. Lifting my heavy balls to one side, the corrupt degenerate whore began her unholy unspeakable act. She pushed her whole face into my bottom and began to lick, worship and finally penetrate my arsehole.

I immediately pulled the red-head towards me from her bent over position beside us and rested my leg on her shoulder. She found my weapon now, and furiously began to suck the whole length.

Then the youngest wench sensed that she was being left out! She used her hands to feel her way round our bodies and started hungrily to suck and lick my balls.

The three whores licked and sucked, sucked and licked, until after a few minutes I grabbed the hair of the three demented creatures and exploded...

10

The morning breeze and the gentle swish of Julie's movements awoke me from a deep sleep. I felt a trifle muzzy, but it was the day the prisoner would arrive, the one entrusted to me on her way to be deported, and I must inspect the quarters that had been prepared.

As soon as I had had a drink of rum, for I was in no mood for breakfast, I walked along the perimeter of the vegetable patch until I reached the outbuilding where she was to be housed. It was a stone-built structure with a small window and large enough to maybe house a couple of horses. The sturdy door was open and I went inside.

I looked around at the simple bed and the basic wooden furniture, and tested the manacle and chain that I had instructed Beatrice to attach to the wall. It was long enough to allow free movement, but only within the room.

All seemed to be in order, so, realising that I had not had sufficient morning medication, I returned to the kitchen where Beatrice poured me a large measure...

A distant rumbling jolted me from my daydreams and I looked at the cloud of dust that could only be the penal carriage approaching.

I was amazed to see that not only had the driver a guard sitting next to him with a gun but four armed horsemen followed the coach. Why the hell did it need six soldiers to escort a single woman? What manner of beast could she be?

I went out as the two-horsed black windowless carriage and its escort thundered to a stop. I instantly recognised the dark blue uniforms of the King's Welsh Fusiliers. The Captain jumped down from the driver's bench and saluted me.

Before I had time to greet him, the coach suddenly began to shudder from side to side, as if some unearthly power within was desperate to escape.

"Why Captain," I asked, "what have you brought me? I was told to expect a single woman prisoner."

"Indeed, Sir," he replied, "that is what you have. She is a black slave that escaped from her Master in the Caribbean and somehow managed to stow aboard a ship returning to England. On board the ship, upon being found, she killed the Captain with her bare hands and a further two sailors before being finally shackled. Arrived in London she was charged with murder and has murdered a further three women convicts whilst in prison. She was sentenced to death, but her owner in the Caribbean has asked for her back and she is to be sent to him."

"Sounds like a handful!" I ventured.

"Totally mad, Sir," said the Captain. "I trust you will allow me to inspect the building where you intend to keep her?"

As he went off with Beatrice I poured another glass and wondered what I had got myself into. I had hoped the prisoner would provide a little light feminine diversion. What the hell was I supposed to do with some crazed murderous devil woman?

After a few minutes the Captain returned.

"The one chain is totally insufficient. I have instructed my men to install additional chains and manacles. Have you a pistol, Sir?"

"Yes," I answered.

"I would most strongly recommend that you carry it whenever you are near her. She is a large powerful creature, and you must observe extreme caution. If you wish to fetch your pistol, we will transfer her to her quarters as soon as the chains are ready, and be on our way."

I went for my leather holster, checked the pistol, and fixed it to my belt.

The Captain positioned three of his men to stand some twenty feet away from the rear doors of the carriage with raised firearms. The other two men were instructed to grab the long chain that was attached to the prisoner's manacled writs in case she would be stubborn and have to be pulled out of the carriage.

When he was satisfied, the Captain unbolted the heavy carriage doors and flung them open. The three soldiers cocked their rifles and waited nervously.

Suddenly a deep unearthly growl emanated from the dark carriage and slowly rose in intensity. The noise stopped abruptly when the prisoner got to her feet and swayed the carriage from side to side.

Then she dismounted in a leap and stood proudly poised before us.

I could not believe my eyes!

She was over six feet in height, maybe six and a half.

She was a magnificent creature! She wore a thin grey dress that exposed her size and power, shining ebony skin and beautiful sinewy body.

Two soldiers seized the long chain and began to pull her towards her new prison, followed by the armed escort and the Captain by her side. She snorted and growled like an animal as the soldiers manacled her wrists and ankles to the wall, then closed the door and bolted it.

When the Captain and his carriage and soldiers had gone, much relieved to be rid of their charge I think, I went up to my quarters, poured myself a hefty drink and sat on the sunny balcony to reflect.

After a while, when I had calmed down a little, I instructed Beatrice to place the woman's food inside the door three times a day, saying that she would be quite safe because the chains that now held her did not reach as far as the door.

When, that evening, Beatrice came to collect my empty supper tray, I asked her about the prisoner.

"Oh, she's as quiet as a mouse, sir. When I took her supper over she was sitting on the bed."

I was intrigued about the calmness of my prisoner and decided to investigate the cause. I strapped my holster to my belt again and went downstairs.

The evening was very quiet and I walked apprehensively in the direction of the stone hut. Even the usual howls and hoots of the omnipresent mischievous spirits were surprisingly subdued. Had her malevolent presence frightened away the ambitions of the demonic upstarts?

I stood quietly outside the closed door. Nothing. Nothing but silence. I took out my pistol, and so as not to alarm her I hid it behind my back and opened the door slowly.

My eyes slowly became accustomed to the pitch blackness and I became aware of two large white eyes that stared at me. Then gradually a faint gruff noise materialised, repeating the same word over and over again.

... um, um, um, um, rum, rum, rum...

She began to shake her chains in chorus to her chant.

Very well! I thought to myself. I'll give the creature some rum, and let us see what happens!

I returned to the house for two bottles and quickly returned. I placed them on the ground and bolted the door. Then I looked through the tiny windows and was amazed at the speed of movement of the creature as she jumped off the bed, pulled off the cap and instantly began to gulp down the liquid.

I returned to the house with the intention of returning later to satisfy my curiosity. In my quarters I pounced upon a half finished bottle and took in the virtuous nectar. As I sat on the balcony, a sudden uneasy thought crossed my mind. What if the pistol were to jam? I would be totally defenceless. I opened the long cabinet on the wall and withdrew a whip which I had used on my plantation. It was some five feet long and made of specially treated black rubber. The grip was firm and hard, gradually loosening in suppleness along its length and diminishing width. The working end was springy and pliant, in all a most veritable avenger. I twisted it into a coil and thrust it into my belt.

I silently left the house and crept in the direction of the beast woman's lair. The outbuildings were behind the house, some three hundred feet away. The closer I got the noise from the night creatures decreased step by step.

Soon the small stone hut loomed ahead and I adjusted my holster and checked the whip. When I arrived at the hut I quietly walked to the side in order to look through the window - the full moon had moved so that now its light upon the little window meant that the interior would be reasonably visible.

To my amazement I found that the glass had been

knocked out and lay in fragments on the ground. Not knowing what to expect, I silently approached the open frame and peered into the moonlit cell.

The superb bitch knelt completely naked on the bed and with one hand held an empty rum bottle which she thrust in and out of her sex! All the furniture was strewn about, broken into small pieces.

I burst angrily into the room.

"What the hell are you playing at you stupid great whore?"

She immediately picked up table legs and bits of chair and viciously threw them at me, narrowly missing my head. When the empty rum bottle splattered above me, I drew my pistol.

"Any more of that and I'll send you to the next Kingdom!"

Even this lunatic calmed down at this confrontation, and collapsed against the wall and sat there laughing at me.

I kicked out all the broken furniture, together with her torn dress, and took the whip from my belt.

"Yus think, white man, that yus can tame me?" she spat out gruffly. "I's bin whupped plenty from a child and I's so used to it I's just laugh!"

With that she turned her back to me, went on all fours, and stuck her arse up in the air!

My John Thomas quivered with intense expectation and my head burnt frantically as I stared at the intoxicating sight. I lifted the whip and with all the force I could muster drove it down on those magnificent black haunches with the speed of lightening.

CRACK!

A throaty guffaw broke into a train of contemptuous deep laughter.

CRACK!

CRACK!

CRACK!

Again her laughter drowned the resounding echo of the lash on flesh.

"Yus white piece of shit! Yus can't break this black queen!" She belched and spat, hitting me in the face. The witch's gruesome obscenity triggered a spasm of sadistic cruelty in me and I let fly as if possessed by the very devil!

CRACK!

CRACK!

CRACK!

I belted that big black arse like a madman. The whistle of the whip drove me into an unstoppable frenzy.

CRACK!

CRACK!

CRACK!

On and on I wielded the whip with every vestige of strength and cruelty until at last I heard the great whore yelp. Any other woman would have been screaming in agony by now and begging for mercy.

She lifted her head slowly and looked at me.

"Maybe yus should find yusself a little white whore to beat up!" she said. "Yus can't break this black queen!"

I threw down the whip, grabbed the loose chains and wound them tightly against the wall to prevent the movement of her arms. She could have used the length to attack me! Suddenly she sank her teeth into my calf, but let go when I kicked her. It was lucky that I was wearing long leather boots under my trousers!

Her animal attack sent me into a frenzy and I rushed outside and picked up a long hefty plank. I'll teach the bitch some respect, I thought.

I raised the heavy wood with both hands and drove it mercilessly down onto her, but she suddenly kicked out backwards and knocked me flying to the floor. I picked

49

myself up in a rage, forced her body to the floor and tightened the chains securely to the wall so that her legs were fully splayed out. I checked her wrists again. Her arms were fully secured and extended by the tight chains.

Her stomach now rested on the floor, and I shoved her waist roughly with my boot and was finally satisfied that she could exert no further free movement. Then I took off my leather belt, placed my pistol in its holster by the door, and sat astride her waist facing her arse.

I raised the belt and began to flay the upstanding flesh.

The bitch started to sway from side to side, then lifted her body off the floor.. She bucked and tossed trying to dislodge me while I rained sharper and sharper blows upon her.

"I'll kill yus with ma bare hands!" she bellowed.

Her angry promise spurred me into a renewed fervour and I increased the strength and intensity of the blows.

CRACK!

CRACK!

CRACK!

The frenetic way she bucked and tossed slowly endowed my John Thomas with an overpowering heat. The sight and smell of the great quivering arse that danced and shook with every blow of my belt swathed my mind with an increasingly intolerable lust.

A rum bottle stood in the corner of the room.. She had smashed the first one but not the second, which still held some liquid.

I got off her and drank thirstily.

The watched me and laughed. "Yus can beat ma black hide and ride ma black back, but yus can never break ma black spirit!" Then she spat at me again!

She didn't know that I had seen her pleasuring herself with the neck of the bottle, and I made up my mind to play a little game with her.

I pulled one cheek aside and instantly shoved the neck of the bottle into her cunt, and began to work it back and forth just as she had been doing.

She began to laugh! The scornful taunting sound drove me into a vengeful delirium. I got to my knees and released my aching red-hot weapon and speared into her in place of the bottle and started to push in and out.

Suddenly the insufferable whore spat out a torrent of laughter and jeers.

"Yus think yus can please a black queen with that little white cock? Ma little boy has more than yus!"

It was too much! I yanked out my cock, picked up the whip and began to flay her bouncing flesh yet again.

CRACK!

CRACK!

CRACK!

It took some time, but the bitch was eventually broken as I whipped away at her in a vengeful fit. She cried, sobbed, and finally begged me to stop.

Then I loosened her chains, brought out my John Thomas, and enjoyed her at leisure.

13

I went upstairs and entered my room after being told by Beatrice that the local magistrate had come to visit me.

A tall man stepped back off the balcony and came to greet me.

"Mr Ashton, I presume," he said hoarsely as he stretched out his hand. "I am Sir Josiah Waldegrave, come to inspect your establishment here."

"You are welcome, Sir," I said. "Can I get you another rum? I see that Beatrice has been looking after you."

51

"Splendid woman, splendid," he laughed. "Reminds me of my dearly departed."

I invited him to sit whilst pouring the drinks, and asked him to call me Percy. He was a tall elderly man, somewhat portly with grey hair and long white side whiskers. His face was quite stern, although he showed his jolly nature when he spoke.

"There you are, Sir Josiah," I said as I offered him replenishment and took a generous helping myself. "How can I be of service?"

I sat opposite him as he lit up his pipe.

"Well my dear fellow," he said, "as you know my legal jurisdiction covers the whole of these townships and I felt it my duty to call on you personally."

"Yes, Sir Josiah?" I prompted him, as he seemed somewhat hesitant to proceed with anything serious. As we drank and exchanged idle banter, I was very conscious that if any unfortunate misdeed or unforeseen accident should occur in this house it would be his sole responsibility to decide on the action to be taken. He could break me like a dry stick, for only recently the Home Secretary had given full judicial discretion over Poorhouses to the magistrates.

He was taking more and more rum as he brought himself to the point of saying something of significance to me.

"There have been stories in the papers about abuses of girls in Poorhouses," he said at last. "One has to take care, Percy, does one not?"

"Yes indeed," I agreed. It was an inauspicious beginning!

"Well, my dear fellow, I am an old man and in my position as magistrate, it would not be prudent to seek out... you know what I mean, you are a man of the world... it would not be prudent to seek out the company of a, er, an unfortunate young lady, let us say, who had to be punished in London... you see, my dear fellow, in short and to be plain, these new regulations that the Home Secretary has just introduced enabling curators of houses like these to chastise any misbehaving wen - their charges, that is to say, they are to be used, are they not?"

"Why yes," I said. That sounded a little better!

"And if they are abused, then it is magistrates who are invoked. Myself in your case, my dear chap."

"Yes, I suppose so."

"And have all your girls been behaving recently?"

"Why, yes," I said.

"Oh!" His obvious disappointment struck me at once.

"As a matter of fact," I said, "there IS one unfortunate girl that I propose to punish. "Are you likely to object to that?"

"No, no, my dear fellow," he said with enthusiasm. "Oh no, not at all. My meaning was that I would protect you should others dare to criticise you for being too severe." He hesitated. "Indeed," he added, "if I can assist in any way..."

One glance at his eager face and I knew what he was after.

"That is very good of you, Sir Josiah," I said.

"So long as the vic - so long as the miscreant does not see me," he added.

"As it happens," I said, "I have a policy of allowing the girl being punished to wear a hood to save her from embarrassment."

"Good, my dear fellow, very good, very humane," he loudly exclaimed, sitting on the edge of the sofa as he nursed his glass which I had just replenished.

"And you would be prepared to help?"

"Anything to make your task easier, my dear fellow!"

"Well, I am rather busy just now. Perhaps I could secure her, and then leave the room whilst you administer a suitable degree of punishment."

"EXCELLENT!" he roared. "And fear not that in future you will have any trouble whatsoever should any complaints arise about your treatment of the wen - the inmates.."
After he had drained his glass he bellowed: "I'll make sure that the Home Secretary's recommendation secures for you a title from the King!"

One could not say fairer than that! I immediately went down to the recreation room where a few of the girls sat gossiping in a corner, and chose one.

"You are to be punished," I said, "Put this hood on and come with me."

She did not ask what the punishment was for. If I decided a girl was to be punished, there was no more to be said on the matter. Be sure they had all come to understand that recently, even if I have not troubled you with the details.

I led her, hooded, to the room. Sir Josiah's eyes bulged from his sockets when he saw her, for she was a favourite of mine, one I chose for her excellent figure and her ability to withstand a beating.

"Lift your dress," I said.

She lifted the hem above her waist, and he gasped in admiration as I tied it there.

"Bend over the sofa," I said, "and do not dare to move until I have finished with you!"

I knew that she would not dare to do so. She would stay there, supporting herself with her hands on the sofa, come what may.

Sir Josiah walked over to her in silence and ran his hands over her bottom, then spread her legs apart, which she meekly accepted, as I had taught her to do. His excitement was almost killing him, so red had he become in the face, just like a turkey cock.

I beckoned him over to the cabinet where the instruments of punishment were neatly laid out, and we chose our implements, then walked silently back. Fortunately I have a thick carpet and she would not have realised that there were two people present.

I raised my hand and slowly began to tease her with gentle slaps from a slipper.

Smack!

Smack!

Smack!

Then Sir Josiah copied me, somewhat harder.

Smack!

Smack!

Smack!

After a few more blows from him we retreated to the table, where we sat and consumed more rum. I was glad to see that he appreciated it. then I gestured to him that I was leaving the punishment to him, and stepped out onto the veranda to savour my drink.

But soon the sounds from within, sounds of slapping and yelping and moaning, made me wish I was participating in the punishment. Well, why not? I had to go back into the room to pour another rum, anyway.

The girl was writhing about and yelling out loud now, for Sir Josiah turned out to have a very string arm and was enthusiastic. But he came and joined me as I poured the rum. He needed a rest, I think, for his face was redder than before and his chest was heaving from his exertions.

When we were ready we both took belts and wrapped them round our fists as we crept up upon the waiting girl. Her bottom was already a nice shade of red, and we had hardly started.

We resumed with enthusiasm and soon had her squirming and wriggling and gasping more than before. The intoxicating view of that tortured bottom seemed to inflame Sir Josiah and he threw down the strap he had been using and started to fondle her whole body as I continued the beating. So now she knew there were two of us, but it really didn't matter, for there was nothing she could do about it since any complaints would be referred to him!

The fingers of his left had began to slip into her cunnie, and soon he was thrusting in and out whilst I belted her bottom cheeks with great abandon, making her wriggle on his fingers. My head throbbed like a drum as I played my part and watched the obscene squirmings and wondered where it would lead to.

I did not have long to wait. When he realised that I would not prevent him from plundering her, he evidently decided to take full advantage of the situation and impatiently pulled at the buttons of his trousers.

As his weapon sprang out of its restriction I nearly fell against the door, for it was a solid monster considerably bigger than mine! I began to fear for the girl as I watched the mighty thing sway about, but it was too late to draw back now.

He threw her down on the floor and was upon her in an instant. She cried out at the sudden massive stretching of her tender flesh, but soon he appeared to awaken in her a newly heightened lasciviousness with his escalating pounding, and before long she had become as enthusiastic for the taking as he was. After a few minutes of tasting the new found pleasure, she started to buck and push against the now fully inserted weapon.

I watched dumbfounded at her ability to accept such a colossus and then realised that her whole body was starting to convulse. She shuddered with trembling spasms and when Sir Josiah began to thrust with all his strength she seemed to erupt with an insane savageness and began to buck and heave her hungry loins up and down the huge length until they both collapsed in a shattering climax...

I sat back, warmed by the morning sun, and sipped my rum. I felt quite quite content with my curatorship of the past weeks. I had got the girls completely under control and made an ally of the local magistrate, the only man who could have interfered with my pleasures. Beatrice had turned out to be a most beguiling mistress, a mistress who was mine to command, and I was growing in my fondness of Julie, ever the temptress. If I tired of all the pleasures of this place, then London was just a few hours away.

I was even tempted to prolong my stay by instructing Charles to postpone his search for a new plantation for a few months.

I stood up and decided to check on the girls downstairs. I was in the mood to punish one or two of them. I finished my drink and walked downstairs past the empty recreation room and was just about to turn to the stairs that led to the kitchen when the Countess Diana came running up the stairs.

"Sir, there is a coach approaching the house," she exclaimed, dropping a curtsey, as I had taught her to do. It always gave me pleasure, as it made the proud creature blush when I was able to look down the front of her dress. I also made her hold up the hem of her dress as she did so, and that seemed to embarrass her also.

"Very well," I said. "You may go." Which she did with great relief, for she knew that I might well have singled her out for punishment. Her formerly haughty manner had made her one of my more constant favourites.

I opened the front door just as the rumbling duty coach pulled into the drive. I was pleasantly surprised to find that it was Lady Cordelia as James jumped down to open the carriage door.

"Well, well, Percy," she exclaimed as she stepped off the coach, "please excuse the unannounced visit."

I hardly recognised her when she smiled and held out her gloved hand. Her grey hair had been transformed into a mass of wavy luxurious reddish-brown that fell onto her naked shoulders. Her deep blue dress, decorated with an intricate white pattern over her bosom and around her short sleeves matched perfectly her little white booties. A thin black neck-band displayed a delicate golden ornament that danced upon her heaving breasts.

She laughed at my astonished look and remarked, "Are we to stand here all day?"

I apologised and invited her in. When she arrived at my quarters she was obviously impressed. "It is very comfortable, Percy. I am quite envious. Well, don't just stand there. Aren't you going to offer a lady a drink after her long thirsty journey?"

I poured our drinks and then pulled a single sofa onto the balcony so that we could sit comfortably in close proximity, and she careful arranged the voluminous folds of her long blue dress as she settled down for a chat.

"It is a great pleasure, Lady Cordelia, to see -"

She suddenly interrupted. "Oh Percy, don't be such an old fogey. In private, call me Cordelia."

"Very well, Cordelia. I was about to say that you look marvellous!"

"It is you I have to thank, Percy. Before your visit I had been for some time in a state of depression, but you snapped me out of it. I bought an entirely new wardrobe from Paris. What do you think?"

She stood and and twirled round.

"The change is unbelievable," I said. It was true. The newly died reddish-brown waves took away her severe appearance. Her better spirits gave her the bearing of a woman of much younger years.

58

She opened her colourful parasol to shield herself from the sun. "Well then, tell me, dear Percy, did the demonstration on Daisy's well developed rump stand you in good stead in your new duties?"

"Yes indeed!" I said. The rum by now had relaxed and enlivened both our senses and I felt I could speak quite freely to my vivacious benefactor and friend, and felt brave enough through the lubricating nectar to ask her a question. "When did you first have an opportunity to exercise your whims against a wanton bottom?"

"Ah, Percy!" She smiled wickedly. "It was at a very tender age. I must have been eleven or twelve. The very first governess I had - I think she was a French woman of about twenty - well, she was a stupid sort of person and I managed to convince her that I could get her dismissed if she didn't let me have my way with her. Every few nights I raised her dress and strapped her on her naked bottom."

I listened to this story with a thumping head and a bloated John Thomas.

"Then there were the other governesses," she continued. "My poor father always wondered why none lasted longer than three months, bless his simple soul. No wench could last longer with the severe beatings I gave them. Except now I have Daisy, and of course she has no choice, poor creature, it is her misfortune to have so fine a bottom. When I first saw her scrubbing floors after a late show at the Royal Theatre, I was determined to have her. I employed a private detective to find out all about her. She is an orphan who had recently been discharged from a Poorhouse. I bought the house where she lived and procured her discharge from her job and soon she was a kitchen maid in my house. I had never in my life seen a bottom such as hers. I just had to have it. The amount of beating it receives is truly wondrous."

I was in an utter state of unequalled bliss. I had long

sought a spirit of the opposite sex that shared my every thought, wish and desires, and here she was!

"Were you ever beaten yourself?" I asked.

"Yes, my uncle used to visit our house every Sunday. He was always boasting how he beat his many children and his wife to keep them under firm control. One Sunday I was particularly disobedient and in the absence of my father, who had stopped strapping me years before, he forced me onto his lap, lifted my skirts, and used his hand on my naked bottom. What a thrill it was! Every Sunday after that he didn't even try to find an excuse, he always took me over his knee and beat me, only now he used my slipper. It was only much later, when I was about twenty and much more worldly, that I realised I had orgasmed every time."

I stood up to stretch my legs and she chuckled salaciously and pointed to my John Thomas. "Just look what I've done to your poor willie!" Then she looked at me with a dreamy expression. "After all this talk of punishment, I need to be beaten, Percy?"

My John Thomas jerked at the invitation and I took her by the hand and knelt her before the sofa.

With her elbows planted firmly in the cushion, I picked up the hem of her blue dress and flung it over her waist. I then ripped at her white drawers and instantly pulled them down to her knees. The sight that met my eyes froze me to the spot. Her fifty year old naked bottom exposed from the confines of her baggy dress was easily a match for Julie's. The milky white globes were perfectly round and slightly fleshy. Her sturdy thighs had the firm muscularity that a woman gains with age. The most stupendous vision of all was the minute size of her waist, which I immediately measured and found to be the smallest I had ever seen in my life. My fingers and thumbs easily circled it with plenty of room inside.

My head swam with unbearable lust as I picked up a

discarded sandal from some previous victim and brought it down sharply on Cordelia's trembling rump.

Crack!

Crack!

Crack!

"Wheeee!" she cried out, "harder, Percy, harder!"

I thrashed her quivering buttocks mercilessly. Again and again I belted the hungry flesh whilst she wheezed and howled.

"Ooh yes ... and again ... harder, harder ... HARDER HARDER!"

She suddenly reached back with both hands and pulled her cheeks apart to expose her crack with her arsehole gushing out a noticeable heat.

Now ... THERE!"

She screamed as I obeyed her, and I pulled out my engorged prick.

"YES!" she howled. "OH YES! NOW!"

I immediately thrust deep into her arsehole and, grabbing her bucking hips, took her as quickly as I could, faster and faster, on and on...

After that we sat and talked for an hour or more on the endless possibilities that a partnership could provide for ensnaring innocent girls for our pleasure. Part of the enjoyment of the art was inflicting humiliation on an unwilling wench, but the other half, equally intoxicating, was finding one who desperately needed to be punished, and in this she had an unsurpassed sixth sense.

At last we realised that the sun was going down.

"My dear Percy," she said, "I really must be on my way. Would you care to visit London tomorrow?"

With thoughts of Daisy affecting my John Thomas I nodded instant agreement.

"Then I shall send a carriage for you tomorrow," she said. "Early!"

As I waved her off I was fully determined to forget the Caribbean, because although I would have an endless supply of unwilling victims there, I would never satisfy my hunger for the willing ones. Even the knowledge that practising the art in civilised England was full of danger as opposed to the absolute freedom of a slave plantation did not alter my steadfast determination. In Lady Cordelia I had found a true devotee, a follower of the highest order, a Goddess at peace in her own temple. Any true thinking man would give his right arm to bathe in the delicious sweetness of her salaciousness.

15

A loud crack of thunder roused me from a reverie. It seemed I was on the balcony and it must be late at night. The bottle at my elbow was empty, and a sudden torrential downpour made me seek the safety of my room.

I poured another drink and gazed out at nature's cleansing vengeance. My pocket watch showed that the time was just after midnight. It struck me that on every occasion I had dozed off on the balcony I had been disturbed at about the same hour. It must have been the midnight congregation of imps and demons that lurked out in the darkness and hurt my head.

The black night with its growling thunder hurled javelins of lightening that were as ferocious as Medusa's gaze turning men into stone.

I drank more virtuous nectar and soon recovered some clarity of mind, especially when I closed the windows against the obscene night. The remaining bottle seemed to be empty, so I took a candle and headed for the kitchen for another.

As I picked my way in the flickering light of the candle down the dark stairs, some peculiar urge drew me to Purity's room One day I would beat the spirits and demons out of her, and the house would be at peace.

I stopped outside. Silence. I was just about to walk away when the infernal chant started.

'... and those who choose to wield the odious sword of misbegotten sacrilege will breathe the dark one's citadel. The unending feast of the last morsel of man's unworthy soul will echo its bloodless chime down the ages. Man will feed upon man and child upon child as the heinous lizard trumpets the beginnings of the eternal state of warfare amongst the dark ones for the souls that will fall into the pit of fire. Every obscenity known to man will be as nothing when the dark ones reveal their secret tortures...'

My head pounded as I listened. One day I would beat the diabolical little wench into silence. But not tonight, for the rum inhibited me, alas it had made my John Thomas too unready to enjoy her properly.

As I clambered up the stairs clutching the new bottle I consoled myself with the thought that her time would come, and her retribution would be all the greater for it!

I was just trying to pour a full glass without spillage when I heard the voice of an angel.

Not an angel, the sound of a temptress from the devil himself!

"I heard a noise and came to the door and it was you stumbling, sir. Are you alright?"

Purity supported me as I slumped into a chair, straight and graceful in her skimpy white dress, so short, with nothing beneath it...

"You look a little unsettled," she said timidly, as she refilled the glass and handed it to me. She could not realise how seductive her throaty little voice was.

"Come here, my child," I said, and she came innocently

63

into my arms for a cuddle and a kiss, such a long lovely kiss, and - believe it or not - I told her I was alright and sent her back to bed with no more than a mild pat on that gorgeously provocative behind of hers, naked as my hand slid up the warm pliant flesh...

I must have fallen asleep at once, because the early morning sun roused me and I realised I had not been to bed even as I heard the rumbling carriage pulling into the driveway.

Before many minutes had passed I was down there. "Good morning sir," James called out cheerfully, a little too cheerfully for the state of my head.

"Morning James," I replied as I boarded the carriage and we promptly pulled out. The morning sun together with the relaxing drink I was now able to take directly from the bottle soothed me into a restful doze and it was only when we hit the potholes on the approach to Streatham village that I fully awoke.

I thought about the long conversation I had had with Cordelia and how she had told me that she was now Administrator of all of the Southern Poorhouses, and how she wished me to become her partner, for only a man could be the Inspector, and that after he had had experience of a curatorship.

Later, as we slowed down amongst the numerous coaches trundling along Oxford Street, I looked out at the many wenches parading their finery, exposing their barely concealed bosoms and smiling saucily at the sight of myself in Cordelia's magnificent carriage.

Soon we turned the last corner and I jumped out into the bright sunshine outside Cordelia's house. She opened the door herself and with a flashing smile invited me in. She hugged me tightly to her heaving chest, then pulled me into the elegant drawing room and handed me a large rum whilst pouring one for herself. She had arranged her richly coloured hair off her face, tied loosely behind her neck. Her low cut morning dress was a dazzling shade of cream unadorned with any jewellery.

"Well," she said, "have you come to any decision?"

"Yes," I replied. ""Our fate is irrevocably intertwined, and that is how it was meant to be."

She jumped up in glee.

"You'll see, Percy, we'll conquer the world, I'll give you as many wenches as your heart desires and no one will be able to stop us."

She sat down and gulped her drink, staring at me with dreamy eyes that seemed already to have conjured up visions of wenches in compromised positions.

"I'll go to Charles later today," I said, "and abdicate the plantation."

"Excellent," she said. "Now let me show you my little collection of playthings." She took me to the far end of the drawing room, where a long cabinet, reaching to the ceiling, rested against the wall.

When she unlocked it and flung open the doors, I could not believe my eyes. On the left hung every size and weight of whip. Some were coiled as if awaiting virgin flesh, others were decorated with adjustable metal notches and a few had tightly interwoven metal ringlets at the thin end. My eyes eagerly scanned the collection and I suspected that there must have been at least twenty.

Further along were restraining straps, manacles of both leather and metal, a few masks, a selection of straps and belts, and a collection of chains and other peculiar looking items.

"What are those thin flexible looking things?" I asked.

"Bougies," she replied. "They are surgical instruments for exploring the passages of the body." She handed me the key in case I might need it during my plundering of Daisy.

"Can I have her now?" I asked.

"Right away. I shall send her to you."

"Does she know what I intend to do with her?"

"Of course not. She will be distressed, she always is when she is to be beaten, but she dare not resist you just because she is not accustomed to being used by a man."

She got up, blew me a kiss and left the room. My mind was spinning with lust as I drunk my rum and waited for my prize.

A gentle knock announced her arrival. "Good morning sir," she softly whispered, with a fleeting glance.

"Good morning, Daisy," I answered. "Please pour me a drink."

She padded over to the drink cabinet whilst I looked at her. She wore her Sunday best, which comprised of a long grey dress cut horizontally below her shoulders, bordered by a thin white fringe. The short sleeves that exposed her arms were level with the cut of her dress. She wore a thin black belt loosely tied round her waist so as not to emphasise her over-large bottom. Her short brown hair was cut in a straight line just above her eyes and was neat and shiny. It was cropped over her small dainty ears and tucked tidily into the bare nape of her neck.

She brought my drink over and stood before me, waiting further instruction, puzzled, I suppose, as to why she had been sent to me.

"Now," I said, "it would be best if you were to take off your dress."

"Sir?" She had not taken it in.

"It would be best," I repeated, "if you were to take off your dress."

"Oh sir!"

"Come," I said, "if Lady Cordelia gave a similar order, would you not obey instantly?"

"Yes sir, but -"

"Because you fear to forfeit your position?"

She shuddered visibly. The fate of a penniless female on the streets was not to be contemplated.

"Yes sir!" she said faintly.

"You are lucky to have held it so far," I said. "With your disfigurement."

"I cannot help the large size of my bottom, sir."

"No," I said, "but it would make it hard to find another employer."

"I know -" She was crying now.

"Or to do business on the streets!"

"Oh sir!" she wailed. "But to undress before a man -"

"Lady Cordelia has commissioned me to ascertain how severe a beating you can endure," I said. "And if it is not sufficient she intends to discharge you."

She gave me a pathetic look as she stood facing me, then began to undo the buttons at the back of her dress, her eyes averted from mine. At last she was able to pull the dress off her shoulders, down to her slim waist. Then she bent forward and dragged it over her extraordinary bottom with some difficulty, blushing about her size as she did so.

Stepping out of her dress at last, she stood before me, ashamed and vulnerable, and totally naked. I stared at the intoxicating vision. Her eyes gazed into mine, seeking mercy, whilst I devoured the sight of her shame like a hungry animal. I had to admire her shapely shoulders, her perfect nubile breasts, and finally the wild sweep of the curvature from her childish waist to those tremendous buttocks, which she considered a blemish on her otherwise considerable beauty, but which Cordelia and I valued so highly - a worthy target for our sadistic inclinations. The great buttocks were set off by the contrast of the tiny almost invisible crack of her nearly hairless little cunnie.

I told her to turn round, and the second vision almost threw me into an apocalyptic fit. The snowy white shoulders blended easily into the smallness of her curvy back and down to her neat waist. Again the curvature of the splendid buttocks swerved outwards, more aggressively than before, encompassing two beautiful round fleshy globes. Her sturdy thighs seemed to ripple against the constant heavy load and only relaxed in her rounded sinewy calves.

I beckoned her to stand between my knees, and she came, even if reluctantly and avoiding my gaze, with her hands clasped behind her back. My hands explored her, particularly those superb buttocks which I was coming to appreciate more and more with every passing moment. Standing between my spread knees, her small stature made the exploration even more erotic as I drew her closer and felt the warmth of her trembling body.

"You understand," I said, "that I am to test your capacity to endure a real beating, such as a woman cannot give, and that if you prove inadequate you are to be discharged?"

"Yes sir," she said. There were tears in her eyes. "You will find that because of the excessive size of my rump I am able to tolerate more than the average girl."

"I am to do my worst, then?"

She bit her lip, then looked me in the eye. I could have sworn there was a twinkle in it, but that of course was impossible. "Yes, sir," she said. "Do your worst. I shall not fail this test."

She was breathing in quick gasps as my hands roamed over and under her buttock cheeks, testing the size and weight of each globe, and the tips of her breasts pressed against my shirt as I drew her further in and set my lips briefly to hers, opening them with my tongue and catching hers for a brief instant.

"Bend over my knee!"

She did so, and taking a deep breath I began to smack the yielding soft flesh with my bare hand.

Slap!

68

Slap!

Slap!

I held her firmly by the hair to stop her forward wriggles and then hit her harder on that springy expanse of flesh. My John Thomas was almost out of control and my head throbbed as I grabbed her soft supple tits and squeezed and pulled them while raining blows onto that unrivalled rump.

I stood up, forced her to her knees and bent her over the sofa. I went to the whip cabinet and pulled out a long sturdy cane of about six feet in length. I tested its springiness, then returned to Daisy. The way she was positioned with bottom high in the air exaggerated the already extraordinary size of it.

"Are you ready for the test?" I asked.

"Oh sir, was not that it?"

"Indeed not," I said. "I am about to commence with this cane."

"Then proceed, sir," she gasped, and I instantly began to thrash her with powerful strokes.

Thwack!

Thwack!

Thwack!

"Ugh, ugh, ugh!" she gasped, her bottom wriggling splendidly, her whole body pulsating.

Thwack!

Thwack!

Thwack!

The cane sang as it bounced and sprang off the squirming target. A slight pinkish hue was slowly starting to envelop her fleshy globes.

My head thumped like a thousand drums when I stopped at last and went over to the drinks cabinet to refresh my glass, leaving her across the arm of the sofa, heaving and sobbing. I noticed that she did not attempt to rise or put her hands to her stinging buttocks, and assumed that Cordelia did not permit it.

Nor had she howled out yet, but I proposed to alter that.

After a while I went to the other cabinet and swopped the cane for a paddle with a two foot handle. I began to belt her flesh with this, and after every stinging rap she let out a yelp.

"Now crawl!" I shouted, and immediately she was on the floor, on hands and knees, crawling away from me. The first blow of the paddle propelled her forward and I watched the flesh of her buttocks jiggle from side to side as I followed her slowly round the room, belting her shaking bottom if she slowed down.

My head pounded with disbelief at the humiliation she was a prepared to lower herself to in order not be be thrown out on the streets. She soon got into her stride as I urged her forward with stinging blows. I hurried her round the room, gradually increasing the speed of the blows until she was scurrying round like a frightened rabbit.

"Stop!" I said. "Fetch me a drink!"

She rose and walked gracefully over to the drink cabinet. As I watched that magnificent arse of hers swaying below the neat waist, my head beat with indescribable lust as I imagined what further indignities I could conjure up. She came back and handed me the glass and stood within reach as I ran my hands over her once again, feeling the heat emanating from her abused bottom.

"Stand on that chair," I said. "And bend forward. I must examine your bottom to see how the test is proceeding."

My John Thomas almost screamed in pain at the incomparable sight. The shaking rump was level with my face and I was able to grasp the two fleshy cheeks and pull them apart. Her deep cleft opened up and exposed her little brown ringlet, and when I let go they immediately sprang back together with the slight sound of a fleshy smack.

I left her there and went to pour a further rum, then told

70

her to sit by the wall on the floor. Cordelia had shown me a little pulley she had installed on the ceiling directly above that place. She said she had never used it. I slowly finished my drink, then went over to the handle and began to turn it, and gradually a rope with two leather manacles descended to the floor.

"Put your ankles in these," I ordered her, "and tighten the buckle for me."

When she had secured the manacles about her ankles, I began to wind the wall mechanism and slowly the rope lifted her legs, then her bottom, until eventually her whole body was completely off the floor and she hung upside down. I cranked the handle until her gorgeous rump was level to my face.

My weapon felt as if it was about to burst out of its confines as I picked up the paddle.

Thwack!

Thwack!

Thwack!

With each strike the suspended body began to swing from side to side and the massive cheeks seemed to come to life in the way each one trembled and shook with each passing swipe. As I increased the speed of my assault her body slowed and then began to twist round. Faster and faster I belted her until eventually the rope speeded her body round in rapid pirouettes. I matched the twirling bottom with rapid blows until she started to scream out.

Soon after that I released my aching cock and thrust it into her mouth. I grabbed her rump and when I buried my mouth into her wet cunnie she suddenly started to buck her head back and forth, quickly engulfing my whole length deep into her throat. As I squeezed and pulled her bottom flesh she speeded up her gobbling action and lifted her hands up to my bottom. She then quickened the motion of her thrusting mouth and pressed my buttocks onto her every

71

swallowing lunge until my head exploded into a ball of fire as she milked my hot discharge to the last drop.

I stayed within her for a minute, until her heavy body stopped shaking, and then slowly withdrew. I buttoned myself up then slowly lowered the pulley until she relaxed on the floor.

She looked up at me whilst she was undoing the manacles and winked! Yes, I swear it, she actually winked at me!

"Oh sir," she said, "I did enjoy that! I do hope I shall be tested by you again soon!"

As I watched her slip the grey dress over her shoulders I was quite envious that Cordelia had caught such a fine prize. Still, I thought, I can share the wench at any time. I poured a rum and fell into a chair, exalted at the little adventure.

11

I slept for most of the journey home - back to the Poorhouse, that is - and when we finally rumbled through the outer gates it was dark and the time was eleven o'clock.

I dismounted, bade James a safe return, and entered the house. Groping my way up the dark stairs I decided to listen outside Purity's door. All was silent, but it did not prevent my John Thomas from twitching in anticipation of the little surprise Cordelia and I had prepared for her on the morrow, or rather later today.

I went to my rooms, unpacked and sat on in the mild night with a glass and a bottle. I was roused from my chair in the morning by Beatrice, and found that I had not actually gone to bed. That is what good night air and healthy tiredness can do to one, and there is no harm in it.

"Ah Beatrice," I said, "pray fetch a new bottle to enhance this excellent breakfast."

When she returned with it, I began to put our plans for Purity's downfall into effect by telling Beatrice that I had met a Mother Superior in London who would be visiting today on the chance of finding an inmate who might be interested in joining her convent.

"Why sir!" she exclaimed at once, "there is Purity."

"Ah yes," I said, "Purity to be sure. Do you think she would be interested?"

"Oh yes, sir, I am sure of it. What time is Mother Superior arriving?"

"About ten," I said. "You had better make Purity aware of this and have her in readiness if she is interested."

"Indeed sir I will," she replied, leaving me to finish my breakfast, pour another rum, and sit on the balcony with Purity's tight little bum in my mind...

... I think perhaps I dozed a little, until my attention was attracted by the sound of an approaching coach. As it drew closer I could see that it was not Cordelia's usual one, nor was James driving it. A good point, Cordelia, I thought. When it was close enough I saw a passenger dressed in the garb of a nun.

I would never have recognised her, so Beatrice was not likely to. However, I went downstairs to open the door to the Holy Mother myself as the black carriage came through the gate and rumbled to a stop.

Cordelia opened the gate and climbed down.

"Mr Ashton," she said, "it is so good of you to allow me this spiritual quest." I bowed as she took my hand and gave me a conspiratorial squeeze whilst keeping up the pretence of a solemn occasion until we were safely hidden in my rooms, then she slipped off her black head garb and hugged me.

"How do I look?" she laughed, twirling around.

"Splendid," I said. "Just like a Mother Superior, I should think, you have the face for it my dear." She did indeed look a picture of holiness with her long flowing black uniform immaculately pressed and with sombre black shoes. Her flowing rich auburn locks, freed for the moment from the oppressive head garb, were the only indication of her true nature.

"I've even got some spectacles," she said proudly, taking them from her prim black bag.

I poured her a hefty rum - which she must finish before Purity arrived - then closed the balcony windows and drew the curtains. We did not want any witnesses to our forthcoming morning's pleasures.

We laughed and drank more rum, then talked as we decided on our plan of action. Presently Cordelia covered her hair again and donned her spectacles while she assumed a fierce gaze which made us both burst into laughter.

Then I went to get Purity.

"Are you ready?" I asked. "Do you wish for this interview?"

"Yes sir," she said meekly, in that seductive little voice of hers. "This is the most important day of my life!"

I hid a smile behind my hand. "Very well, child," I said, "if you are resolved you may follow me."

She obediently accompanied me up the stairs. When we approached my rooms I said to her: "The Mother Superior is waiting inside. Go in now and be a good girl." I then left her as she entered after knocking timidly, and then I quickly walked back to the glint in the door.

I could hear every word and see all.

Cordelia started by explaining to Purity that the age of entrance to her convent was eighteen years due the the fact that sixteen year old girls, such as Purity, normally do not appreciate the need and necessity of total obedience.

"But Mother Superior," pleaded Purity, "I do understand

fully the reasons for obedience. If we are to pray for salvation then our minds must be trained in subservience."

"If that is so," said Cordelia sternly, "why is your dress so indecently brief?"

"We were only given a certain amount of material," said Purity, "and I thought it important to conceal my breasts adequately, then I found too little left."

"That was thoughtless, child."

"We were not allowed long enough -"

"Be silent!" thundered Cordelia. "It ill befits one so young to make excuses for such carnal laxity! Rather you should be pleading to be purged of your evil."

Purity burst into tears and dropped to her knees.

"Forgive me, Mother Superior, forgive me!"

"The penance for misbehaviour in our order is physical chastisement," said Cordelia sternly. She looked over Purity's bowed head and winked towards the door.

"Then let me be chastised!" said Cordelia. "Oh please let me by chastised, do not reject me for my sins, chastise me as severely as you see fit!"

"Very well," said Cordelia, standing up. "Bend over with your hands on the settee and close your eyes."

Purity immediately complied, and Cordelia came round to the back of her and lifted the white dress to her waist.

My head swooned with lust at the sudden naked exposure. Her milky white little bum was firm and round, standing atop lean curvaceous thighs that melted into slim sylph-like legs.

Cordelia began to smack the tender flesh.

Slap!

Slap!

Slap!

She hit each cheek in turn with increasing severity until Purity started to whimper, still keeping her eyes tightly closed as she had been ordered to do.

After a few minutes of this, Cordelia paused and looked towards the door, and I entered stealthily and stood next to her as we had arranged.

Now I took over, hitting harder than Cordelia had been able to do.

Smack!

Smack!

Smack!

My John Thomas shook with lust as I spanked the firm little cheeks, listening to Purity's moans. I gloried in the soft warm springiness of her. I continued for several minutes, then Cordelia took over again and I retreated quietly to the balcony, from where I could spy on everything through the curtains.

"Now then, my cherub," said Cordelia, raising Purity and letting her dress fall over her sweet reddening bottom and returned to her seat, leaving Purity standing before her, "now we have to find out if you are strong and healthy for a lifetimes work in the order."

"I understand," replied Purity, wiping a tear from her eyes, "what must I do to show you?"

"I have to determine if you have a strong but supple body with good sinews. I will need to test the strength and flexibility of your little frame. Normally it is not common practise, but because of your apparent fragility, I could not allow you to enter the order unless I am satisfied. It would not be fair to you."

"What must I do?" repeated Purity.

"Stand before me and close your eyes again, and you must keep them closed no matter what I may do."

Then Cordelia lifted Purity's white dress by the hem and lifted it over her head and off to leave her standing completely naked.

Again my John Thomas shook wildly at the seductive sight, she was so small and appealing, such a spankable morsel. Her boyish round rump shivered silently and her petite trim legs quivered with anticipation, and she was biting her lip hard.

Cordelia led her by the hand to a tall chair and helped her to stand on it, then made her cover her eyes with her hands as a further precaution. She proceeded to test her back by running fingers up and down her spine, then squeezed her bottom and kneaded her small firm breasts until the nipples hardened.

When Cordelia looked in my direction I entered silently and my hands took over from hers. The flesh beneath my fingers was warm and shrinking from the touch, so shy was Purity. I stroked her round shoulders, rubbed her titties some more, grabbed the firm warm flesh of her bottom cheeks and played with it for a few minutes, I explored at length both the front side and the back side of her slim body, and stroked her all over. The girl was shaking and cringing from my touch, holding her hands to her face and whimpering.

Then Cordelia took over the sport whilst I poured myself a hefty rum to quell my pounding head before returning to the balcony to spy upon them.

She told Purity to step down and open her eyes. She did so in a very distressed state.

"May I dress now?" she asked.

"Patience, child, patience," rejoined Cordelia. "You realise I trust, that in order to give the whole of your life in the hope of salvation you must forsake all worldly pleasures."

"Oh yes, Mother Superior," came a trembling little voice. "I have already done that. I just want to give my whole being and soul to the Lord."

"And what would happen," pressed Cordelia, "if at some later stage you might be tempted to taste the fruit?"

Purity looked confused. "I do not understand, Mother Superior."

"In every order there is eventually always an instance where one crosses the path of a male. Sometimes it is whilst purchasing provisions from a village or maybe coming into contact with a gardener or workman. There have been occasions where unfortunate situations have arisen."

"I would do nothing wrong!" cried out Purity adamantly.

Cordelia looked at her sternly, and behind the curtain my John Thomas sprang to attention. "I have to find out these things, child, before I permit a novice to enter our walls."

"What must I do then?" Purity sobbed.

"I assume you are of course a virgin?"

"Oh Mother Superior! Oh yes, yes, I fought them off!"

"Who, my child?"

"My step brothers!"

"I see," said Cordelia. She appeared to ponder. "Very well, I shall break you in today."

"Break -"

"You see, my cherub, we cannot take the chance that your lubricity might be woken when it is too late and you are already a member of the order. Why, a child might be the result! What I need to find out is if your constitution can withstand an insertion of an object similar in size and strength to that of a normal healthy man and to see if you are capable of withstanding the feelings that lead to an explosion of passion. If you can resist your feelings in this way then I shall know that you will be able to trust yourself in the future."

Purity gazed at her in dumb horror.

"If you wish," said Cordelia, "You may dress and return to your duties. I have an appointment elsewhere shortly."

"You intend to insert something into my - into me?"

"I must if we are to proceed."

Purity seemed frozen to the spot in mute distress. Then at last she spoke in a voice that trembled and could hardly be heard. "It is my lifelong ambition to enter an order. If my salvation depends on such a test, then you may proceed."

"Very well."

Cordelia picked up her bag, searched inside and pulled out a ten inch long wooden object. It was phallic in shape and covered tightly in pig skin. Purity stared in amazed dread at the monster that was about to test her lasciviousness.

"Oh but Mother Superior," she cried in fear, "I am only a small girl, how could I possibly manage to take all that!"

"There are some men who equal this size -"

"Oh no!"

"- and therefore I have no choice but to use it on you if we are to succeed."

As I put down my glass and stared hungrily at Purity's shaking body my head throbbed at the thought of what was to follow.

Cordelia stood up, took hold of the trembling girl by the hand, and led her to the back of the sofa. She bent the slim naked body over the back, so that her tight bottom protruded up and her dainty toes barely touched the floor.

"You will not wish to see this," said Cordelia. "Bury your head in the cushions."

As the girl did so, it was my cue to creep back into the room and stand against the wall where I had a clear view of Cordelia standing over Purity's outstretched little bottom, which exposed her tight pink rosette and inviting little cunnie.

"Remember what I told you, my cherub," repeated Cordelia. "I am testing to see if you can withstand the type of passion that a man might give to you."

She placed her left hand onto Purity's bottom cheek, pulled it to one side, and placed the bulbous head of the instrument to the entrance of her cunnie.

79

My head pounded like a drum as I watched Cordelia first tease the tight crack, then ease the first massive inch into the virgin flesh.

Purity lifted her head for a moment, with a cushion clenched in her teeth and her eyes screwed up tightly, realising that any sound might give the impression of a sign of lustfulness.

Cordelia pushed in another three inches, then began to slowly withdraw and then push back in again. Purity flexed her body tensely, so that the sinewy muscles of her slim legs stood out distinctly.

Now Cordelia ventured six inches and unconcerned at Purity's heaving and moaning, began a rapid frigging action. Purity involuntarily lifted her straining legs off the floor and then started to jerk up and down in rhythm to the thrusts.

At this Cordelia motioned to me, and my head pounded like a thousand drums as I released my stiff weapon and advanced forward. I squeezed into Cordelia's side as she slowed down the frigging, and as she pulled the instrument out I entered instantly, pushing in by four inches and continuing the back and forwards motion.

As I pushed, I steeled myself against the sudden tight warmth until the overpowering flush of lust had subsided. Then I began a gentle rocking motion whilst Cordelia started to smack the tight hot cheeks that squirmed beneath me.

After a minute of regaining confidence in my staying power, I increased the speed of my thrusts, now pounding in a full seven inches of my weapon. Purity kept her teeth tightly clenched against her inner grunts, but had no control over her kicking legs. Cordelia, red faced, smacked the inviting fleshy cheeks with increasing tempo, and I began to push in harder and deeper.

I withdrew to the first inch, paused, then suddenly rammed the whole of my cock into her!

"AAAAAGH!!!" she screamed. And then she gasped: "Absolution and s-salvation will be my redeemer!"

I could not believe what I was hearing. The little wench had started to chant! I slowly withdrew and again pushed all the way in, then with every jerking jerking thrust the little bitch spewed out obscenities.

"AAAAAGH!!! Surrender and s-s-sacrifice will be my s-s-salvation!"

As I perked deeply to the sound of her broken gasping words, I looked at Cordelia, who, stricken with shock, had stopped beating the girl. But the little witch had inflamed my senses and I pounded away more furiously than before.!

"AAAAAGH!!! The dark one's fire and d-dam-damnation will scourge m-man's evil s-s-soul!"

The scurrilous little sorceress had unknowingly awoken my deepest insanity and her every utterance invoked in me a mightier sadistic plunge.

"AAAAAGH!!! The name of the d-dark one will echo and re-resound in every cit-cit-citadel!"

Cordelia's worst savageness now also seemed to have been wrenched out of her darkest depths and with the vengeance of the whore of Babylon riding on a beast with seven heads, she suddenly unleashed a ferocity of blows the likes of which I had never seen before.

"AAAAAGH!!! Ter-terrible will be h-his fiery look when he re-returns to claim his thr-throne!"

The madness burning in my mind, to the chorus of the girl's diabolic rantings, provoked in me the vision of the God of War's last stand and I began to throw the longest and most cruel javelins at my earthly prey.

"AAAAAGH!!! L-lions with l-lambs and and saints with sin-sin-sinners will stand at the dark one's gate!"

Cordelia's bursting face and stricken eyes testified to her hidden sadistic obsession and with increased combustion she flayed Purity's shrinking flesh.

"AAAAAGH!!! The tr-tr-trumpets from the p-pit of fire will ring out their AAAAAGH!!!victory in every c-corner of the universe! AAAAAGH!!! AAAAAGH!!! AAAAAGH!!!"

I suddenly spewed the eternal flame and falling off the fouled creature I seized the bottle and stumbled onto the balcony...

12

Next morning Purity came to me.

She knocked timidly, then crept in and stood meekly enough before me, looking as unintentionally seductive as always. But she was trembling and had been crying. Then she started to cry again I opened my arms to her and she came into them, her cheek burrowed in beneath my shoulder, my hand gently caressed her smooth warm bottom beneath the short dress as her slim body heaved with her sobs.

"What is the matter, my child?" I asked gently, wiping the tears from her cheek. "Did not the Mother Superior accept you?"

"She said she would be writing to you, sir," she sobbed. "Oh sir, it is not that which troubles me."

She lowered her eyes and looked to the floor. Her hands were round my waist, clutching tightly, and her whole petite figure was trembling as she clung there in her short white dress, making my John Thomas rise at the knowledge of her nakedness beneath. I cannot deny that her innocence and her pixie face was part of what had caused me to welcome her to the privacy of my rooms.

"I am evil!" she gasped, to my total amazement. That throaty little-girl voice again! "I am! I am! I am a wicked girl! I shall burn in hell for my sins!"

"What?"

"To hell!" she suddenly shouted. "My soul will go to eternal hellfire for my lewd wickedness, for I do not wish to join the Mother Superior in her order! No, no longer wish for it! In my mind I failed, in my flesh I am changed now that I have foretaste of carnal knowledge, oh I am changed, I have become wicked and I am glad of it, glad, glad, glad!"

She was sobbing wildly now, her childish face screwed up in some terrible distress. It set my John Thomas further on fire!

"I am unclean!" she said. She had slipped down a little and was clasping me round the knees, her tearful cheek turned to my crotch, the tip of her pink tongue touching those pouting little rosebud lips. "I have indulged in carnal excess! I must be scourged for it, but nobody will cleanse me!"

I licked my lips. "I will do it, my child," I said. I assuredly would! My John Thomas was almost overflowing in anticipation already. "I will do as you desire and save your poor soul from the hellfire that is coming unless you are punished for your wickedness." I paused. "But changing your mind about your calling is surely no great sin. Even the enjoyments of the flesh do not condemn you! Very few are called, but it is not only they that are saved."

"No, no, it is also my step brothers!" she wailed. "I have told no-one before, but you are so kind to me sir!"

"Your step brothers?" I asked. "What of your step brothers?"

"They tempted me, Sir, since I was little, but I resisted, but, oh sir -"

"Yes? Do not distress yourself so, my child."

"They - they - I do not know the word for it sir, they took me the other way -"

"They buggered you?"

83

"If that is the word, sir, they did, I could not prevent it sir."

"And that is what drove you to your chanting and everything?"

"Yes sir. I see now that it was, for I came to permit it in the end. I should have known that I have no true calling, sir, I am naught but a harlot. I came to ask you to inform the Mother Superior, sir, that I cannot come to her."

"You enjoyed what she did to you yesterday?"

"Oh yes sir. And I think I would enjoy to be - to be -"

"To be fucked?"

"Yes sir, to be fucked properly."

"And beaten?"

"Oh yes sir, it has always been my greatest delight to suffer punishment, though I tried to conceal it from myself."

"And buggered?"

"Perhaps, sir. Yes. Perhaps I have acquired a taste for it."

"Very well," I said. "I see that I must investigate all these matters."

"Oh yes, sir!"

What a tasty morsel she was, so delightful in my arms. She had stopped sobbing now, and her eyes sparkled through tear drops, her lips were warm as she stretched up to mine, her tongue an invitation, her flesh smooth and warm beneath my fingers as I eased that skimpy dress up and over her head until it fluttered unwanted to the floor.

She dropped naked to the floor at my feet, and her fingers were at my buttons... I seized her by the hair and dragged her to her feet.

"Fetch me a drink," I said.

She pattered to the cabinet and brought over a bottle of rum, settled me into my seat, and poured me a full glass.

"Master!" she said, and the word was music to my ears.

"What shall you do with me?"

"I shall beat you first," I said.

Her eyes gleamed with excitement as she acknowledged this with an eager little nod.

"Stand in the corner until I am ready." She walked over to the corner. She was very graceful in all her movements, like a neat little elf. "Face me," I commanded, "with your legs apart and your hands upon your head."

I took a sip of the delicious nectar in the glass, to reinforce what I had had before and ease my pounding head a little.

"Stand straighter," I said. "Legs wider! On tiptoe!"

As I rose to my feet, a little unsteadily I think, so great was the force of my anticipation, I set down the glass, which spilled over on its side I seem to remember, and I started to unbuckle my broad leather belt..

EPILOGUE

"An unexpected surprise!" exclaimed Charles when I called upon him. "Your visit is most fortuitous. I was about to write to you today."

We sat on the plush red leather sofas and exchanged simple pleasantries.

"Charles," I said when the opportunity arose, "I have decided not to proceed with the purchase of another plantation."

His face dropped at my words, and he looked at me in distress.

"But Percy, my dear fellow, I have already purchased one for you! It was in part exchange for the larger one."

"Well, you will have to sell it again."

"It is not as easy as that," he said. "The power of the

85

abolitionists is gaining so much influence that not many a business minded person sees a plantation as a viable proposition any more. If I were to sell in haste I fear I would deplete your resources to an unmanageable level."

"So what would you advise?"

"I have purchased the slaves you asked for also - female labour, dear boy, supervision and constant discipline will be required. You must go out and manage it until I can find a purchaser or it will deteriorate and you will loose too much."

So that is what I confronted Cordelia with.

"My dear Percy," said that indomitable woman, "all is not lost. I have always dreamed of being Mistress of a plantation! I shall join you there!"

The next two weeks I began to put my life in order. I frolicked with Julie every morning and became even fonder of her. I used Cordelia's influence to secure the curatorship of the Poorhouse to Beatrice. Cordelia and I spent a few days together in London and it became obvious that she would not be able to wind up her affairs in time for my departure and would have to obtain passage on the next frigate.

Charles sent for me at last and I went to see him.

"Percy my dear fellow, do come in," he exclaimed, inviting me into his library. "So you sail in two day's time."

He produced a list of slaves that had been purchased to my specification. With a few exceptions all were females under nineteen years of age. He then produced another list: "These are the white women being deported to your plantation."

There were ten of them. As I looked down the list I kept a serious and solemn demeanour, but my John Thomas physically shook as I looked at the last two on the list.

"these are in addition to the fifty I have bought to supplement those already there?"

"Yes my dear fellow. Of course if you decide that you have too many you are fully entitled to sell off any you do not require." Then he gave me all the necessary contracts and such, and bade me farewell and wished me a safe and pleasant sailing.

When Cordelia saw the list of deportees she was convulsed. "I know exactly what I'd do with those last two!" she chortled. "Oh Percy, I can't wait to meet them!"

PART TWO: PLANTATION PUNISHMENT - VOODOO

1

I gazed at the distant shore. Instead of edging nearer it seemed to fluctuate back and forth. The journey from London Port had taken four weeks and in the past days as we sailed closer to the Caribbean Island the heat had become almost unbearable. The Captain had said that it was a passing phase due to the time of the season.

Cordelia would join me in about two weeks. I hoped her voyage across the punishing Atlantic would be less severe than mine, and blessed the day that fate had decreed that two people who were devotees of the art of chastisement had been brought together through the administration of a Poor House - that is another matter, with which I will not soil this story: however, I append an account of it at the end for those perverse enough to enjoy such cruelties. Suffice it for now that when she had heard of the type of female slaves that would work on my plantation she immediately agreed to sail once her affairs had been put in order.

Maybe it was fortunate that I would have two weeks to myself with the fifty young African slave girls and the ten white ones who had been sent to the colonies to pay for their crimes in England. Slaves were used to being punished by their lawful master, but I wasn't sure how they would take to a visiting English female aristocrat, and so severe a one at that, for Cordelia was apt to beat girls at the Poor House so sadistically that even I became somewhat unnerved.

The coast line was drawing ever nearer and eventually I bid the Captain farewell and was transported by boat to the deserted landing stage where I was to meet the housekeeper who would take me to my plantation. The arrangement had been for the woman to attend every day with horse and trap, mid-afternoon, because of the uncertainty of the ship's arrival, but when we arrived at the wooden jetty I couldn't see a soul.

As the two sailors began rowing their boat back to the ship, I looked around and wondered if I had been left at the correct landing place. Apart from the dusty track leading from the jetty there was nothing to be seen but thick foliage intermixed with jungle trees.

I sat on my luggage and swatted the interminable insects that seemed to be attracted to the novelty of a European skin and gave no respite. The glowering sun tortured me with its never ending scowl and I began to wonder what would become of me if indeed this was the wrong jetty.

But after only about twenty minutes I heard a distant rumble coming down the track. I stood up and through the dense trees appeared the nodding head of a horse pulling a trap with a colourfully dressed driver.

They suddenly burst through the thick overhanging trees and came to a stop.

"So you've finally arrived sir," said the woman as she jumped down.

She was about twenty-five years of age, of medium height and with short black crinkly hair. Her skin was medium brown and I suspected that there must have been some white blood somewhere in her ancestry. Her features confirmed this, because they were straight and regular and not at all Negroid in appearance. She wore a knee-length baggy dress with short sleeves and her chocolate skin contrasted sharply with the harsh red, yellow and white bands of the material. As she loaded my heavy baggage the strain exposed magnificently shaped breasts and a splendid bottom.

"What's your name, my child?" I asked.

"Barbarella sir," she answered with a cheeky flash of her coal black eyes. "I learned English from the missionaries sir. They've long been gone now."

After she had loaded the last of my luggage she turned to me. "May I just have a quick wash sir, the journey has made me all filthy?"

"Take your time my child," I said as I climbed onto the trap and took a bottle of rum from my bag. I pulled out the cork and drank thirstily, hoping that further refreshment awaited me at the house.

After a few long gulps I looked down to where I assumed she was washing her brow, or wetting her arms and legs - and I nearly choked! She had discarded her dress and stood totally naked in the shallow water with her back to me.

My John Thomas swiftly rose to attention after the long sea journey as I watched her splashing water onto her firm brown shoulders. The long drips fell down her curvy muscular back and danced off her round bottom cheeks. She appeared to be totally unconcerned as she bent forward to wash her face, and inadvertently pushed her bottom out, straining her shapely thighs with slight tremors. Then she reached back with both hands to wash and wet those generous cheeks and with the occasional pull exposed her light brown anus and pink cunnie.

Then she turned round, picked up her dress and slipped it over her wet body.

My mind reeled at the quick glimpse of her goodly bosom and the curves of her broad womanly hips. I detected a faint black down covering her cunnie, but it was almost hidden by the shadows from the sun behind her.

Totally unconcerned, she climbed onto the trap next to me, clipped the old horse with the reins and turned it round for the return journey.

As we travelled along the bumpy track my thoughts, after the long sea journey, were concentrated on the lewd naked exhibition I had just seen. She sensed that I was deep in thought and suddenly remarked "I hope I didn't embarrass you sir but here on the plantation we aren't that concerned with nakedness. You'll find that most of the girls in the field don't bother that much with clothing, especially because you don't have any male slaves."

My John Thomas shook in expectation, and I decided to question her further.

"How did you find yourself on the plantation, Barbarella?"

"I was brought here as a young slave girl sir and after a few years the previous master put me in charge of the house when his old housekeeper died."

"What sort of man was he?"

"Oh sir, he was very old and, er, tired." She hesitated. "When he left, he told me to look after the house until a new owner would be found for the plantation and all its slaves. He had grown very slack and over the past two months the girls have grown lazy and even insolent."

My head swam suddenly with the many possibilities I would have in setting the girls to work. I half wished that I had Cordelia by my side. She would surely relish such an interesting start to her first experience of a plantation.

As we travelled along the dusty path, the overhanging trees jostled and hit our heads with their flaying foliage and every so often we had to duck sharply to avoid being hit. The bumpy trap together with Barbarella's constant bending drew my eyes to her low cut dress, which exposed more and more of her naked bouncing breasts. I remembered her description of the previous master as old and tired and wondered if her lubricity and obvious passion had manifested itself in her lewd exposure at the edge of the sea.

The sun was rapidly sinking now, and eventually, after a seemingly interminable length of time, we approached the plantation in near darkness. She pointed out the two large canefields where the slaves worked and the long row of huts where they slept. At last we turned the path past the fields that led to the house.

Barbarella said that she would stable the horse, then bring my luggage upstairs.

The house was typically colonial with large white pillars fronting the entrance. Its medium two-story size befitted the modest dimensions of the plantation. The whole building was slightly dilapidated, but in its day, with the grand structure of its white stone walls and tall windows, it would probably have impressed.

I walked through the imposing entrance and was immediately stirred by the rather magnificent drawing room. It was large and had an abundance of leather sofas, rich mahogany cabinets against each wall, and the wooden floor was strewn with Chinese and Persian carpets. The back of the room held a dignified looking library, separated in the middle by a single door.

There was a large kitchen with a huge table against one side, above which hung numerous pots and pans.

By the entrance to the kitchen another door led upstairs. There I found a grand bedroom with a large balcony that opened to the full width of the front of the house. Another room behind the bedroom housed the washing facilities, and a further couple of store rooms which had been changed into sleeping quarters.

I came back downstairs to find Barbarella. She had just carried my baggage in through the front door.

"Can I get you some refreshment sir?" she asked.

"Thank you," I replied, and tested out one of the leather sofas. She poured me a large rum, then carried my luggage up to the bedroom. When she came back down she poured herself a rum and sat down.

"What is the meaning of this behaviour?" I barked.

She looked at me in shock, and recoiled.

"How dare you act and behave as if you are a lady of the house, when in fact your station is the same as the other girls on this plantation!"

It was obvious to me that the blame for the lax conduct of the slaves which she had mentioned belonged not only to the disinterest of the previous owner but also to her.

"I will not tolerate this slovenly attitude," I exclaimed sternly, standing up.

She was very shaken and accidentally dropped the glass on the table.

"Your place is in the kitchen and only if you are invited to sit and take refreshment will you do so."

She suddenly stood up and shook visibly. It was quite a contrast to her lewd naked display with her haughty teasing manner and the way she had spoken to me on the journey to the house as if she had been a friendly cousin that I hadn't seen for a long time.

"Bend over!" I thundered.

It was a defining moment! The last thing I wanted was to have to try to subdue her physically.

But, thank God, she hardly hesitated before padding over to the sofa I was pointing to. Then, with a frightened glance over her shoulder, she bent over with a supple movement and laid her body over the top so that her hands rested on the soft cushion and her rump and legs fell off the back. I went over to her, grabbed the hem of her dress, and with one move I flung it up over her waist so that it fell onto her trembling shoulders and covered her head.

My head started to pound as I stared at the lush brown cheeks that spread out before me, and the muscular thighs that strained to keep her toes balanced on the floor.

Without warning I began to slap her twitching bottom. It obviously knew what to expect, and that encouraged me.

"You belong to me," I said. Smack! Smack! "I shall beat you" Smack! Smack! "or take you" Smack! Smack! "whenever it suits me to do so."

"Yes sir," came a whisper from under the dress that covered her head, and she started to whimper. I took another refresher from the rum and she waited there, naked from the waist down, until I was ready.

Smack!
Smack!
Smack!

I went to my task with zeal, and she started to gasp and moan as my hand alternated from cheek to cheek. After a few minutes I bent down and took one of her slippers from her feet.

Crack!
Crack!
Crack!

The leather sole loudly resounded around the room as I increased the strength of my blows onto the brown springy flesh. As her arse started to vibrate and buck from the pain, I grabbed her left orb in my hand and concentrated on her right. Whacking at her flesh, I gently pulled the cheek to

93

one side.

I had had opportunity to inspect and delight in the secret sanctuaries of many a whore, but never had I seen so large an opening to an anus. As I belted her arse, even though I held her cheek fully outstretched and pulling her anal ring to one side, I was stunned to see that the muscles of her entrance still had the elasticity and strength to expand and dilate it of its own accord. I released her cheek whilst still belting the right orb and slowly inserted my fingers into her muscular anal opening.

My John Thomas jerked noticeably and my head pounded with a new ferocity as suddenly the inner walls of her greasy tube started to flex and squeeze against my fingers, compressing and contracting against its newly caught prey. As I pushed in to the knuckles, the pressure of her squeezing muscles increased to such an extent that my John Thomas felt as if it would break free and go on the rampage with a life of its own. I quickly released it from the tight restriction of my trousers and, still belting her lush brown cheek, I pushed half of my ten inches into the enticing entrance.

Immediately the pressure re-started, squeezing and squashing against my hardness. My head pounded ferociously as I slowly shoved in the remainder of my cock, then began to belt her twin cheeks with a new vigour as I stood embedded within her and allowed the pressure of her squelchy clamping compressions to milk and squeeze my rock hard weapon.

The sensations were unusually intoxicating. It felt like a wet soft hand pumping and siphoning its trapped fruit. Unable to withstand the maddening milking, I threw down the slipper, grabbed her slippery writhing bottom and started to thrust and stab to the sound of her loud moans. After a few minutes of vigorous deep pounding she suddenly screamed and I finally spewed the elixir of life into her hungry chasm!

When I withdrew she immediately burst into a flood of tears, picked up her slipper, and ran into the kitchen. The wanton hussy had been taught her first lesson in subservience and I doubted if in future she would look to me as if I was a friendly cousin!

But I was determined to make sure.

"Barbarella!" I shouted.

She came out apprehensively. "That dress is dirty," I said. "Take it off!"

When she had done so and cast it aside, I walked round her, examining her closely. She was a magnificent specimen of succulent womanhood and would suit me well, fore as well as aft, and for beating sessions also.

"Go upstairs," I said, "and fetch one of my shirts."

When she brought it down I told her to put it on. When she had done so, I made her walk up and down before me. She looked delightful in it.

"Hold your hands above your head," I said, "and walk around."

That was excellent. It now came nicely to just above her swaying hips.

"In future," I said, "that is what you will wear in this house."

"Yes sir," she said meekly.

"And," I said, "you will stand very straight at all times, and hold your hands above your head when I you are not using them and I am present."

She straightened up even further, although her posture was, in actual fact, excellent already, and stretched her hands up into the air, watching me all time in fright.

"Otherwise," I said sternly, "I shall beat you."

"Yes sir."

"Very well," I said. It was a little victory won. I went upstairs with the bottle of rum and sat on the balcony. Four weeks of starvation had been released in a few short minutes of torrential lust and I made up my mind to explore her obvious talents again very soon.

Suddenly a distant noise similar to a beating drum broke my thoughts. I stood up on the dark balcony and looked out in the direction of the abominable booming. It seemed to come from the distant wooden huts that housed my slave girls. As suddenly as it had started it abruptly stopped. The only sound that remained was the incessant low croaking of the numerous demonic frogs.

I went back into my bedroom, turned up the oil lamp and began to unpack my luggage. The wall cupboards were soon full of the usual paraphernalia that a gentleman needed for a life on a plantation and I saved the last cupboard for my collection of instruments necessary for instilling obedience on unruly buttocks. The collection housed a number of whips of differing lengths, a few paddles and bats and an assortment of masks, leather restraining bands and other peculiarities.

After I had finished I poured another rum and sat on the balcony. I glanced at my silver pocket watch. The hands were approaching eight-o'clock.

I decided to have an early night, but before retiring I picked up the lists showing the types of slaves that had been bought with my instructions. The first list indicated fifty African girls. The second list comprised ten white girls who had chosen a life of slavery as opposed to the death penalty in England, or at least a lengthy prison sentence.

Mary Stokes, age 20 - Wilful murder of husband.

Jane O'Reilly, age 19 - Child murder.

Annie Banks, age 21 - Arson endangering life and limb.

Susie Watts, age 18 - Lewd behaviour with a Minister of the Crown.

Betty Trimble, age 18 - Persistent absconder from the Poor House.

Elizabeth Pendle, age 19 - Blackmailer of Church Minister.

Rosie Siddal, age 20 - Treason.

Pauline Dench, age 19 - Wilful murder of husband.

Sissy Smith, age 18 - Incurable nymphomania.

Patsy Edford, age 18 - Untreatable lascivious perversion.

The Caribbean agents had been instructed to purchase only young slave wenches and the additional ten white girls that the agents had provided were an additional bonus - because of a recent act of Parliament any new purchaser of a slave plantation was forced of necessity to undertake acceptance of white women.

As I glanced down the list - and especially the last two! - my mind pounded relentlessly with imaginations and possibilities.

When I finally retired to bed I was impatient of the new day.

2

I awoke at five in the morning with the already warm breeze wafting from the open balcony over my brow. I quickly dressed, poured a glass of sweet nectar and stepped onto the balcony.

In front of the house was a grassy stretch of open land of about five hundred feet in length and sixty feet wide.

On both sides the thick foliage of the jungle reached back almost to the edges of the house. Beyond the open land, a fence partitioned the plantation of tall sugar canes that were so thickly interwoven as to give an impression of a vast sea of impenetrable greenery. On the left of the sugar canes I was just able to detect a long row of dirty huts that were the slave's sleeping quarters.

I wiped my brow, stepped into the bedroom and poured a further refreshing rum and then went downstairs to the kitchen.

Barbarella greeted me with a surprisingly cheerful smile, considering that she was wearing only a shirt and was holding her hands over her head so that it rode above her hips.

"Tiptoes!" I ordered.

It was a distinct improvement, and her ready obedience was pleasing. She really looked very erotic like that and I congratulated myself on my good imagination.

"Will you have breakfast in the kitchen or the drawing room sir?"

I indicated the drawing room, and shortly she placed ham and eggs on a table. Then with a mischievous glance she went back into the kitchen. As she left, I watched her swaying cheeky bottom that held such an unusual talent. Her morning demeanour gave no indication of what had transpired the previous evening and I assumed that she must have welcomed the lewd intrusion.

When I finished eating I took the tray back into the kitchen.

"Where do you sleep?" I asked. "Is it in the huts by the sugar canes?"

"Oh no sir," she replied. "The old master allowed me to use one of the huts next to the stables behind the house in case anybody would try to steal one of the horses."

"How many horses do we have?"

"The old one that pulls the trap and two others sir."

A noise at the front door interrupted our conversation.

"That must be Justine sir. She is the overseer."

I went back into the drawing room and looked at the newly arrived woman.

"Justine, I presume?"

"Yes sir," she replied. "I am pleased to meet you."

98

"I am the new owner, Mr Ashton. Take a seat and tell me your duties."

As she sat down I went over to a cabinet and poured myself a rum. She looked to be about forty years of age with short crinkly hair that showed the first signs of greying above her temples. Her face was quite plump and jolly with jet black skin and typically negroid features. She was taller than Barbarella and wore a grey dress that fell to her knees. I was slightly taken aback by the coiled whip that hung from her brown belt.

"Do you find the need to use that very often?" I asked as I sat down opposite her.

"No sir, not really, all the slave girls are young and strong and do their work well."

"When was the last time you had to use it?"

"Er... two days ago, sir."

"In future, if any girl is slovenly in her work I will take care of the punishment myself. Is that clear?"

"Yes sir," she nodded meekly.

"You must not hesitate to send them for punishment. Indeed, it would be well to make an example soon, as a warning to the others. I will not let you down on discipline, you may be sure of that."

"Thank you sir," she said, and appeared to appreciate my help.

She went on to tell me that she had been on the plantation serving different masters for about twenty years. She only had the need to administer the whip on rare occasions, because the past two masters had introduced a system of reward where groups of five girls worked together in competition with the rest and at the end of the month the most industrious group were given two days off with as much rum as they wanted and ten shillings which they were allowed to put by towards eventually buying their freedom.

"How long would the girls need to save if their group

were to attain the prize every month?"

She thought for a moment, then started counting on her fingers. "About six years."

"I will increase the sum to ten pounds!"

Her eyes suddenly widened and her mouth dropped in astonishment.

"Justine," I said, "I believe in fairness in dealing with my fellow human beings. I think it is only right and proper to give the girls some light at the end of the tunnel."

I sent her into the kitchen for her breakfast, then went upstairs, poured myself a rum, and sat on the sunny balcony, considering life with a certain contentment. The paltry sum of ten pounds was only a minute percentage of my monthly profit. I had learnt from the experience of my first plantation - that too is another story, but in this case I must ask you to wait, as it might be over strong - that incentive not only produced a stable efficient work force but also opened up various other possibilities. Any slave can raped, of course, and doubtless many would be, but sometimes to be seduced with ardent passion makes a pleasant change.

No time like the present for planting rumours. I hastened downstairs and found Justine just leaving the kitchen.

"A moment before you go."

I poured her a rum and spoke to her of other duties that were her responsibility. As she opened up and seemingly established a friendly rapport towards me, I steered the conversation round to the solitude of my position as a plantation owner. I mentioned a few examples of previous plantation owners that I knew in London, who had successfully taken kindly to a young girl and eventually married and settled happily. When I finally asked her if she thought I might have the same good fortune here she replied with enthusiasm, saying that any girl would give their right arm to find themselves chosen by so kind a master. I had sown the seed successfully, then, and sent her on her way with the news that I would conduct my first inspection in two hours. Then I returned upstairs and sat on the balcony with a rewarding rum as I watched her scurry off towards the cane fields.

As I took my first steps into the sweltering heat to commence my inspection the sky was totally cloudless, and after only a few yards I developed a moist sweat upon my brow and wondered how the slaves managed to tolerate such a fierce temperature. I walked along the perimeter of the open field and after a few minutes entered the gate into the sugar canes. I made a note that next time I must bring a long cutting blade, because the density of the canes meant that I had difficulty in picking my way through. After a few yards I came to a part of the field that wasn't so concentrated and suddenly detected voices and the sounds of swishing blades.

A few steps further and I numbed momentarily, rooted to the spot!

Three young black slaves, naked to the waist and wearing short grey skirts, flounced their arms back and forth as their long blades cut at the tall cane. All three briefly turned to look at me, then with cheeky grins continued to work whilst my eyes feasted on their firm bouncing breasts and sweaty backs. After four weeks on the ocean it was a most welcome sight and my John Thomas responded to the sight of their supple semi-nakedness.

I eventually tore myself away and was sure I felt their eyes following me. I picked my way through another section, then I heard a humming sound to the accompaniment of a swishing blade. The noise grew louder, until finally I pushed my way through a shield of cane and stepped into a small clearing.

I froze immediately as I saw before me a totally naked woman with her magnificent back to me busily cutting cane.

She was extremely well built and I watched her glorious black arse as it shuddered and shook with the exertion of her flaying arms.

She suddenly sensed my presence, turned to face me and said, "Oh, good mornin' Bwana." She looked directly at me and took the opportunity to wipe the dripping sweat from her splendid bosom, which matched her strong frame.

My John Thomas throbbed madly as I watched her lewdly squeeze her heavy breasts. Then she picked up a dirty cloth and said, "Bwana could I's ask yus to wipe me back?"

I took the cloth from her hand and she immediately turned and bent forward. I started to dry her shoulders, but my eyes were fixed on her shiny black bottom that trembled slightly. I transferred the cloth to my right hand and with my left slowly moved down her hot sticky flesh until the palm of my hand felt the heat from her straining anal orifice.

Still wiping her back, I carefully pushed three fingers into the steaming wet tightness. When I eased them further in, up to my knuckles, she slowly began to move her arse backwards and forwards and I responded by frigging her wet bum hole with faster sturdier movements.

A sudden noise of a blade cutting cane made me withdraw and I left the lusty wench and walked on into the cover of a large patch of cane. I stopped after a minute to recover my breath. I couldn't believe what had just happened - if I hadn't been disturbed, I could have taken the wench where she stood!

After I regained some composure, I decided to proceed further. Forcing my way through the inflexible close knit bushes, I eventually stumbled onto a pathway than ran along the outside of the cane field. After a minute, the sound of chattering mixed with giggles tempted me back into the canes and I stumbled upon a clearing where the recently cut cane was piled onto a low waggon.

Again I froze with my head pounding like a drum as I found three young black naked slaves cutting cane. They looked no more than seventeen or eighteen years of age. They acknowledged my presence with furtive cheeky smiles then continued to work as I stared at their slim sinewy backs, lithe waists and solid little bottoms. They swung their blades to the left and right, totally unembarrassed at my lecherous piercing gaze.

My John Thomas raged painfully as I tore myself away, encouraged by the constantly increasing lewd discoveries.

After a couple of minutes more progress I heard European voices and broke through a wall of cane to find two white girls of about eighteen years of age. They worked naked to the waist, exposing white bouncy bosoms. Both had shoulder length scraggly blonde hair that contrasted against their dirty grey skirts.

"G'mornin' sir," they both suddenly called out, glancing over their shoulders. As I watched them working away, one of the girls placed her blade on the ground then stretched her arms out and complained to her friend of the heat. I stared dumbfounded when with a muffled giggle from the other she began to undo the buttons of her waistband and then pulled her skirt off, picked up her blade and began cutting cane totally naked!

I watched her firm breasts bouncing up and down in rhythm to her trembling large fleshy rump, then finally tore myself away.

Four weeks of absence from the pleasures of the flesh had sent my mind into a spinning turmoil, but I knew I had to restrain myself and choose my time.

After a minute I came across another black slave. She stood alone and attacked the cane as if possessed by some abominable demon. As I stared at her massive naked frame, I instinctively dropped my hand to my belt and realised I had forgotten my pistol. I stood and watched her flay the cane with hulking shoulders that rippled and shook in unison with her muscle decked bottom and powerful legs.

I eventually tore myself away from the intoxicating spectacle and decided to return to the house for refreshment. Maybe later, after the demise of the midday sun, I would attempt another inspection, but this time on a horse and with my pistol.

As I entered the house I heard the clatter of pots and pans from the kitchen and went upstairs. I pulled another bottle of rum from the cabinet and sat on the cool balcony. I drank the first glass straight down to quench my thirst from the intolerable heat of the day.

3

A sudden noise downstairs roused me from my slumber. I looked at my pocket watch. Two thirty p.m. The obnoxious heat of the day had felled the constitution of an English steadfastness and I got off the whicker chair and poured a rejuvenating glass of nectar.

I went downstairs to find Justine, with a white slave girl.

"What is the meaning of this intrusion?" I barked. "Shouldn't you both be at work?"

"I'm sorry sir," Justine replied, "but when Patsy found out that a new master had taken over, she pestered me all morning to be allowed to see you on a private matter."

I looked at the scruffy girl who stood meekly beside Justine panting visibly, lifting her chest up and down.

"Very well," I said with seeming reluctance. "I have a spare half an hour. I'll see to the girl, Justine, you may return to the others. Come on, girl, up the stairs."

"Ooh its y'bedroom sir!" she gasped as we entered.

"Yes, its cooler here," I said. I told her to sit on the sofa across from the bed and went to the cabinet to pour myself a rum. I then instinctively decided to give her one as well.

"Justine says we aint allowed sir." She recoiled blushing as I held out the drink.

"That's alright," I answered. "You have my permission."

As she took the drink into her grubby hand I looked closely at her. She seemed very young and could not have been more than five foot two or three. Her short blonde hair, matted with sweat, fell about her freckled face in short yellow strings. Her large ears protruded through the lanky strands and her two front buck teeth flashed gawkily as she slurped from the glass. Her dirty flowery dress hung loosely from naked shoulders and exposed all of her freckled arms.

I came away from the common looking wench and walked over to my lists on the cabinet. When I checked the reason for her punishment in the colonies, I choked on my drink and my John Thomas instantly began to throb. She was the 'untreatable lascivious perversion'.

I sat opposite her. "What can I do for you my child?"

"When I 'eard the old master 'ad gone, I knew I had t'see you sir," she gulped. "I should never 'ave been sent 'ere, sir, I've done nothing wrong."

"Then how did it happen?"

"I was in th'employment of a gen'leman called Sir Waldegrave, a magistrate sir."

I gagged on my drink. I instantly recognised the name of a rake and usurer I had had dealings with before my departure from London, but I couldn't believe that fate would deal such a coincidence.

I remembered how the devious hypocrite had found an excuse to come to the Poor House then in my charge and blackmailed me into letting him chastise one of my inmates on the pretence of protecting my good name and the reputation of the institution. He had thoroughly belted and taken advantage of the girl, and I should be the only one to do that!

"'E came to the poor 'ouse an told th'mistress 'e was lookin' fer a kitchen girl, an 'e chose me straight away and took me home with him."

"And what happened then, Patsy?" I prompted.

"After two days I broke a plate and 'e pushed me over his knee and belted me bare bum."

"Carry on, Patsy. I'm listening."

"Well sir, first time it 'urt, but when 'e did it two days later, well it wasn't so bad. I was surprised it didn't 'urt as much as afore."

"So what is the problem, my child?" I was trying to keep a solemn demeanour.

"Well sir, after a while 'e did it more'n'more regular 'an after a while I didn't mind it at all! In fact, sir, it ended he was doin' it nearly ev'ry day!"

My John Thomas was beginning to feel painfully uncomfortable and I stood up and refilled our glasses. When I sat down she continued. "One day, sir, 'e told me that because every time he punished me 'e was tearing my dress, I must take it off when he punished me." She looked at me with a straight face as I tried to hide my discomfort. "I didn't mind sir, I told him!" she suddenly burst out.

"How do you mean my child?"

"I told him sir, I told him 'twas alright 'cause its costing 'im money."

My John Thomas throbbed painfully and my head reeled at the way she spurted out the last few words in total innocence.

"I suppose sir," she continued, "after a while I suspected that 'e might be taking a bit of an advantage, but you know sir 'is wife died recent and I thought to myself its not doing any harm to anybody is it?"

Again I nearly choked at the words of the stupid wench who spoke innocently and with obvious sincerity. She gulped her drink and I quickly poured her another.

"You see sir 'e was only an old man and 'e gave me a job and everything and I thought to myself its only harmless fun it's not as if he's trying to give me a little brat or something is it sir?"

I nodded in agreement, paralysed with lust.

"I know that from time to time 'is fingers might 'ave slipped into... you know where sir... but I just ignored it 'cause I'm sure 'e didn't mean it."

I listened with a determined steel-willed composure, and if it hadn't been for the supporting backbone of the rum I would have fallen on the wench then and there!

"One day e' come back an said 's taken a fall from 'is 'orse. 'E said the top of his legs are painful and could I rub 'em with the lotion 'is doctor gave 'im, so 'e put on 'is dressing gown 'an asked me if I'd be embarrassed and I said no and 'e gave me the lotion an showed me where 'e wanted it put. 'E pulled open his gown -" She placed both hands over her mouth and eventually managed to suppress her giggles.

"I couldn't believe it! It was all long and soft like a sausage! The only ones I'd seen afore was my little brothers an his friends. I didn't believe a grown man had such a long one. Anyway sir 'e got me to rub in the lotion by side of 'is thingy, on both sides, and slowly -"

Again she clamped her mouth.

"It got bigger and bigger and bigger!"

She fell back against the sofa and burst into peals of laughter. While she shook from side to side, I quickly poured myself a drink. After a few moments she calmed herself and hoisted her quivering body to the edge of the sofa.

"Well sir, then 'e asked me to put some lotion on 'is - on 'is thingy, you know sir, and I thought it can't do any harm with an old man, but I had to use two hands sir, it were such a monster!"

I realised that I had lost all purpose of the conversation. But the wench had me totally enthralled and I told her to continue.

"Well sir -" she spoke sitting on the edge of the sofa and leaning towards me - "- after I had rubbed it up an down a bit 'e told me I'd been a good girl and just like you kiss a babe sweet dreams after you've sung to him, could I kiss his thingy good night."

I choked on the rum, thinking that I'd heard everything, but unbelievably the scurrilous demented whore wouldn't stop. I wiped my eyes to make sure I had full clarity, not believing her innocent demeanour.

"Well sir what 'e said were quite true. Every time I sung my brother to sleep or when I rubbed his little hand after he had a fall, I always kissed him better. So I saw nothing wrong and kissed his plum. 'E sort of gave me 'ead a little push and it just seemed sorta natural, so then I took 'im proper like, in my mouth you see and just let 'im use my head like a little toy."

I stood up again and stepped onto the balcony. After a minute, when I had recovered from the fire that had threatened my sanity with a sudden demonic fiery combustion, I returned, sat down and poured myself a cleansing elixir.

"Well sir," she continued, "after that 'e wanted me to do the same thing to his friend who would be visiting the following day -"

She went on to explain that she didn't really mind helping out Waldegrave, but when she had refused his friend he dragged her into a court of law on a trumped up charge and had her sent to the colonies and maybe I could help her out?

The now drunken dimwit girl was sprawled against the back of the sofa. She looked mischievously at me, then slowly raised her left leg and placed her foot on the edge. Her dress fell down and exposed the whole of her thighs. Then she slowly lifted the half finished glass to her lips and amazingly started to sway her naked fleshy leg from side to side, exposing the whole of her open cunnie lips on every outward swing.

When she finished the rum she rested her thigh against the arm of the sofa, opened her legs wide, displaying her moist cunnie, and whispered: "If you could help me out sir I'd be ever so grateful if you know what I mean..."

She set down her glass, pulled herself to her feet and turned her back to me, whilst giggling cheekily. Then she bent forward and grabbed the hem of her dress and unhurriedly pulled it up, inch by slow inch, up her thighs and over her naked bottom.

Finally she slipped it off completely!

My head pounded like a drum as I stared at her smooth round shoulders, her curvy back, her puppy-fat waist, then the broad sweep of her hips and fleshy cheeks.

She stood naked for what seemed like minutes, glorying in the exposure of her lewd nakedness, then with a quick giggle knelt on the seat of the sofa and pushed her splendid arse up and wriggled it in the air.

My head felt as if it was about to explode and I immediately got up and started to spank the obscene wench!

Smack!

Smack!

Smack!

I alternated from one bum cheek to the next as my hand bounced off the warm springy flesh. After a minute she began to respond to every stinging blow.

Crack! Wha!

Crack! Whee!

Crack! Phwee!

When I speeded up, her voice started to blurt in rasps.

"Ye-ye-yeah! More! Harder!"

I continued smacking her right cheek and my other hand dived into her left fleshy balloon. I began to twist and turn clumps of her bottom into distorted shapes. I pulled, squeezed and bent the puppy fat flesh into every contortion imaginable.

"Oh yes sir!" she moaned in short stabbing gasps. "Use it, do it, oh yeah, stretch it, twist it, do it!"

Quickly releasing my bloated ten inch cock, I brutally speared her anal ringlet with a mighty lunge up to the hilt.

"Wheeeeee!!" she screamed

The dimwit hussy had teased and cajoled me for far too long and I was determined to extract revenge. I began to plough and plunder with long demanding stabs. I jabbed, butted, rammed, lunged and skewered her pestilent chasm.

Finally she gave a long torturous scream and I cleansed her secret sanctuary with a vengeful fire. Then I pulled off her shaking body and buttoned myself up. She wallowed on the sofa, moaning and groaning then finally got up, pulled her dress back on, and gulped the rum I had poured her

"You will help me out, won't you sir?" she asked.

"Yes my child, when the next ship delivers the mail from London I shall send a letter about you. Now, back to work with you."

She gulped the remainder of the drink and skipped out of the room. I went to sit in the cool breeze on the balcony.

The dimwitted girl had unknowingly provided me with ammunition I could use against the conniving rake Waldegrave. I now had a witness who could easily be persuaded to testify against him, if upon my return to England he should attempt his devious blackmail against me. Upon the sale of the plantation I would take her with me and put her in my employment in case I needed her.

The other charms that she had so willingly provided

would also be most useful...

I drank more rum, well satisfied with the promising start to my first full day on the plantation.

4

A sudden torrential tropical storm awoke me. Where the hell was I? I glanced at my pocket watch - nine p.m. I reached for my glass, but it was empty as was the bottle. Damn, I thought, this unbearable heat seems to provoke endless sloth!

I wandered downstairs into the kitchen, where Barbarella was preparing some cold meats. She worked away at the kitchen table in silence with her back to me.

Her shoulders were shaking!

"What's the matter child?" I asked.

"You've t-taken over the p-plantation at a b-bad time sir," she stuttered. She stood in my short shirt facing the kitchen table, and now she put down some implement she had been using and raised her hands as I had commanded. Suddenly she turned to face me and blurted out: "It is said that in two weeks Exu will appear in these parts."

"Who the hell is Exu?"

She looked at me with trembling lips. "Oh sir, he is the voodoo Satan of Quimbanda," she whispered.

"Oh, no, Barbarella!" I laughed. "Not voodoo! You're a civilised woman brought up my missionaries!"

"I'm not so sure sir. Every year around this time strange things happen."

"What strange things?"

She looked at me, frightened. "If I tell a great evil might fall upon me," she whispered, and there was terror in her tone now.

111

"Don't be stupid!" I said angrily. "Go upstairs and fetch the belt that is on the chair beside my bed."

When she brought it to me I swished it through the air. "Now," I said, "bend over and take hold of your ankles. Be careful to keep your legs straight and your feet well apart."

It was an erotic sight but my mind was not really in it, for this talk of demons was disturbing. I just gave her a few half-hearted swipes to prove that I could do so whenever I wished and drew no more than a gasp or two from her.

"You may wear the belt," I said, "so that it is always to hand."

Then I left the stupid wench to her superstitious beliefs and took my supper tray and a fresh bottle upstairs. I poured a refreshingly large tot and sat on the balcony shielded from the worst of the storm.

Suddenly it stopped and after a further couple of flashes of lightening, silence fell over the plantation. As I drank, the cacophony of croaking frogs began again until it pervaded every corner of the house.

As I listened to the abominable croaks and cackles of the demons of the night, the humid air which had been still as a graveyard unexpectedly began to rustle the nearby jungle trees and suddenly the black thundery clouds lifted to expose a huge yellow moon. I drank the sweet nectar that seemed to be my only sanctuary in this dark god-forsaken place and then, somewhere in the distance, I heard the unearthly booming that I had heard briefly the previous evening.

I stood up and looked into the night. All I could see through the blackness were the faint flickers of the oil lamps dancing through the open windows of the slave huts. As I strained my ears trying to detect from which direction the booming noise came, it stopped suddenly, as if someone had chopped it off. I sat back down, drank more rum, and decided that it was probably only a harmless innocent noise

112

that always seemed to permeate out of jungle's still inhabited by grotesque nocturnal beasts.

On impulse I decided to go downstairs to the library and check on the books that the previous owner had left. When I came to the bottom of the stairs all was quiet in the kitchen and I presumed that Barbarella had gone to her hut. I must make her sleep in the house, I thought, so that she was always to hand when needed. Maybe I would let her sleep on the floor by my bed: I had often thought that a slave girl there would be useful at times.

I flicked my fingers along the many volumes of wisdom, the various encyclopedias and the travels of cultured men, until at the very end of the shelf I came across a torn dirty book entitled 'The Curse of Voodoo'.

I went upstairs with it and pulled out a fresh bottle and settled on the comfortable sofa on the balcony. The first page said 'Translations from the Yoruba language of West Africa' and continued:

'It is said that when the European calendar holds within it three 8s, then the God Exu will appear to find a wife who will cleanse him of his evil, but before she does so she must sate his hunger of the earthly flesh. She will not know his desire until he appears. He will be known by his three horns and by his half black and half white body, signifying darkness and light. His appearance will be preceded by the 30 loa or lesser gods over 30 years and only if they advise him the time is befitting will he come.

Otherwise the the 30 year cycle will start again.'

I drank from my glass and wondered how many of the slave wenches believed in this abominable sorcery. The three 8s in the date jumped out at me suddenly. It was mid July. It was with quite a shock that I realised that in two weeks it would be the eight day of the eighth month of the year of

Our Lord eighteen-oh-two!

I was actually frightened for a moment, my hairs stood up, then I laughed to myself at my stupid reaction to this mumbo-jumbo and poured myself another rum. The unearthly night with the endless chorus from the frogs and the thunderstorm seemed to have taken their toll on my sanity.

I sat back on the balcony and continued to read:

'The preceding weeks before the evil god Exu appears will be signified by one or all of three earthly apparitions that will come by night: these are the loup-garu (werewolves), the vampires (red-eyed demons on human form), and the zombies (walking dead). The period before his appearance will also be known by the letting of the blood of the sacrificial white chicken and the emergence of black pigs whose forms will have been taken over by the spirits of dead black magicians.'

I slammed the damnable book shut and picked up my rum. The demonic night with its croaking frogs and the disquiet of the tropical wind had finally taken its full toll. I stood up and stared towards the black-hearted distant canes and the ungodly flickering light from the slave huts.

Suddenly the low incessant drum beat radiated out from the black night with all the malevolence of the scurrilous prophesy I had just read. Then, as before, as abruptly as it had started it ceased.

I poured another protecting glass and decided to banish the omens of doom once and for all. I took out my faithful pistol and attached it to my waist. From the cabinet I withdrew a long black whip, curled it and pushed the trusty servant into my belt. Finishing the rum, I felt confident in my armoury against the vilest of two-legged monstrosities that might cross my path.

I went downstairs into the oil-lit shadows of the huge drawing room. It threw out ghostly silhouettes like a cold blasphemous catacomb. Finally I stepped out into the moon-lit night.

Instinctively, I unholstered my pistol and placed my right hand over the handle. As I walked through the grassy field, turning left towards the boundary path that led to the huts, I soon became enveloped in pitch blackness. The only indications of my direction were the eerie pricks of light from insects that danced around the curtain of the beginnings of the jungle. Underneath I could just about make out the long snaking grey path. The noise from the frogs and the other nocturnal demonic creatures seemed to gradually pale into the distance with every searching forward step. It was as if they knew that I was too big a prey for them and had decided to leave my soul to be devoured by a more sinister predator.

I finally reached the safety of the path only to find that all the fiendish eyes had deserted me into the dark womb of the jungle. The only lights that beckoned me onwards now were the shadowy dancing glints that fell out of the distant slave huts. The full moon played out its own game of deceit as it hid its ghostly face in and out of black clouds.

I stood still for a second and turned back to look at the dimly lit house that seemed like a distant speck of light on a dark ocean and suddenly realised that all around me was deathly quiet! Not a sound or a moan could be heard from the multitude of inhabitants of the night.

Then suddenly it started again, that deathly far-away booming!

I listened for a few moments, half expecting the first onslaught of the loup-garu, and as soon as it did the multitude of frogs and other abominations began again to spew out their incessant croaks and moans.

I decided to complete my journey as the huts were only

about a hundred feet or so away.

As I picked my way along the path, a sudden rustling noise came from behind the jungle trees. I stood deathly still as it grew louder and louder and suddenly three black pigs jumped out of the thick foliage like bats out of hell! As they screeched past me I managed to kick the last one. It ran off with a demonic squeal, snaking its ugly little fat body from side to side. They may have housed the souls of long dead black magicians but it sounded to me more like a hog in pain than a malevolent spirit, which cheered me up somewhat.

Eventually I came closer to the huts and wondered what I would find. The low timber shacks, according to Barbarella, were each divided into three rooms. As I came to the first, I could tell that there must be about twenty shacks stretching into the distance.

As I picked my way through the blackness I stood on a twig and awoke two white chickens that fluttered in panic into the air, then fell into the cover of the foliage.

The light from the first hut beckoned to me and I slowly stepped up to the windowless frame. I became suddenly transfixed at the incredulous sight that met my disbelieving eyes!

Three young black slaves, totally naked, sat in a circle on a dirty brown carpet. Each one held a phallic shaped black instrument of some twelve inches in length in their mouth and they each pushed and pulled the monstrosities in and out!

My John Thomas instantly reared up at this lewd exhibition of self debasement. Were they practising some strange ritual? Or was it a voodoo rite? I watched as suddenly one of them reached over to her friend, grabbed the end of her instrument with one hand and began to push it forcibly in and out of her gagging mouth...

A sudden noise caused them to hesitate and I backed

away. I moved along the path past the next dark huts until I came to another dimly lit shack. Peering through, I was astonished to see a young black slave lying naked on her back with her feet held high in the air. She had a similar instrument to the first three, and jabbed it deeply into her cunnie. As I stared in fascination she suddenly pulled it out and immediately transferred it to her anal opening. Again she began to thrust the object deeply within herself, then after a while started to move it from side to side as if she intended to stretch herself as wide as possible. My mind was now incensed with the lustful visions and I dragged myself away to the last of the huts that was still lit up.

Here, two young slaves had just pulled out similar phallic tormentors from their mouths and, after exchanging a few words I could not hear, one of them turned her body and knelt on her elbows and knees with her tight neat rump thrust obscenely into the air. The other pulled out a small silver palm sized casket and opened it. She then pushed her fingers inside, twirled them round then pulled out her hand and smeared some red dusty substance into both palms, then started to smear the powder over the tight rump of her kneeling friend.

After a minute she took her hands away and incredibly I saw that the girl's little arse had grown larger! The dose was repeated and now I stood frozen in disbelief!

The girl's buttocks now stood out, out of proportion with her slim girlish back and waist. But what happened next sent my mind spinning with torturous intensity! The girl who had applied the mysterious concoction bent over her kneeling partner and pulled and squeezed the over-ripe buttocks as if testing their newly found firmness. Then she picked up a slipper and began to smack the sturdy brown flesh.

I suddenly realised the meaning of all the obscenity I had witnessed: the scurrilous wenches were preparing themselves for the coming of Exu and because they didn't know of his sexual preference they were practising for every eventuality.

The girl wielding the slipper had stood up and was belting her kneeling friend with ferocious stinging blows.

Crack!

Crack!

Crack!

Suddenly the last brutal impact propelled the girl down to the floor. I watched as her friend stood over her, looking down at the body writhing and shaking on the ground. After a little while she stood up. They exchanged affectionate kisses, then fell into their sleeping bunks and blew out the oil lamp.

I staggered away and with my mind in a state of fiery combustion, I walked back towards the first hut. The lights had been turned off here too and I reluctantly decided to return to the house.

After some twenty minutes I entered the sanctuary and went upstairs to the balcony where I poured a rejuvenating rum.

Eventually sanity returned and I picked up the discarded voodoo book and flicked the pages to where I had left off. A passage referring to Exu drew my eyes.

He will be recognised by the faithful by his three horns.

Each will be identical in size and only two will be on his

head.

I turned the page and was astounded to see a drawing of a demon sitting on a rock. He was totally naked, black to the waist and white below. His face was horribly contorted and appeared like some devilish mask with wolf-like features that resembled disguises I had seen used in pagan satanic rituals in England. On his head he bore two black horns that appeared to be about fifteen inches in height.

The obscenity which gave him a monstrous appearance was his huge rampant penis that jutted out horribly from between his thighs. It was identical in size to the horns on his head.

I turned to another page and came across a sober warning:

It is said that the last time Exu appeared in Haiti in 1772
    when the European calendar held the three sevens it would
        precipitate the destruction of all the great plantations.

I read the words attentively because I was fully aware that at its peak, Haiti's five hundred thousand slaves had been worked by some forty thousand Frenchmen. Soon after the French revolution, a mysterious figure, Boukman, found a strange influence over the slaves who eventually began to rise against their masters.

Before my departure from England, the newspapers had been full of the altercations on that island and some learned men even spoke of their vision of the total overthrow of the French and the imminent setting up of a Republic.

I slammed the damnable book shut! All it spoke of was destruction and the end of civilisation. I poured another rum and went to bed.

5

I awoke late in the morning because of the previous night's exertions. The old clock chimed ten as I dragged myself out of bed and quickly washed and dressed. I had just taken a seat on the balcony with a morning nectar to dispel my headache when Barbarella knocked and walked in with my breakfast tray.

"Good morning sir. I heard you walking about so I made your breakfast."

"Thank you, child." She raised her arms and turned to walk away and I suddenly called her back. "Come here."

She faced me with frightened eyes, maybe thinking that I would find some fault with her, maybe beat her.

"D'you remember our conversation last night?"

Her demeanour changed and she looked at me solemnly, still keeping her arms above her head and standing very straight. I saw that she was wearing the belt, but did not have a mind to use it on her at that moment.

"How many girls on the plantation believe in this voo-doo nonsense?"

She brought a hand to her mouth in thought, then after a while replied, "Oh, not so many sir. Maybe seven or eight."

"And what do the others think of those seven or eight?"

Again she looked pensively at me, then replied, "Some just laugh at them, especially those that come from different tribes."

"What about the rest?"

"Some, like me sir, don't know what to believe and others are simply terrified."

"I see." It was a worrying situation. "Go and tell Justine to assemble all the girls on the field in front of the house in one hour," I said.

I finished my breakfast and took my bottle onto the sweltering balcony. I had had the opportunity to meet some of the girls, although a few had been spied upon furtively. It was my second day in the house and I intended to see the remainder. As I drank my rum thinking of the lustful looking wenches that soon may gaze upon me and wonder if I looked at them as a potential wife? I stepped off the balcony and opened the drawer. I'd had a fake but impressive gold embossed certificate made up some time ago. I pulled it out and hung it on the wall: 'Professor of Gynaecology and Doctor of Medicine.'

I had studied for a while at Oxford but left before completion. I'd gained enough knowledge to pacify most enquiries and had developed the remainder in my study of the whore's mentality over many years. I looked at the impressive certificate - I had even had a fake signature of King George added.

I sat back on the balcony thinking of the lascivious acts I had been witness to last night and especially of the wench who had had her bottom so erotically enlarged with a magical concoction: I confess that I am a lover of large bottoms.

Voices in the distance roused me from my thoughts - more time had passed than I thought - and I saw that the slave girls were beginning to congregate on the field in twos and threes. I picked up a telescope that I had pulled out of a drawer for this purpose and put it to my eye.

As I scanned the field from left to right I noticed that all the wenches were dressed. Not one flashed a naked breast, a tantalising back or any other sultry flesh. They all wore tatty clothes drenched in sweat. I focused on a group of black wenches who walked together. Yes! I thought to myself, those are the little sorceresses that have been exercising their lewd orifices in preparation for Exu's coming.

So it was true what Barbarella had said - eight believers!

Scanning the field further I came across the simple wench Patsy, who walked with two girls that looked even more simple in demeanour. Looking onwards I spied a large black woman walking alone, who I remembered had asked me to wipe her back in the cover of the canes.

121

Glancing haphazardly around, I saw that my agents had followed my instructions to the letter and had bought mostly lithe nymph-like girls with a few exceptions of large meaty women. The white girls I had had no choice in and they were a motley bunch. Apart from the dimwit Patsy with her two gawky friends the others were of differing stature and appearance.

Finally, when they were all assembled and sitting down, I left the balcony and finished my rum. I holstered my pistol to my belt so that if any disruptive wench might want to waylay me at night she would know that I was prepared.

I went downstairs, stepped through the door and was met by Justine. We walked into the field where the girls had gathered in a semi-circle. When I stopped before them, Justine sat at one side.

"As you all know," I began, "I have taken over the plantation. I'm sure Justine has told you all that I have decided to increase the payment to the most hard-working group to ten pounds. I don't want any of you thinking that your new master is a fool, because if I find you slacking in your work I will stop the payments, put up barriers around the plantation and employ a strict taskmaster who would have my authority to deploy the whip freely.

"Furthermore, I do not want to hear of any voodoo mumbo-jumbo on the plantation. If I do you will bear the consequences. You don't need to turn to sorcery or magic with your ailments, because I am a trained medical practitioner and any girl who falls ill can come to me."

As I continued speaking of the need to adhere strictly to the rules and regulations of the plantation, I noticed that most of the wenches glanced far too often at my John Thomas, which because of the unbearable heat strained uncomfortably against the confines of my trousers. I finished my talk more quickly than I intended because towards the end most of the girls stared unashamedly at the object of their lewd desires.

I told Justine to set the girls to work and returned to the house.

No sooner had I poured a drink and sat on the balcony than I saw Justine approaching the house with a young slave girl. I went down to the front door.

"Sir, this girl says she is suffering from fever," said Justine. I looked at the girl and realised that it was the same one whose bottom had been expanded by the magical red powder last night.

"Very well, Justine. Return to your work now. Come, girl, follow me up the stairs."

My John Thomas was still fired up after being in close proximity to so many wanton young women. Of course I could beat any one of them at any time, abuse her in any way I wished, the thought was always tantalisingly there, but for the present my clever strategies appealed to me more. Yes, the thought of examining my prey gave my lusting mind no respite.

As she followed me up the stairs I asked her name.

"My name is Susie, Bwana. It was given to me my the missionaries who raised me."

When we entered my bedroom I instructed her to sit on the sofa and went to the balcony to collect my drink. Rum is not an extravagance in these parts, being a blessed product of the sugar cane it is cheap.

As I finished the glass I looked at the girl and licked my lips in anticipation.

She couldn't have been more than seventeen and looked younger because of her short cropped black ringlets. Her face was quite tiny, almost pixie-like with neat European features. Her body was slim and lean but slightly muscular with svelte chocolaty skin hidden by her sleeveless grey knee-length dress. Her feet were bare and the tiniest I had ever seen.

"So what is your problem, my child?" I beckoned as I sat opposite her. "I see no signs of fever?"

She looked at me, deep in thought, then replied in a soft voice. "Bwana, I may have done wrong in coming here but I could not tell Justine because she would not understand."

"You may tell me, my child. Anything you tell me will be in confidence."

"Bwana, I am now past sixteen and eventually if I save enough money to buy my freedom I want to be ready to find a husband."

"Well, you are a very pretty girl," I said. "I don't think that you will have a problem."

"Bwana - you don't realise!" She hesitated. "I was born into the Manunga tribe and the men of that tribe will only consider a girl for wife if she has a large strong bottom." She became agitated. "As you can see I am small and unless I find a way" - she faltered again as if trying to find the right words - "a way to make my bottom bigger, the, the men, the men won't look at me."

Exu, she meant. She was speaking of her chances of enticing Exu, I was sure. But I decided to allow her to continue with the charade. It was certainly engaging my interest, my John Thomas was witness enough to that: I would examine the seductive little creature shortly. "Do the men of your tribe look for other qualities in their women?" I asked.

"Bwana, because you are European you may not understand our ways. I was raised by missionary sisters and after they left I was found by the women of my tribe. They instructed me in the traditions of the old ways. They told me if I am unable to keep my new husband then I would be banished from the tribe for ever. I was shown what I must do to keep a man after I became a woman."

"And what is that, my child?"

"When a young woman reaches sixteen in the Manunga tribe she is given a Banga stick with which she must practise for the next year until she is finally ready for a husband... This is a Banga stick."

It was, of course, the same phallic monstrosity that I had seen being used by her and her friends the previous night. My John Thomas began to burn even more fiercely and my head started to pound, so that I had to take a soothing glass of rum before I steeled myself to regain my composure.

"And what must you do with your Banga stick?" I asked, a trifle unsteadily due to a tightness of breath caused by the heat.

She held the black object upright on her lap, twisting it between slim fingers. Her reply was very soft and hesitant. "Bwana it is not just me. I have some friends also. We are all sixteen and over and every night we practise the Manunga traditions."

"You must tell me what you do, my child."

She looked at me apprehensively. "You must understand, Bwana, that this is the way of our people."

She then rested her pixie head against the back of the sofa, opened her mouth wide and lifted the head of the Banga stick to her lips. It was at least two inches wide and twelve in length.

When she had positioned it over her mouth, she slowly inserted it inch by inch, until eventually she had swallowed the whole length deep into her throat. I watched as she held the end in her tight fingers and noticed the contortions of her throat muscles gulping at the intrusion. After a minute her neck muscles stopped pulsating and she began to quickly jerk the monster fully in and out. She pulled the head out to her tight ringed lips, then pushed it back in with increasing speed until the actions of her thrusting hand became a blur. After a minute she pulled it out and burped loudly.

Then she lifted one slim leg onto the edge of the sofa, pulled up her grey dress, and slipped the head of the instrument into the pink lips of her small cunnie. Again she repeated the quick frigging action, pushing the black instrument quickly in and out. After a while she withdrew it, slipped down the sofa and pulled her naked legs up to her head.

As I watched her expose her round bare chocolate bum, my head felt as if it was about to explode!

When she was satisfied with her position she held the phallus to her anal entrance and with a single lunge buried it completely in her deep passage. After a moment's hesitation she slowly withdrew it, then began to drive it in and out with faster speed. She didn't slow down and after a minute with each lewd thrust she started to sway the monstrosity from side to side, as if intentionally trying to open herself up. I looked at her pixie face between her shaking legs and noticed that her eyes were closed whilst her mouth was open, gasping with loud breaths.

Suddenly she opened her eyes, looked at me and probably became conscious of exceeding the length of time of the demonstration and quickly withdrew the instrument and sat back up on the sofa.

I stood up, poured a quick glass of rum and gulped the cleansing nectar in one go, then poured another and turned to face her with better composure.

"Yes, my child, you have interesting traditions, but what did you say about the size of your bottom?" I didn't know who was taking who for a fool any more, but I'd stopped caring some time ago. I sat down as she continued.

"Bwana, these are the ways of my people, but my fear is that because of its small size I may not find a husband. One of the other girls uses a powder to anoint my bottom. When she first began it helped, but after a while it didn't work any more unless she smacked me to make it hard."

I watched the girl as she spoke. Her tiny brown frame was almost lost against the back of the huge sofa. Her black eyes looked at me innocently and her pixie face was solemn and sincere.

"Perhaps, then, it would be wise if I were to examine you, my child. Do you happen to have any of the powder with you?"

She reached down into her bag and rummaged around until she found the small silver casket that I had seen yesterday.

"I shall rub some of this into your bottom," I said, "and then try to keep the flesh firm by using a spare boot paddle that I have with me."

I explained to her that an English gentleman's servant, after he had applied polish to his master's boots, would finally use a special paddle to keep the leather firm. I stood up, went over to my cabinet, and handed it to Susie. She examined both surfaces, then ran her fingers over the rough brittle side that was covered in a mass of tiny projections.

"Do you think this might help me?" she asked, looking up at me searchingly.

"If you will be so good as to take off your dress, my child," I said, "that is what we shall endeavour to discover."

I sat back as she stood up and put the paddle on the sofa. Then, in a matter of fact way, she lifted her hem and pulled the grey dress easily over her shoulders and stood waiting, naked.

My head instantly numbed as I stared at her lean slim frame with smooth round shoulders, her small pointed nipples sitting on neat firm breasts, the steep angle to her tiny waist and the gentle outward flow of her boyish hips. Her tiny cunnie was sparsely covered with a thin black down that melted into her beautifully sculptured thighs and slender shapely legs.

127

When she considered that I had feasted enough on her naked brown nymph curves, she slowly turned round.

My eyes devoured her straight shoulders that swept downwards in a long loop into the tightness of her waist. Her firm round boyish buttocks quivered in anticipation of the beating to come.

Sensing that my appetite was sated, she knelt on the floor and bent forward onto the sofa.

What a sight she was! I licked my lips and poured a drink, in no hurry to proceed. The silver casket was almost full. I suppose they had enough to replenish it at will. It seemed to gleam in the lamplight, beckoning to me. I took the clean handkerchief from my pocket and tapped the casket until a reasonable amount fell upon it, folded it, and put it back in my pocket.

Then I took the casket and sat on the carpet facing her bottom. Feverishly, I smeared a little of the red powder all over her firm round rump and inadvertently stroked her moistening cunnie lips.

Then I stood up, took up the rum I had poured and sat back waiting as she remained in her erotic position. Initially I thought I hadn't used enough powder, because by the time I had half emptied my glass the brown hue had returned to her bottom, but when I looked more closely I realised that the red powder had been absorbed by the gleaming flesh.

As I stared at those boyish buttocks, I noticed some swelling. I rubbed my eyes. It wasn't swelling, the damn shape had grown a fraction already! I gulped down the remainder of the rum and picked up the bottle. Empty! I stood up, went to the cabinet and searched for more rum. Damn! I thought, what a time to run out! I rushed downstairs and entered the kitchen. Barbarella turned from her cooking and raised her arms and gave me a warm smile. Quite amazing! Anyway, I found another bottle and climbed back upstairs as I uncorked it.

I went back to my chair and sat down in more amazement!

Susie's small boyish buttocks had changed into beautiful large ones that set off the remainder of her young figure to perfection!

My head pounded painfully as I got off the sofa and knelt down to run my fingers over those splendid orbs. Then I picked up the paddle as I had promised and set out to make the flesh firmer, so that it would not shrink away again - for my sake as well as for hers!

Crack!

Crack!

Crack!

On the third blow she gave a loud gasp, then began to breathe heavily, wriggling but remaining in place. It was too much for me. I began to flay wildly backwards and forwards, left to right, unconcerned at where the paddle fell.

Then, regaining a little sanity, I decided to concentrate on the right cheek. As I prised the left one outwards with the palm of my hand, I whacked the right one with all the force I could muster. As I belted her I detected a slight wetness on the tips of my left fingers and realised that they had slipped into the confines of her wet bum hole. So as not to alarm her, I started to shake the left cheek, jerking it from side to side whilst increasing the speed of my blows on her right one and this soon had the desired effect of sucking my fingers into her.

I doubt if she noticed, because her beautifully expanded rear must have throbbed in pain from the power of the red ointment and the beating I was inflicting upon her.

I took my fingers out and, whilst continuing to flay her shaking rump, I quickly unbuttoned my trousers and released my engorged cock. I increased the force of my blows onto the crown of her bottom and again slowly pulled her left cheek aside. Then I gradually slid my weapon through the open cleft. When my helmet touched her anal opening, I forced her left cheek further out and slid myself into her.

I began to flay the flesh harder and faster whilst slowly moving my cock in and out of her. Her heavy breathing had turned into low moans upon my entrance, but I suspected that it was due to the increase in force and speed of my blows.

As I used her, I marvelled at the surreptitious advantage I had been able to benefit from by first belting her bottom into a raging painful distraction. It probably throbbed with such intense heat that my intrusion was unnoticeable. Nevertheless, I played safe with long but gentle movements, as I knew it was only a question of time before her natural wet clamping action would have its desired effect upon me.

I continued to whack the crown of her bottom as I moved my buttocks slowly backwards and forwards. Gradually the heat built up, second by second, moment by moment, until fearing that at the last instant I might be tempted to lunge into her madly, I stopped and waited for her wet squeezing sensation to slowly draw my madness out. With a final clamp of her soft tightness she extracted the first spewing fire, then the second, neverending, until my last drop was gone.

I continued to belt her ferociously whilst I pulled out and buttoned my trousers. Finally I stopped hitting her. "Yes my child," I said, "I really think that this new paddle will help to keep your bottom strong and firm." I stood up, now fully composed.

She turned her gasping head, saw that the treatment of her bottom was over and slipped to the floor. She was highly agitated and her whole body shook from the effect of the painful torture her throbbing bottom had just endured. She finally came to her senses, staggered to her feet, and covered her nakedness.

She sat back on the sofa and after a minute when she'd calmed down said, "Bwana, do you really think that treatment with this special paddle will help?"

"Well, my child," I replied, "the best thing to do is to take it with you and try it for a few nights. I'm sure it can't do any worse than your friend's hand."

My intention, of course, was to spy secretly and see what might develop.

She put her new saviour into her bag, thanked me for my kindness, and went downstairs.

As for me, I poured a hefty rum and went out onto the balcony. I wondered for a while - if I had taken her forcibly, would she have protested? My vast experience of the workings of a whore's mentality had taught me that there are many women who prefer to be taken, apparently without the need of giving permission, so as to be able to enjoy their natural lustful inclinations without feelings of guilt.

Was she really practising for Exu's coming or was she genuinely training her body for a Manunga marriage? Had she used the pretence to satisfy her lustful cravings by obtaining guiltless pleasure at my expense?

I poured another rum to alleviate the merciless scorching heat of the interminable sun and my mind drifted away on a cloud of debauchery...

6

I awoke from a torturous sleep swathed in sweat and with a thunderous pain in my groin! My head pounded and my bones ached. I looked down to the source of the tearing discomfort and found to my horror that my John Thomas

131

was swollen and reached down my trouser leg almost to my knee!

What the hell was happening? Had I been struck by some infernal tropical disease? Had Exu the demon Satan thrown a curse upon me? As my pounding head fought for an explanation I suddenly realised that it must have been the red powder from Susie's arse!

I pulled myself up from the sofa and in a panic went downstairs to see if Barbarella might have a remedy. When I entered the kitchen she turned around in surprise and noticed my bloated John Thomas. As she raised her arms she gave me a knowing look, knowing that Justine had brought Susie to the house.

"Barbarella," I said, "the stupid girl came to see me with a swelling that she had developed and I examined the lotion she said had caused it - and now I find that it has spread, through my hands, to me."

She was careful not to laugh as she replied. I would certainly have beaten her if she had!

"Susie and her stupid friends have a herbal mixture that does seem to have the effect of enlarging flesh," she said. She was still concentrating hard on keeping a solemn look upon her saucy face, her arms in the air, and a straight back. "I shouldn't worry too much sir, the best cure is to drink plenty of rum."

She pulled out a half finished bottle left over from her cooking, poured me a glass and brought it over. As she walked towards me her eyes fell and she stared lewdly at my straining John Thomas. It didn't matter to me, because in my painful condition she was the last thing on my mind. All I wanted was to ease the blistering pain.

When she handed me the glass, her searching eyes pulled away from my John Thomas and she said quietly, "You know sir that reputedly the dark prince Exu has a size very similar to that."

Normally I would have considered that a compliment and sought to find a way for a little adventure, but with the searing pain I ignored her and drank the medicine in one go.

"They do say sir," she said, "that it is only the first application which is painful and the flesh becomes accustomed to the herbs."

"That is enough," I said, "go back to your work." Many times in the past I had allowed a whore to tease and cajole me and through bitter experience I found that they only appreciate a man who remains forthright and masterful.

I went upstairs carrying the case of rum that Barbarella had given me and sat on the balcony. Looking at my watch I saw that it was ten. I pulled the bottle to my lips and drank deeply of its medicinal properties. A glass was for socialising and my pain was the immediate priority.

After about fifteen minutes the discomfort seemed to ease slightly and I was able to think more clearly. I wondered if Barbarella through her lusting eyes imagined my distended organ spearing her. She had tasted my normal ten inches and maybe... I had a thought. Why not measure the damn thing before the rum reduced it to its normal size?

I stood down from the balcony and pulled out a tape measure. I didn't dare drop my trousers because I knew I might have difficulty encasing the iron monster back in. I was astonished to record fifteen inches exactly! I checked the width - nearly three inches. No wonder the damn thing had been so painful. It was a miracle that it hadn't exploded!

A sudden flash of lightening opened the tropical sky and I returned to the balcony as a deluge of rain came pouring down. I peered through the teeming blackness at the distant flickering lights from the huts and wondered is Susie and her friends were busy practising their lewd abominations. A flurry of shaking trees just below the balcony drew my attention and I thought for a second that I saw two black figures slinking through the undergrowth.

Then the croaking began.

I finished the last of the bottle and went to the cabinet for more medicine. As I walked I found that the pain had gone but my John Thomas remained fully enlarged. I suspected that time and further medicine would do the trick. When I picked up the bottle I found the voodoo book from last night and decided to explore a few more pages.

I soon came to a passage describing Exu's coming:

'... this evil demon's practices on the dark side of the world equal his greed to finally find the light. The only wife who can rescue him from his perverted deeds is one who before his coming will show her depravity and lewdness of the flesh.

Before his coming he will look down upon his followers and search for a wife whom he will recognise by her lewd obscene behaviour, be she a whore, a sleeper with many men or an insatiable nymph.'

I picked up the bottle and gulped the drink, realising now why Susie had come to me. I am the only man on the plantation. If what I had just read was true... my mind suddenly went into an apocalyptic fit when the implications sunk in! It slowly entered my mind that I might be amongst a coven of the most depraved and lascivious whores ever to be found from time immemorial!

The chime announced eleven. I wasted no more time but stood up to find my holster and pistol. The pain had gone. I looked down and found that my John Thomas had returned to his normal length. I went downstairs - the kitchen was quiet as I stepped out into the night air.

The immediate cacophony of frogs and the numerous dancing insects was soothed only by the forgiving light of the huge moon. As I walked quickly down the left path, the shaking rustling trees seemed to forwarn of some demonic impending doom. I ignored all the prophetic signs, for my lusting mind drove me onwards towards the huts. I wasn't concerned if I were to meet a pack of werewolves or a horde of zombies as I strode purposefully along the path. Eventually I came in sight of Susie's hut and slowed down. The oil lamp flickered invitingly from the open window and as I approached it, the wooden door suddenly opened and Susie came out.

"Oh Bwana, it's you!"

She was framed in the open door, holding the wooden pillars with outstretched arms.

"Do you want to meet my friends?" she asked, beckoning softly as I followed her into the hut.

"These are Danda and Aenga."

I looked at the two girls as they jumped to their feet. Both wore the same grey dress as Susie. Danda offered me her hand. She was much taller than Susie and had a slim curvy body. Her hair was short and decorated with a black sweat band that covered her brow. Her face was attractive with typical negroid features.

"Pleased to meet yus, Bwana," she exclaimed with a quick smile.

The third girl also now greeted me with outstretched hand. She was much smaller than her tall sister, about the same height as Susie. The difference was that she had full womanly breasts and a shaking bottom that strained noticeably against her grey dress. Her hair was short with tight black ringlets, and her round face with its flat nose and heavy lips was somewhat similar to Danda's.

They all sat down on the straw covered floor in a corner and whispered furtively whilst I looked around.

The low hut with its wooden-planked walls was some twelve feet by ten feet with two single beds facing each

135

other and covered in colourful bedding. the rest of the sparse furniture comprised a broad cupboard pushed against one wall on top of which were a few pots and pans with a spatter of cooking utensils.

Susie turned to me. "We were just about to start our practice with the Banga sticks. You can stay if you wish." Her two sitting friends lifted their hands to stifle their nervous giggles when I nodded to Susie's invitation.

After a momentary hesitation, Aenga, the full-breasted girl, stood up and pulled her dress over her head, throwing it to the floor.

My head reeled as I stared at her voluptuous nakedness, and I watched with incredulous eyes as she began to rub and massage the front of her shapely body. She stroked her fleshy shoulders with quick circular movements, then moved her hands to her breasts. She bent forward slightly and stroked her hips, dropping her hands occasionally onto her strong thighs.

As Aenga kneaded herself, Danda, the taller girl, stood up and pulled her dress off, immediately followed by Susie. I was transfixed as I watched Danda, who although taller than the others displayed a lean curvaceous body with small but firm breasts. She started to stroke and squeeze her brown flesh in much quicker jerks than the slower Aenga. She lifted and pulled at her firm breasts, separating them then allowing them to spring back into shape. Bending slightly, she then crossed and rubbed her sinewy legs from her ankles up to her strong thighs, then rotated her palms all over her tight flat stomach.

Susie had joined in the fray and was caressing her long arms and shoulders. She began to stroke the whole front of her tiny frame, alternating with each hand on the up and down movements.

As I watched the lewd exhibition, my head thumped like a drum, but when they all turned round and started to rub their backs and bottoms, I thought my John Thomas would explode.

I stared unbelieving as Aenga, the tallest of the three, rubbed her back as if washing herself and with the other hand frenziedly scraping at her firm rump as if trying to disgorge a troublesome insect. Susie and Aenga followed her and both frenetically tortured their flesh with quick rubbing movements.

Then Danda bent forward and picked up her Banga stick, and the others followed. Soon I was watching one of the most obscene exhibitions I have ever seen in my life!

I needed fresh air...

I went outside into the cool night air and sat on a fallen tree trunk behind the huts. I pulled out a bottle from my shoulder bag and gulped the refreshing nectar. After a few minutes my mind became clearer as I thought of the three lewd wenches.

My hand went to the little wooden box in my pocket, which contained that amount of the red powder which I had kept for myself when treating Susie. As I drank more rum and was assaulted by the devlish croaking of the innumerable frogs, the thought of what it could do was eating at my mind.

I opened my bag and took out the box. Before reason caused me to change my mind, I quickly stood up, pulled out my John Thomas, and swiftly massaged in a generous portion of the powder. Then I quickly buttoned myself and sat back on the sturdy tree and added further lubrication by quenching my thirst.

The stirrings in my loins soon became distinctly uncomfortable and I stood up. The thing that met my eyes was truly frightening. It throbbed and pulsed almost all the way to my knee. I drank more rum and pondered upon my decision. There was no going back. I threw the empty bottle

137

away and walked back to the hut.

As I stood in the doorway, the three naked girls turned. Their eyes widened at the sight of the huge growth within my trousers.

Susie was the first to break the spell. She came over to me, grabbed the monster sitting on my leg and stroked her little hand up and down. Then she went over to Danda and grabbed her by her short curls. She pulled the terrified girl to the centre of the floor and forced her to her knees.

"Naaa," shrieked Danda.

"If you want a Manunga husband you have to learn!" said Susie. Then she pulled me in front of the quivering kneeling girl and proceeded to undo the buttons at my waist. Soon my trousers were down at my ankles.

As my John Thomas sprang into Danda's terrified gaze she wailed in panic. I was not surprised as I looked down at the apparition that had arisen like a vengeful sword. I doubted if even Susie with a mouth like a bottomless chasm could swallow the full length. The bloated dark head was nearly the size of a small man's clenched fist and if the terrified Danda could stretch her lips over the pulsating ogre she would still have a veritable length remaining.

When incredibly she had taken in half, Susie finally gave up on her and allowed her tearful friend to disgorge the tormenter. Then she pulled Aenga to her feet and forced the small quivering girl to her knees. Aenga knew she had no choice and made a spirited effort by instantly lifting up her open mouth and, with some difficulty, she took in the huge plum - but even with Susie pushing she could go no further.

Susie pulled Aenga's head off my weapon and looked round. "I'll show you how it should be done!" she proclaimed.

She took Aenga's place in the centre of the room and turned me sideways to give the others a full view. She grabbed the base of the monster, spread her legs and bent forward. When her eyes hovered just inches away, she repositioned her legs again and bent her head forward at an angle.

Then she stretched her lips over the plum as if to test it out and slowly fed it into her open mouth. She eased her head down, swallowed about half and, satisfied with the angle, lifted her mouth back up to my helmet. She took a few long breaths, waited few seconds, then with an almighty thrust shoved her head down in a sudden move into my pubic hair and stopped!

I looked down with incredulous eyes at the vision below me. It was as if Dante's inferno had suddenly combusted onto the face of the earth! Compared to this, the whole of life and death meant nothing!

Then, suddenly, she started to move her head slowly backwards and forwards. She gradually speeded up, until eventually she was swallowing the whole length. Then amazingly her lips began to hit my pubic bone with painful blows. On and on she gorged, her appetite insatiable, then her small body started to rise off the floor! In my demented mind I hadn't realised that the other two were lifting her up.

Having her physical body detached from the floor, she seemed to increase even more her stupendous speed, ramming and jamming the massive John Thomas further into the depths of her frame.

Now her friends started to chant some unearthly voodoo abomination, which grew slowly in its intensity, louder and louder, until it reached a crescendo of all-consuming fanatical howling!

Then, just as the unremitting noise was about to drive me mad, Susie pulled her mouth off and stood down to the floor.

She picked up the paddle and forced Aenga and Danda

139

onto their hands and knees before me. Both girls knelt with open mouths and terrified eyes.

Susie looked down at Danda, then suddenly began to flay the girl's bottom with scorching blows!

"AAAARGH!" screamed Danda. Then she abruptly stopped when Susie used her feet to push her onto my monstrosity. She started to suck on it as if possessed, whilst Susie flayed her shaking bottom with tremendous blows to the shrinking brown flesh.

Aenga was frozen to the spot like some captured beast as she strained her eyes with a horrified expression at the severe punishment her sister was receiving.

The ferocity of the blows forced Danda's tortured mouth forward, inch by inch, until after a few minutes she was sucking and swallowing the whole length!

When Aenga saw the monstrous projection fully embedded in Danda's mouth she started to howl and wail like an injured animal because she knew that the same fate awaited her.

Susie's muscles strained and shook as her arm flayed up and down, painfully and relentlessly. Her eyes shone with demonic zeal as she scourged her prey, who looked up at me with screaming tortured eyes straight out of the pit of hell.

Suddenly Susie kicked aside Danda, who scurried to her feet and ran off into the jungle. Susie immediately began to flay Aenga's bottom and had roughly kicked her onto my cock before she could even cry out.

Incredibly, she then threw the paddle to one side and fell to her knees behind Aenga. Like some infuriated beast she started to slap the girl's bottom with both hands. She hammered, bludgeoned and pounded in the most horrendous display of sadistic insanity I had ever seen.

Aenga's flood of saliva dripped down my legs, whilst her bulging eyes pleaded and begged as her tortured mouth slid up and down my monstrosity.

Suddenly Susie began to scream and shout, finally having lost her mind. She stood up and started to kick Aenga with a maddening ferocity.

Then she raised her head to the sky and let out a loud scream and pushed Aenga away from my cock. The petrified girl quickly got to her feet and ran out of the door.

Susie fell silent and picked up the paddle. She dragged me out into the open and pulled me by the hand to a tree with a low branch. Then she jumped up and hung by her hands.

As I watched with incredulous eyes, she somehow managed to hang by one hand and began to hit her small cheeks with the other.

I picked up the paddle and pushed her hand away.

Slowly at first, I hit her quivering bottom and watched her beautiful naked brown body start to sway. As her lithe frame swung more and more, she repositioned her hands and clamped them tightly onto the branch.

I lifted my arm to its full extent and began to thrash her bottom with painful sideway blows, backwards and forwards.

She kept her mouth closed as I increased the speed of the swats, whilst her body flew faster to the left and right.

The combustion in my head slowly built up in unison to the rising impact of the stinging blows. I had seen the severity of the punishment she had dealt out to her unfortunate sisters and her clamped mouth meant that she wanted the same.

I was determined to hear her begging sobs and I started to lunge at her flesh with the most painful blows in my armoury. I thrashed those helpless bottom cheeks as she swung from side to side, almost losing her grip.

Not a sound escaped her lips!

Then I took off my heavy leather belt. As the metal

fastening tasted the air, I began to beat her with it, aiming at her wildly swinging bottom cheeks.

The scurrilous unearthly whore, the demented creature from hell, the filthy heathen barbarian, had finally awoken my spewing madness and with a ferocity and insanity born in the depths of hell, I hit harder and harder until finally she screamed in pain.

"EXUUU! See me! Hear me! Take me! I am yours!"

The horrendous unearthly howl filled my head with a cataclysmic inferno and I stumbled away from the clearing.

7

A torrential downpour roused me from my sleep. I was very relieved to find that my cock was back to normal. I got out of bed and quickly dressed.

Barbarella had left breakfast. She slept naked on a rug on the floor of my room now, but she kept out of my way as much as she could. Maybe I took too much pleasure in beating her, or did it too often. Or maybe I was giving her too many humiliating orders, like the one about holding her hands above her head. When I surprised her not obeying, I have to admit that it was my custom to beat her rather hard. And, of course, the fact that I could take her to my bed whenever I wished, day or night, meant that I had no need to force any of the other slaves, as you may have noticed.

Anyway, she was gone about her duties and I ate ravenously. The old clock chimed ten thirty a.m. No matter. I deserved my long sleep after last night! I poured my morning rum and sat at leisure on the balcony.

I had never seen such a torrential downpour as I now

witnessed. Pools of water had collected on the field and the jungle trees shook and heaved from the onslaught of the pounding rain. It was almost as if the heavens wanted to cleanse the earth of its damnations and curses. The canopy above my head released the occasional load of collected water over the wooden fencing of the balcony. The humidity was slightly more bearable now, but the tropical air was still clammy and moist.

Barbarella's timid knock broke my thoughts.

She looked gorgeous in my short shirt, the broad leather belt I made her wear setting off her slim waist, her hands held up obediently into the air, palms forward. She was trembling as she looked at me, and went on tiptoes before she spoke, for that was one of my latest commands, one I was quite pleased with.

"Good morning sir -"

"Come here," I said. The sight of her was already exciting my John Thomas.

She came and stood close to me on tiptoe, her eyes looking into mine. Was there an excited gleam in her's too? I put my hands on her hips and slid them up to caress her splendid jutting breasts, under the thin material of her shirt.

"Belt!"

Still with her eyes fixed on me, she unbuckled the belt round her waist and held it out. "Bend!" I said as I took it into my hands, and she adopted one of the first poses I had taught her, legs wide apart and straight, back straight also as she bent forward and clasped her ankles, then shuffled round so that her bottom was towards me.

I swished the belt in the air and saw her flinch.

"Well," I said, "why did you disturb me?"

"J-Justine is waiting downstairs sir," she said between her legs, her saucy face upside down.

"If I am not back within the hour," I said, "you may resume your duties."

I laid the belt over her shoulders and went downstairs.

Justine had two soaking white girls with her. They were in need of medical attention, she said.

"Very well, Justine, you may leave them."

As they stood dripping on the floor, I offered them a glass of rum each to warm them up.

"It is cooler upstairs," I said, and they followed me meekly enough.

This very morning I had repositioned my bed to the back of the the room away from the sounds of the frogs and persistent storms as the raining season began. I'd placed the two black leather sofas facing each other by the open balcony to make my bedroom resemble a sitting room.

"Barbarella!" I shouted.

When she came in from the balcony and offered the belt to me, as my orders dictated, before bending over again, their eyes nearly popped out of their heads, though they said nothing.

"A towel each for these girls," I said, "then you may go about your duties."

Barbarella straightened up, glancing at them proudly rather than in shame I thought, put on the belt, brought the towels, and left on tiptoe with her hands above her head.

"So!" I said, bringing them back to earth. "And what are your names?"

"She's Betty," said the tall one. "And I'm Sissy."

As they started to dry themselves I opened the cabinet to check my lists. I nearly dropped my glass when I saw why Sissy had been sent to the plantation: incurable nymphomania!

At that moment she turned on Betty. "Do it properly!" she exclaimed, snatching the towel away from her and starting to rub her hair with her own. "She's useless, this one, sir. She can't do nothing properly."

They both wore thin sleeveless dresses that were so dirty and soaked that it was only just possible to make out the design of multi-coloured flowers against a pale cream background. The material hung loosely to just above their knees and both wore saturated slippers.

Betty was about five feet in height and shapely, with short brown hair that fell in wet strands onto her freckled face. She had big innocent eyes, round cheeks and lips that seemed to have a nervous twitch.

Sissy was a good few inches taller. Her long blonde hair was plaited down her back and fell to her eyes in a fringe. Her nose had a slight kink in the end, causing it to perk upwards when she spoke.

Both had good breasts and chubby inviting bottoms, quivering and shaking as they strenuously dried themselves unashamedly.

Finally they sat opposite me. They sipped their drinks and looked at me with big open eyes.

"Well girls, what seems to be the problem?" I asked.

"Well, sir, Patsy told us that you might be able to help us out," began Sissy. "You see, sir, me and Betty got to know Patsy when we arrived here and found out that we had all worked for Sir Waldegrave which got us into trouble and she says she's been to see you about his goings on and you're going to help her."

She paused, breathless, and I couldn't believe what I was hearing. The damnable rake Waldegrave was obviously scouring the Poorhouses of London and taking advantage of of unfortunate girls.

"For the first few days," she continued, "he was a perfect gentleman. Then he complained about the cleaning and he spanked both our naked bottoms! And a little later sir I found he was washing Betty."

She opened her eyes wider and repeated what she had just said, as if to emphasize the statement.

"He was washing her every night, sir, all naked."

I turned to Betty. "How did this situation occur?"

"Well sir," she squeaked in a baby voice, "the old man in the Poorhouse washed me on my first night and I thought it was alright because he said he washed all the other girls too. So when we got our position and Sir Waldegrave said he was going to wash me I just didn't think anything of it."

She looked quickly at Sissy and stifled a giggle.

"Tell the master," interrupted Sissy. "Tell him what else happened."

"I didn't think anything of it, because the old man at the Poorhouse did it too."

"What was that, Betty?" I gently encouraged.

"Well he washed my titties then, er, my bottom and, er, in between my legs!" She clamped her hand over her mouth to suppress another giggle when Sissy looked sternly at her.

I poured another rum to calm myself and asked Betty to continue, but Sissy interrupted. "When I found out what he was doing to her I didn't blame her, because she's a bit simple you know sir. But I told Sir Waldegrave to leave her alone and wash me instead if he must. And then, sir, well I couldn't have him taking advantage of her could I, so anyway when he asked me to take his thingy into my mouth, well I did, so he'd keep his filthy hands off of her."

I turned back to Betty. "Didn't this sort of thing happen with the old man at the Poorhouse?" I asked.

"Well sir, yes, er, well, I suppose it did a bit."

"How many times is a bit?" I asked.

Betty sat demurely staring at the floor. Then she looked up, stifled a giggle with her hand, and whispered quietly, "Every night I suppose."

"Whaaa!" cried Sissy in surprise. "You're nothing but a filthy whore, that's what you are!"

Her small friend sat deeply in the sofa with a red face

trying to hide her twitching lips behind her glass. Both appeared already to be half drunk as they twisted and turned awkwardly, unknowingly exposing their naked sun-browned thighs.

"You're jealous!" shouted Betty aggressively, "because you're not half as attractive as I am!"

"Show us then!" shouted Sissy in a rage. "Stand up and let sir see what you've got to boast about!"

I thought Betty would back down at the provocation, but she insolently stood up and lifted her grubby hem up to her shoulders. Sissy followed immediately. She stood beside Betty with dress also raised, blatantly displaying herself.

What a sight! After admiring their excellent firm breasts, tight waists and womanly hips - I gestured to them to turn round and they both stuck out their pale round bottoms which quivered with a hint of ripe puppy flesh.

"Anyway," said Sissy, when I made no choice between them, "I bet I can take a cock deeper in my mouth than she can!"

"Prove it then!" Betty retorted indignantly.

They both turned and stared at my John Thomas.

I somehow forced myself to compose my pounding head. "If I can help settle your argument, then I'll do what I can," I said.

"You see!" exclaimed Sissy. "Because he's a gentleman, he's willing to help out!"

"Come on then," replied Betty, perching herself on the edge of the sofa. "You go first!"

Sissy gestured to me to stand before her, then fumbled with my buttons. When my straining cock suddenly sprang out Betty gasped and put a hand to her mouth, whilst Sissy stared hungrily at the bloated head. Then she dropped her lips and immediately started to swallow the whole length into her mouth. I looked at Betty's unbelieving eyes as she

147

watched her friend gobble my weapon with increasing speed.

After a minute, Sissy pulled off. "Now, let's see you do better!" she gasped to her incredulous friend.

I moved over to Betty, who, not wanting to be outdone, grasped the base of my cock in hot little fingers and began to slurp and lick from the bottom to the top.

"Never mind all that," cried out Sissy, "let's see you take it in!"

Prompted by the challenge, Betty suddenly sucked in my whole length and started to push her head back and forth greedily as Sissy watched closely.

Eventually Betty pulled her head away and rubbed my cock up and down with her hand. "See, I told you I could do it better!"

They both picked up their glasses and gulped greedily. "So what!" Sissy blurted out. "I can take a belting better! What about the time when I saw you being belted by Waldegrave. You were crying all the time."

"That's nothing!" replied Betty. She turned to me. "I once saw that brute doing it to her, and she was shrieking at the top of her voice. But after a while she went all quiet like and then I heard her begging for more. More, more, more. the filthy cow was begging him to thrash her stupid arse harder, can you believe it?"

"Oooh she's a little liar!" protested Sissy, gulping her drink. "She's only jealous because he preferred me. He always said I've got the best bottom."

"It's not true. He always said my arse could stand punishment all day."

"Alright then. if you think you're so clever," replied Sissy, haughtily taking off her slipper and handing it to me, "Let Sir decide who can take the most punishment."

As I took the slipper from her hand I couldn't believe what I was hearing. My head throbbed as if being hit by a hammer. Suddenly Betty stood up and sat on the arm of my sofa. "Come on then," she said, "get your arse on the sofa and let's find out!"

Sissy immediately put down her drink, twisted round and knelt on the sofa, pulling her dress up over her waist with her left hand.

"Go on sir," prompted Betty, "give her a good belting. She's a filthy cow and she deserves it."

I stood up and looked down at Sissy's naked bottom. It was bigger than I expected, with round white fleshy cheeks that shook and quivered before me.

Crack!

I hit her right cheek quickly to test her out. Her muffled response showed no sign of pain, so I belted her faster with three more sharper whacks.

Crack!

Crack!

Crack!

"Ugh!" she responded to the last one. I continued to belt both cheeks with harder blows. I had her wriggling now. She began to moan through her closed mouth, then after a few more let go of her lungs.

"Whaaa!"

As I continued to beat her she reacted with jerking gasps and began to squirm much more.

"Ugh, ugh, ugh, ugh!"

I looked at Betty who was now standing next to me watching closely. She put her mouth to my ear and whispered, "Go on sir hit her hard, she's nothing but a dirty slut."

Prompted by the traitorous little wench, I renewed my belting with a new vigour.

Crack!

Crack!

Crack!

Sissy's bottom started to shake and sway from left to right, until after another minute or so she began to utter choking noises, then a muffled word that sounded like 'more'.

Betty put her mouth to my ear again. "I told you she enjoys it, sir. I've seen her belted afore, harder'n this."

With the full knowledge that the scurrilous wench savoured each blow, I hit her harder and faster. I beat each fat cheek, then I lifted the slipper to the crown of her swaying arse and cracked down there until she displayed her true shameless vulgarity and began to spew out obscene curses.

The coarse language drove me to new heights of lustfulness and I raised my hand higher in the air as I thrashed the lewd whore's arse on and on and on.

Now Betty bent to me. Another whisper. "Let me do it sir. She won't know any different, my arm is fresh." I looked at her in amazement when I saw that she waited with a lifted slipper she had just taken from her own foot. I quickly stood to one side to recover my breath as she cracked down on Sissy's red-hot bottom.

I watched incredulously as she attacked the reddening flesh with a sudden vengeance. I wasn't sure if it was in retaliation to her friend's lewd accusations or if she simply enjoyed what she was doing.

She belted that naked bottom relentlessly, experimenting with each new blow. After a few minutes she started to concentrate all the stinging shots onto Sissy's right cheek. Then having tired of that, she moved to the left one and belted it with renewed fury.

Sissy's whole body was writhing about now, as erotic a sight as I have ever seen, and little gasps and moans were being wrenched from her.

At last Betty gestured for me to continue, but I was content with what we had done and to watch. I took another refresher from the bottle whilst that abused bottom gradually slowed and stopped, and our victim lay there gasping and sobbing.

"Up!" I said at last.

Sissy rose with tears in her eyes, pulled her dress down and fell into the sofa, still gasping and shaking. I poured a hefty rum for her, which she gulped greedily, then, after another minute, when she had regained some composure, she hissed at Betty. "I told you I could take my punishment! Can you?"

"Of course I can!" replied Betty scornfully. She then swopped places with Sissy, who sat on the arm of my chair whilst Betty climbed onto the sofa, bent forward, and without shame lifted her scruffy dress over her waist.

My mind was still in a state of delirium from spanking Sissy, but when I saw Betty's shapely frame spread lewdly on the sofa my John Thomas throbbed faster than before. She was plumper than Sissy and because of her smallness the width of her spread cheeks was greater. They melted into her soft sun-browned thighs that quivered with anticipation.

I went forward and stood behind the steaming flesh that still gave out a humid rainy vapour. Then I started to belt the firm bottom with rapid blows, marvelling at the springy sensation of the slipper as it bounced off the firm young buttocks.

Suddenly I realised that Sissy was standing next to me and was slowly stroking my hip. As I continued to thrash Betty's quivering flesh, she moved her hand with the gentlest of movements until eventually it held my straining cock through my trousers. When she began to squeeze softly, moving her hand up and down, it made me belt Betty's arse even harder. As I struck her cheeks more viciously, she started to grunt and moan loudly.

I could see that the thrashing Sissy had just enjoyed,

together with watching her friend being soundly strapped, was having an effect on her. She began to fumble with my buttons, then, when she had freed my bursting hot weapon, she grabbed it and started to rub it up and down, matching the speed of my blows onto Betty's shaking arse.

Suddenly she dropped her hand and disappeared from my side. A few seconds later I felt her warm naked body squeezing itself through my spread out legs.

The thought of what she was about to do drove my mind into an insane frenzy and I hit out with fast piercing impacts. Betty sensed the increased intensity of the onslaught upon her and began to gasp heavily with intermittent yelps and shrieks.

Eventually Sissy wriggled through my legs and started softly to massage my hardness whilst she positioned herself in from of my bursting cock. When she was comfortable her sudden plunging lips testified to her lust and wanton greed. If must be true, as Betty had said, that Sissy was always doing it, for her expertise showed in the way she immediately swallowed the whole length past her throat muscles.

She increased the speed until her whole head was jerking back and forth, gulping my whole length. Betty's convulsing yelps and moans forced me to thrash her squirming bottom even harder, whilst Sissy drove me on with her greedy lips. After a few minutes I reached a new level of torturous madness and allowed her plunging wet mouth to draw out my spewing fire.

She kept me in her mouth for a while after that and savoured the wetness, then reluctantly pulled her lips off. She buttoned me up and slid underneath my legs. When I saw that she had put her dress back on and was sitting back on the sofa, I gave Betty a few final belts, then stopped and picked up my glass.

Betty stood up, pulled down her dress and gasped breathlessly, "How was that sir? Can my arse take a good beating or not?"

"Indeed it can," I replied.

"So who won?" they both wanted to know.

"I shall tell you later," I said. I really didn't know. "Or perhaps we shall have to try again."

"Ooh yes sir!" they chorused enthusiastically as they rushed out of the room, apparently the best of friends. I took my drink onto the balcony and watched them run through the rain.

As my mind slowly cleared and I watched the heavy tropical rain pour out of the grey skies, I suddenly realised that they had said they had come to seek my help. The scheming whores hadn't even bothered to ask!

I decided to clear my mind of the devious hussies and wenches that always permeated my life and instead drank the life-saving nectar and listened to the incessant swishing and battering of the merciless rain.

8

I was just nodding off when the canopy above my head shook with the weight of the rain water and sent it cascading in a sudden torrent over the balcony. I looked towards the cane field, barely visible through the heavy curtain of pelting rain, and thought of Cordelia out at sea. I would have to have a lookout soon because if her ship had favourable winds behind it, it might make the long crossing in record time.

The last thing I wanted was for her to be stranded on the jetty!

Time had somehow passed. The clock showed the hour of three and I decided to see what Barbarella was up to and

153

maybe give her a beating to keep her on her toes.

"Oh!" She turned sharply and raised her arms in confusion. "I didn't hear you because of the rain," she stammered. Then she went on in a rush, "I've just finished preparing your food, sir, will you have it upstairs or here sir?"

No doubt she expected a beating, but I decided to surprise her.

"In the drawing room," I said. "Will you join me?"

It was nice to have her sitting there, knowing that I could do anything I wanted to her at any time, and that all she was allowed to wear was my short shirt. We both sat down to the kingly feast she had prepared of wild pig and vegetables. As I chewed on the tender meat I wondered if I was eating the demonic soul of a dead black magician. She somehow read my thoughts and laughed.

"Why look so worried sir? You don't think that you'll come to any harm eating the pig do you?"

"What does voodoo tradition say about that?" I asked.

"Well sir," she looked at me in some amusement, "I don't want to spoil your meal sir."

"I really want to know, Barbarella," I said. "We are both civilised people and not to be frightened by other people's superstitions."

"Well sir, apparently Erzulie the voodoo goddess of love who was rejected by Exu on her attempt to seduce him will take possession of the unbeliever's soul in revenge and transform that person into an insatiable lustful being."

"And what would happen if a believer knowingly ate some?"

"Oh," she looked at me more seriously, "that is the worst thing that a believer can do. It is a most sacrilegious act, because Exu is being deprived of the eyes of his black magicians who bear witness to him of his kingdom on earth. Tradition states that he will change the person into a werewolf, a vampire or a zombie. Strict believers would

154

rather die than expose themselves to this curse, because they know they would never rest peacefully and for all eternity would wander the earth aimlessly."

"It's just as well," I laughed, "that we are not believers."

"Yes sir," she interrupted, "but it does mean that Erzulie will possess our souls and endow us with an insatiable lustfulness."

She looked at me mischievously as she ate her meat, and I noticed that from time to time her eyes studied me with a mysterious glint.

"Damn the rain!" I burst out. "When is it going to stop?"

"Last year around this time it rained for over two weeks."

"Thank you Barbarella!" I said. "Bend over! Belt!" After I had relieved my frustrations with a vicious attack upon her beautiful bottom, which soon had her howling, I returned upstairs to calm down and sat on the balcony.

After a while I went to the drawing room and collected all the ledgers and documents relating to the past five years of the plantation's history. My intention was eventually to sell it and return to England, and this damnable rain provided a good opportunity to ascertain its true worth.

Once I sat by the table and delved into the intricate mysteries of book keeping I became so involved that I didn't realise it was seven o'clock until Barbarella entered with the evening supper.

She put the tray down and stood looking over my shoulder.

"You see these entries sir," she suddenly remarked, "these are mine."

"Really?"

"Yes sir. After the old master found he could trust me in the running of the house he persuaded me to do the book keeping, because his eyes were failing."

"And he rewarded you well, did he not?"

"Yes sir."

"I hope you've got your money in a safe place?"

"Don't worry sir," she answered with a smile. "It's buried in a safe spot in the jungle. That is the best way to keep valuables secure around here." How erotic she looked, standing on tiptoe with her arms above her head and a mysterious smile on her cheeky face. As I sipped my glass I was pleased to see that I still had her under good control.

After she left I finished the meal then continued to work. I was astounded at the accuracy of her entries. Each figure and number was meticulously registered, clearly and logically.

Finally, when my eyes began to feel the strain from the flickering oil lamp, I closed the books, poured myself a rewarding rum and sat on the balcony again.

I awoke to the sound of the clattering windows being pounded by the never ending rain. Somehow I had got myself to bed, then. I looked at my watch. Eight o'clock. Due to the overcast sky the daylight had only just reached the bedroom.

I was soon washed and dressed.

"Good morning sir." Barbarella walked in with my breakfast tray, and quickly left. I ate quickly, then sat by the desk and returned to my work. I studied the ledgers for the rest of the day, glad of the opportunity to make my own assessment of the true value of my investment. My constant companion, the noise of the rain on the balcony, pervaded every part of the house, until by Tuesday I had got used to it and it didn't bother me any more. Wednesday and Thursday passed and my only confidants were ledgers, the never ending rain and the sound of Barbarella cleaning the house.

Friday turned into Saturday and on Sunday I realised that we had had a full week of rain. As I sat on the balcony late that night I suddenly remembered in surprise that I hadn't molested Barbarella in any way for all that time.

So I allocated a couple of very pleasurable hours to teaching her new poses and punishing her when I considered her to be slow.

Then, exhausted, I told her to stand in the corner and picked up the bottle. Damn! Who's drinking all the rum in this house, I thought to myself. I knew that it was the last one in my bedroom, so I tore myself away from watching the pounding rain and sent Barbarella for another case.

She looked so good in the corner again. I had made her turn round and face into it.

I opened a new bottle and settled into the chair to gloat over what was to come when I took her into the bed, but unfortunately I remember no more of that evening.

9

I awoke on Monday morning to the clock chiming eight and felt the warmth of Barbarella. Of course, I had tied her wrists behind her back the previous evening the better to take her. It had been most enjoyable as she had kicked and thrashed about beneath me. I determined to it again this very night. I released her and pushed her out of the bed and she put on the shirt and rushed off to prepare my breakfast.

I climbed out of bed myself and looked over the balcony in the direction of the plantation and saw the canes swaying from the movements of the workers.

The sun was shining and the damnable rain had stopped!

So, I thought, finally back to normal! I had grown so accustomed to the rain that I was even beginning to look forward to the croaks of the frogs.

I dressed and went down to the kitchen. Barbarella actually bowed to me. She was becoming more and more submissive and loving it!

Just as I was finishing my breakfast with her standing close so that I could stroke her if I wished - I enjoyed running my hands up her flanks to her breasts under the shirt as she stood on tiptoe with her hands raised - a young lad ran through the open front door and stood gasping. It was the lad I had hired to watch for Cordelia's arrival.

"Bwana I's seen a ship coming far away in the sea!"

I jumped up in excitement and told Barbarella to prepare the horse and trap. I had told her that my sister was paying a visit from England. Although I trusted her to a certain extent, I thought it wise not to be too forthright at the present time.

After a few minutes she brought the old horse and trap to the front of the house and I set off down the dusty track. When I arrived at the jetty I tied the horse and sat waiting as the frigate sailed closer and closer. Finally it dropped anchor and the crew launched a rowing boat.

There was Cordelia, waving to me excitedly!

"Peeeercy!" She hugged me ecstatically. "How are you, you old devil? Oh how I've missed you! How's everything?" As the two crew finished lifting her luggage onto the trap she put her lips to my ear and whispered wickedly "How are your little slave girls, are they keeping you busy?"

I gave the men a few shillings and helped Cordelia onto the trap, turned the horse, and we started on the return journey.

"You look very sporty," I laughed as she fumbled with the buttons of her loose brown shirt that matched her black trousers. She tossed her flowing reddish-brown hair with a flick of her hand as she listened to my escapades, at most of which she screeched with laughter.

But when I got to Exu and the red powder she became serious and told me to stop the horse.

"Have you thought about it?" she demanded. She

laughed out loud. "Take Exu's place, Percy! All you have to do is fix yourself a mask with horns and paint your body half black and the powder will do the rest!"

At last the horse pulled up before the house and Barbarella came out to meet us. Cordelia certainly admired the way I had her dressed and trained. I could tell that by the expression on her face.

"Well well Percy," she complemented, as we finally sat on the balcony with a glass of rum each. "This is the life, is it not? Servants, sunshine and sex!"

Barbarella knocked and came in carrying platters of food. When I asked her if they contained portions of black pig she nodded mischievously. I suspected that she doubted if Cordelia was my sister, but she was too diplomatic to say anything.

"What was that about the meat?" asked Cordelia, and I told her of Erzulie, the voodoo goddess of love, who would possess an unbeliever's soul and endow it with insatiable lust.

"Are we not there already?" she laughed, eating the pig meat ravenously with glinting mischievous eyes.

I looked at her as she ate. When I had first met her in London, she had been a completely different person in appearance. She had worn long black dresses with her greying hair piled into a severe bun. After I met her some weeks later, when she arrived unannounced at my Poorhouse, she had changed her dowdy old fashioned mode of dress into one befitting an elegant aristocratic lady. She had changed her hair into the reddish-brown I now watched dancing around her shoulders. It took away her previous severe appearance and made her look younger than her fifty years. She didn't have any wrinkles on her face and the addition of the lightly coloured powder on her cheeks made her look quite ravishing.

159

"Percy, what are you looking at?" she laughed, glancing at Barbarella, standing in her exotic pose as she waited upon us. "Don't tell me this delightful housekeeper creature and all your other young slave girls haven't seen to your needs yet?"

After she finished eating, she took some of her luggage into the back bedroom to unpack, whilst I sat on the balcony drinking rum and contemplating life.

"Percy," she called out, "come and see my collection of playthings."

I walked into her bedroom and stood in amazement at the twelve whips she had hung in the open cupboard. Half were coiled as if awaiting virgin flesh and the remainder were of different lengths. A couple had tight notches at the working end and one even had interwoven little metal ringlets glinting viciously. Next to these hung six paddles and underneath were sets of leather and metal manacles.

"What do you think?" she asked, seeing my admiring gaze.

"A princely collection. All we need now is bodies to test them on."

"We can always start with this Barbarella of yours," she said, taking the glass of rum I had poured for her, "but I might prefer some of the others." When she had finished the rum, she decided to saddle a horse and take a look at the plantation. I had told Barbarella and Justine that she had put up half the money for the plantation, so as far as they were concerned she was part owner and could do as she liked.

I sat on the sunny balcony and waved to her as she rode off in the direction of the canes. She had insisted on going on her own and I wondered if her intention was to scour the plantation for easy prey.

After about an hour of quenching the hot sun's rays with glasses of rum, I saw her returning. As I sat up and focused

160

my eyes, I saw that a black woman was following her horse. When they came closer I was a astonished to see that it was Justine.

When I heard them climbing the stairs to my quarters, I decided to hide in one of the bedrooms.

Beads of sweat dripped down Justine's chubby face, making her broad nose glisten and her lips quiver. Her short black crinkly hair was wet and shiny from the exertions of keeping up with the horse.

Cordelia turned to her. "You know why I have brought you here?"

"Yes madam."

"Tell me."

"Because I asked you how severely I should punish the girls who misbehave and when I did not understand very well you said that you would show me."

I could hardly believe what I was hearing. Justine had obviously been attracted to Cordelia - I suspected already that she imposed upon some of the prettier girls - and was using the play to tempt her into seduction. I had already instructed her to bring any slave requiring punishment to me. I wondered if Cordelia's sixth sense in these matters had picked out Justine as a willing participant in punishment or if she was simply taking advantage of the situation.

Cordelia pulled out a long white handkerchief from her trousers and tied it around Justine's eyes. I knew that she was going to play a game with the wench. It was one in which I had seen her indulge with the girls at my Poorhouse.

Justine didn't complain of the blindfold, in fact she even adjusted it herself to make sure her eyes were masked.

"I am covering your eyes," said Cordelia, "to save you embarrassment, because I shall have to take your dress off to prevent it becoming torn."

"I understand madam," Justine replied, and began to breathe faster with a husky anticipation. She had obviously found Cordelia instantly attractive and would probably have agreed to anything in order to gain favour with her.

Cordelia then told Justine to stand up. Justine was easily six inches the taller, standing close to six feet in height. Cordelia turned her round and began to unbutton her dress from her shoulders. I knew that she realised that I was spying from the bedroom and she stood to one side so as not to obstruct my view.

Eventually Cordelia undid the last button and slipped the dress off over Justine's head, then stood aside and slowly folded it.

My John Thomas instantly reared up at the sight of the naked woman. Her muscularity was truly Amazonian, from her strong sinewy shoulders that melted into a sculptured back, rippling with strong fleshy tissue into a tight small waist. Her firm shiny bottom cheeks quivered slightly, whilst her chiselled thighs melted into slim athletic legs.

Cordelia now did something strange, as she had never indicated to me any attraction to her own sex. She started to stroke and squeeze Justine's fleshy muscles from her shoulders down to her waist. She grabbed at her bottom and swiftly kneaded and pulled at the strong flesh, then she bent down and savoured the bulky thighs in long swooping strokes. After she had sated her impetuous hunger, she slowly bent the breathless woman forward, so that her palms rested on the seat of the sofa. She then again massaged the heavy cheeks roughly and turned to me with a signal.

I walked silently from the bedroom and stood next to her groping fingers. We immediately swopped hands and I began to squeeze and pull at the warm brown bottom cheeks. Justine started to wheeze and puff as I contorted the heavy bum flesh into every shape imaginable. I twisted, wrenched, buckled and bent it into every possible contortion.

I then suddenly let go and the heavy arse instantly bounced back into its original shape with a slight fleshy sounding smack.

Cordelia began to slap the sweaty wench's right cheek, whilst her other hand slowly pushed into her crack. When she met the warm anal entrance, she pushed her fingers in and started to frig her wet bottom hole with quick sharp jabs. Then she lifted Justine's legs onto the sofa and gently pushed her up onto the seat, making sure her hands rested on the back.

Justine's shiny bottom now blatantly stuck out and stared us in the face. Cordelia motioned to me to stand back and rippled the long whip on the floor. Then she slowly raised her hand to its full height and swung the whip down sharply across the protruding arse.

Crack!

"Ugh!"

Crack!

Crack!

Crack!

I looked at Cordelia's face. It had hardened noticeably. Her eyes stared strangely out of her sockets at the quivering flesh before her as she stepped back and attacked the shaking bottom with a demonic fury, each blow drawing a resounding yelp. She used the full repertoire of blows that only a true Mistress and devotee of the highest order possesses.

At last she handed the whip to me and I continued where she had left off, lashing the writhing flesh and listening to the yelps and moans. When I stopped momentarily I was amazed when Justine steeled her back against the settee and pushed her arse further out. She began to shake and tremble from head to toe and when I restarted with the whip across her cheeks she finally choked out "more - more - more - harder - harder -HARDER!"

Then, after a few more minutes of painful lashes, she screamed out a torturous howl.

"Aaaeeeooouuu!"

I stopped hitting her and stood back watching her shake and splutter, whilst her wet shiny bottom and legs quivered with decreasing spasms, allowing thin sweat rivulets to snake in strings down her flesh.

I went to pour myself a much needed rum. After I had drunk that and poured another, I looked back and froze at the sight that confronted me!

I stared unbelieving, more than if Lucifer himself had appeared to claim my soul, or even the damnable Exu surrounded by his entourage of werewolves, vampires and zombies. What I saw was Cordelia with her trousers pulled down to her knees, thrusting her penis into Justine's sex!

HER PENIS!

What was she? Was she half man half woman? Had she always been a man? Had the feast of black pig empowered her with a man's attributes?

The full force of it hit me like a thunderbolt. HER-MAPHRODITE!

Never in a million years would I have suspected her secret! I reeled away in need of a very large rum!

"Percy," she said softly as I turned and saw that she had dressed and dispensed with Justine. "You would have found out sooner or later. I desperately don't want to lose your friendship."

With that she fell into a chair and began to sob into the handkerchief she's taken from Justine's eyes.

"P-percy, dear friend," she stuttered in between tearful gasps, "I-I was b-born this way. Believe me, I'm all woman, its just that I have this thing between my legs."

I certainly had proof that she was indeed more woman than most, because I had seen her magnificent breasts flowing out from the top of her gown.

And yet -

She must have guessed what I was thinking.

"Percy, look at me and tell me I'm not a woman!" She quickly began to undress.

When she had thrown her clothes off, I looked at her nudity for the first time. I couldn't believe I was looking at a fifty year old woman, for she had the springy voluptuousness of a newly flowered eighteen year old. Her milky white shoulders were straight and true, melting into large full breasts which sat atop the smallest waist I had ever seen in my life. It curved out into the roundest most gloriously shaped hips, supported by long nymph-like sculptured legs.

I dragged my eyes from her intoxicating beauty and looked at the now thin bedraggled penis that fell over her womanly crack.

She saw my look and lifted the sorrowful object. "See Percy, I don't posses a sac, just this inoffensive little monster."

We both laughed and started to dress. She explained how her disability had precluded her from enjoying married life and how she had discovered that she could obtain sexual relief from the chastisement of real girls...

A|t that moment Barbarella's knock interrupted us.

"Here is your supper sir and yours madam." Black pig! I suddenly wondered if Erzulie had entered Cordelia, but when I challenged her she shook her head.

"Unfortunately not!"

After we had eaten our fill we watched the sun go down, spoke for another hour, then Cordelia decided to retire for an early night to recuperate from her strenuous journey.

I sat back, drank more rum and listened to the awakening sounds of the ever present frogs. The moon appeared from behind the trees and the whole evening became wrapped in an aura of sensuous magicality. I blessed my good fortune in discovering the true Cordelia, one who would be indispensable to me. I understood now why she had insisted on separate bedrooms.

Maybe I would not need Barbarella. Anyway, I sent her back to her hut with little regret.

10

A rustling in the room woke me.

"Yoohoo, morning Percy," sang Cordelia, opening the windows. It was eight a.m. "I'll go down and fetch some breakfast."

I jumped out of bed, stretched on the warm sunny balcony, then washed and dressed. Just as I finished, Cordelia walked in carrying the breakfast tray. She lifted a small table onto the balcony and we sat down to eat the ham and eggs.

"What, no black pig?" I laughed.

"I thought you might have had enough yesterday."

She was joking, but I was not so sure.

"The demon Exu is due to appear in four days," I said. "Supposedly he makes his choice of a bride after experimenting on all the believers. They have picked a place which they have cleared of trees and they have built a mound of earth for him to sit on. Barbarella says that for a week before his coming they light a fire on the mound so that the dead magicians in the form of black pigs can see it and tell him where to appear, and at midnight they dance and cavort and practise their lewdness for his coming."

"Have you seen this?"

"No," I admitted.

"Midnight tonight, then!"

We finished eating, then she poured two glasses of rum. I watched her as she came back onto the balcony. She wore light brown jodhpurs with black riding boots. Her loose cream blouse contrasted well with her reddish brown locks. I myself wore the most comfortable uniform I could find, consisting of baggy trousers and airy shirt.

"Come on," said Cordelia. "Let's get the horses saddled and explore the island."

The time was certainly over due for this, for it was only the rains that had stopped me. The only outsiders on the island were supposed to be two old men and a boy who manned the shack by the sea that had once served as a trading post. It was now only used for collecting the supplies and mail from the regular monthly frigate. The plantation was situated in the centre of the mile long island and apart from the thick jungle there was only a narrow sandy beach which could only be reached by riding down to the wooden jetty where we had arrived.

We were soon on our way.

As we entered the tall crop of sugar canes, we saw Justine patrolling the land and she smiled secretly to Cordelia. We slowed down when we came to a small clearing and suddenly Cordelia grabbed my arm and stopped the horses.

"Wow! Just look at that!"

It was the same black woman, naked now and shining with sweat, who had asked me to wipe the sweat off her back and then allowed me to frig her bottom.

"Just look at the size of her! She must be over six feet! Oooh Percy, the way that magnificent bottom shakes! This I have to see!"

She dismounted and went over to the slave woman, and walked round her, reaching out to pat her bottom as she stood meekly waiting.

"I'll give you a nice surprise later," she said, as we proceeded on our way. I didn't tell her of my previous encounter for fear of spoiling the surprise.

Soon we encountered Sissy, Betty and Patsy. They were

167

all completely nude as they worked. When they heard us approach they turned round, giggled, and continued working. We stayed a while to watch their shaking bottoms and bouncing tits, then with a throbbing head I gestured to Cordelia and we rode on. If I had stayed any longer I would have been tempted to perform some ungodly act, and the middle of a plantation with sixty slaves was not the most prudent of places.

After a couple of minutes we came to another clearing, where three young black wenches worked. They also were naked, and I recognised one of them as the little temptress Susie who had demonstrated her Banga stick to me. The other two I vaguely remembered from their lewd practices in their huts in the middle of the night. One of the slender girls flashed a toothless smile and I remembered that Barbarella had told me about a girl who had persuaded her friends to take all her teeth out in case Exu's preference was to have the whole of his monstrous weapon swallowed inside a tight mouth.

As we trotted towards the end of the cane field we spied more wenches, but because they wore their skirts we turned off onto the path that led to the jetty. Galloping past the jungle trees, I looked at Cordelia who held her noble chin high and seemed mesmerised by what we had just seen.

We soon arrived at the wooden jetty. Barbarella had told us that if we entered the trees to the right we would find a single track that would take us to the sandy beach. After ploughing through the hot sticky undergrowth for some minutes, we came to an opening. We pushed past the trees and stepped onto the golden sand.

"Oh Percy," Cordelia called out, "this is absolute paradise! Just look at the blue sea! Who needs England with its petty laws and restrictions?" We sat in the sunshine and listened to the harsh sounds of the parrots. The close gently lapping sea gave off a welcoming breeze that cooled our brows.

I pulled a bottle of rum from my bag and poured us a glass each.

"Yes indeed," I said, "but there is a growing feeling against slavery, so I must consider selling in the near future."

She was fully aware of the growing abolitionist movement. "One thing we really must do before we return to England," she said, "we have to get a supply of the enlarging powder. Or, even better, let's find out how to make it. It has to be a mixture of herbs or plants that grow in the jungle."

I was in full agreement and already intended to give the matter high priority. One thing I hadn't told her was that I still had some hidden in my bedroom.

We spent the next few hours drinking rum and watching the gently lapping sea break onto the sandy shore in ripples and crests. The hot sun threw down its rays in continuous fieriness. Only the cool breeze offered any respite from the afternoon heat. Drowsiness finally got the better of us and we awoke to a distant crack of thunder.

It was already six o'clock!

We rose quickly, untied our horses and set off through the trees to the track. On the way back we agreed to look for the clearing that the girls had prepared, because we planned to take a clandestine walk there at midnight to spy on the demonic wenches.

As we approached the cane fields all was silent. The slaves had finished their twelve hour working day. We followed Barbarella's directions and found the clearing some five hundred feet beyond the plantation. It was just as well that she had given us clear instructions, because even though some daylight remained the thick cover of the jungle trees would have hidden it completely to an unsuspecting passerby. The clearing was some thirty-five feet across and a mound of earth about three feet high had been built in the centre.

Eventually we reached the house and Barbarella came out to stable the horses, reluctant as she was to appear outside in my shirt, and soon after that told us that supper was served. Cordelia gave her a slap on the arse for good luck and we picked up the trays and went upstairs to sit on the balcony.

"Pig meat again," laughed Cordelia, "I'm sure that woman is trying to fatten us up with Erzulie's lust!"

After we finished, she poured out the rum with a twinkle in her eye. I knew she had some surprise in store for me.

"Put me out of my misery," I implored. "Tell me what you have planned for tonight?"

"You won't believe it!" she said. "There is a wench coming who will do anything, I mean anything your heart desires!"

"Anything?"

"Absolutely anything," she said, as I searched my mind for a logical answer. Her sixth sense might have allowed her to find out a wench's preferences, but that was all. Why should any of them be willing to do anything and everything? Had Cordelia the power of casting spells upon her own sisters?

"Anything at all that you want," she said again. "And here she comes!"

I looked over the balcony. A tall woman in a short grey dress was walking towards the house.

I gulped my rum in expectation as Cordelia looked at me with salacious eyes. When the figure approached the house, Cordelia went downstairs to meet her. After a minute they both walked in and I stepped off the balcony and sat on the sofa.

"What is your name, my child?" I asked.

"Mandy, Bwana."

"And how old are you?"

"I's eighteen Bwana," she replied in a deep seductive voice. I noticed that she kept her eyes subserviently on the floor.

She was easily six foot two, with short crinkly black hair. Her face was round and attractive. Her thin grey dress exposed well moulded arms that hung loosely at her side and set off her uplifted breasts, which were further exaggerated by the tight belt that made her short dress stand out at an angle without touching her muscular thighs and legs.

I gestured to her to turn to face Cordelia and looked at her graceful sinewy back. It was half exposed by the deep V-shape cut of her dress that matched her front. The tightly belted dress further emphasised her straining bum cheeks that pushed against the inadequate material.

As she faced Cordelia, I gave her her first instruction.

"Bend to the floor and keep your legs straight."

She immediately complied and I stood up and flicked her short dress over her belted waist. Like all the others I had seen, she was naked beneath. I sat down to gaze at the sight that was revealed.

Then I smacked her glorious arse and told her to stand up.

"Now, Mandy," I said as she looked down to me with soft trusting eyes. "I want you to twirl round until I tell you to stop."

She raised her arms above her head and started to pirouette, twirling on one foot and pushing herself with the other. She built up an urgent speed and her short dress spun up to her waist exposing those naked bottom cheeks again. Just a shadow of black matted hair covered her cunnie. I watched the dark flesh shake and shudder for a further minute, then told her to stop.

Cordelia handed her a rum and I watched Mandy gulp it down breathlessly, then I gave her a few seconds to calm down.

"Take your dress off!"

That broke her composure! She began to fumble with the buckle of her belt and when it dropped to the floor she bent forward, grasped the hem of the dress in both hands, and pulled it over her head and off in one go.

My head pounded as I gazed at the gleaming brown flesh. She stood there breathlessly, with her magnificent tits lifting up and down.

"Play with yourself!" I demanded.

My head pounded like a drum as I watched her right hand lift to her cunnie and slowly start to stroke it up and down. Her other hand began to lift and massage her breasts, and after a minute the lascivious wench closed her eyes, lifted her head, and started to rub and massage the whole of her body from shoulders down.

Cordelia jumped up and sat beside me to watch the flagrant obscene exhibition.

Mandy slowly increased the rubbing and kneading until after a while she was furiously squeezing and pummelling her beautiful brown body from top to bottom.

When she opened her eyes she saw Cordelia holding out a glass of rum and stopped. She took the glass and again breathlessly gulped it own.

Cordelia bent towards me. "How are you enjoying your present so far?" Then she looked at my straining John Thomas and knew that no answer was necessary.

"Bend over and smack your own bottom!" I commanded Mandy.

She slowly bent forward and I stared at the straining brown cheeks as they tightened. Then she placed her right hand onto one fleshy orb and began to knead as if checking its springiness. Then she let go and started to smack herself with sharp stinging blows.

Smack!

Smack!

Smack!

Cordelia and I watched disbelievingly as she gradually increased the speed and power, then, gasping in quick breaths, lifted up her other hand and began to assault both cheeks together.

We were paralysed with lust as we watched the shameless degenerate vulgarity. As the noise of the self flagellation increased in intensity, the girl even started to thrust her bottom backwards and forwards. We continued to stare at the unbridled vision of torrential lust as she entered upon a frenzy of unrestrained insanity.

I was so enthralled that I hadn't noticed Cordelia slip away and return with a round wooden paddle. She pushed it into Mandy's fingers and the cavorting creature began to beat her straining flesh with renewed vigour.

Crack!

Crack!

Crack!

Mandy suddenly fell to hands and knees in front of us, and, resting on her left hand, restarted the torturous procedure. The noise increased in volume to a high-pitched penetrating cracking then, incredibly, she bent forward, rested her head on the floor and brought her left hand round to the quivering divide of her thrusting bottom.

As we watched, totally numbed with lust, she buried her searching fingers into her dark orifices and began to thrust them in and out. We could not see the target of her stabbing fingers because her insane thunderous fury rocked her body with lustful spasms and contortions. After another minute of madness she suddenly cried out 'Yaaargh!'

After a few minutes her moans and groans subsided and she fell onto her side, then picked herself up and sat shaking and breathing heavily with her back to us.

Cordelia broke the spell. She swiftly poured a rum and

handed it to the drained young woman, then quickly gave me one, and, as I gulped it down, my throbbing head slowly recovered some sanity. Cordelia looked at me without a word as she quenched her own thirst. I leaned over and whispered to her: "Go downstairs and wait for my call, and when you return I shall have a surprise waiting for you."

She looked at me in astonishment but said nothing, just rose and went out. Maybe she thought I wanted to try something with Mandy that I didn't want her to see? I made sure that she wasn't peeking before I told Mandy to rest her body on the sofa opposite me with her bottom stuck out.

I took my secret supply of the powder in its little casket from its drawer and knelt in front of Mandy's quivering bottom. I rubbed red powder all over the gleaming brown flesh and then poured another rum. I had seen the growth of Susie's boyish bottom and wondered what would happen to Mandy's already large one as I settled down and waited for the swelling to start.

After about five minutes I detected a sweet aromatic fragrance in the air. Dusk had finally fallen and the sounds of the croaking frogs began to penetrate into the room. A distant throbbing sound of drums seemed to come from beyond the plantation.

I tore my eyes away from the balcony and focused on Mandy's bottom. As I rubbed the cheeks with my fingers I saw ripples gently vibrating through them. The ripples slowly started to swell and, second by second, spread gradually over the whole of her bottom. It steadily expanded with the slow minuteness of a floating feather, bigger and bigger, until filled with absolute amazement I dropped and broke my glass.

"Percy," a voice called from downstairs, "can I come up?"

I didn't hear her enter, so fascinated was I with Mandy's big bottom.

"Jesus Mary!" Cordelia exclaimed from behind me. She snatched the rum bottle and lifted it to her lips. She was gazing avidly at the flesh before her and I feared for what she might do to it.

The bottle fell from her hand and rum ran all over the floor as she stood up unsteadily and picked up the broad leather belt that Mandy had dropped. I jumped out of her way as she began to flay the unfortunate girl.

Even I could not stand seeing the pain she was inflicting on her innocent victim. I went downstairs and sat there nursing my rum and listening to the horrendous screams and cracking of the belt on the enlarged bottom that could writhe about but not escape it. On and on it went until I feared for the poor girl's life.

At last I poured another rum and went out to sit in the porch. I gulped lungfulls of fresh air and looked out towards the distant swaying canes until at last the beating stopped. Then my mind became engulfed by the rising cacophony of the frogs. Just as the incessant noise reached the pitch of its tormenting crescendo, the abominable distant noise of the drums began.

As I looked at the dark curtain of jungle trees with its projecting dancing eyes of the fireflies and moths, I was convinced that I saw the movements of unearthly beings who would probably soon expose their obscene faces in the shape and form of an army of demons and fiends. Only the rum was holding them at bay. A scourge of numerous black bats that had appeared from nowhere after the week long tropical rain seemed to have congregated over the house as if prophesying some approaching demonic madness.

My mind reeled and spun from the endless taunts of the night, and fearing to tempt the howls and cries of the numerous supernatural beings that I fancied surrounded me, I went back inside.

175

Still the beating continued upstairs! On and on. Never ending. I was convinced that Cordelia was by now flogging a corpse.

I ran upstairs with a raging anger, determined to stop the obscenity once and for all.

I immediately froze to the spot.

It was Cordelia who was being beaten by Mandy!

I poured myself a hefty rum and sat down. Mandy's bottom had regained its original size. Nevertheless, my John Thomas soon reawoke as I listened to Cordelia's gasps and moans. Mandy had substituted the whip for the belt and Cordelia was calling out for more. More, more, more! Harder, harder, harder!

Suddenly she let out a resounding scream.

Yaaaaoooooow!

Mandy stopped whipping her and picked up a glass of rum.

Cordelia fell off the sofa moaning and groaning.

I watched the two scurrilous wenches who had so depraved and dehumanised their femininity. So it was true, I thought. Give a lustful wench a hint of the fruit and instead of feasting on it they instead devour it like demented wolves.

After a few minutes Cordelia slowly dragged herself up off the sofa and pulled up her jodhpurs. Then she gave me a wry smile and slumped into the sofa next to me and poured herself a drink.

Mandy, being unused to rum, was now quite drunk and stood in front of us swaying invitingly as she sipped. My John Thomas reared up at her flagrant lustful movements and her roused smell invaded my nostrils, making my head reel. When she finished her drink she looked at my straining member and lifted two fingers to her lips, then pushed them in and started to thrust them in and out of her mouth.

Cordelia was captivated by the new lewd exhibition and as I stared transfixed I felt her soft fingers at my trouser buttons. After a few seconds she had opened them and my ten inch weapon sprang out.

Mandy, seeing my cock quiver eagerly, slowed her swaying and pulled her fingers out of her mouth. Then she stopped moving altogether and stared with open eyes at the object of her desire.

"Into your mouth!" I ordered and she slowly advanced towards me. When she was standing between my legs she looked down, then gradually sank to her knees.

The sudden wet warmth that engulfed my rock hard cock jerked my head back and I found that Mandy had begun a slow sucking. As she swallowed deeper and deeper and deeper, Cordelia leant forward and whispered something in her ear.

Mandy continued with her deep wet sucking motion, then, after a minute, she gently lifted first one of my legs and then the other slowly over her shoulders.

I looked down at her in a sensual trance, then felt both of her palms steadily push their way under my buttocks, until finally she held both my cheeks in her hands. Still sucking with long wet plunges, she gradually arched her back upwards until she had lifted me off the sofa by about a couple of inches.

My head throbbed insanely at the sudden realisation of what she was doing and I instinctively grabbed the back of her neck.

Still sucking, she slowly stood up and lifted me with her until I balanced on her strong shoulders. I looked down and saw her black crinkly head bobbing quickly up and down.

I had never before sat on top of a standing wench and speared her from above! It was quite an experience! She held by buttock cheeks tightly and started a faster action until my helmet pushed through her gulping throat muscles. Then she increased the speed of her milking mouth until

177

her head almost became a blur.

Mandy suddenly began to sway from side to side and as I opened my eyes I saw that Cordelia was standing up and was driving her round the room by using the bat on her bottom.

"Dance!" I heard Cordelia say, and Mandy started to jump up and down to the sound of the stinging raps of Cordelia's flaying bat.

The sensation on my cock was indescribable, because every time she landed on the floor with a heavy foot my weapon speared her wet gaping throat deeper and deeper. I crossed my ankles firmly behind her shoulders and clamped my hands onto her neck for fear of being thrown off the bucking horse.

"Higher!" shouted Cordelia as she increased the speed of her stinging blows. Spurred on to a new level of excruciating insanity, Mandy clasped my buttocks in a painful grip and jumped as high as my weight would allow.

My body slithered backwards and forwards on her shoulders and after a last thunderous clap from Cordelia's bat, I nearly overbalanced but finally, with a fierce thrust, spewed my demonic fire deep into Mandy's throat.

11

Throughout the night I dreamt a thousand dreams, a thousand obscenities, and a thousand tortures. As I burnt in the pit of fire, surrounded by horned imps, laughing goblins and screeching demons, Exu floated down screaming vengeful curses with Cordelia dressed in white and Barbarella in black, both metamorphosed into small spitting horned imps speared bodily onto the massive horns on his head.

As he floated down and danced before my eyes, he was joined by his fiendish army of a thousand werewolves, vampires and zombies, each one chased by a white clothed whore that I had seduced in my earthly life. As each one beseeched and begged to be taken they were cast into the pit of fire. Erzulie appeared, riding a beast with seven heads surrounded by black winged pigs, each one holding a clutch of fluttering white chickens, and as they floated towards me they chewed off the chickens' heads and spat them into the pit of fire.

Then Lucifer appeared with his hordes of black angels -

"Percy - Percy - wake up!"

I was being shaken.

I thought for a second that the hellish horde had finally begun to devour me, but as I came to my senses I realised that it was Cordelia who was shaking me.

I finally awoke and opened my eyes, and took the glass of rum from her hand.

"Was last night a dream?" I asked, as she poured me another. It was nine thirty. I stretched, finished the rum and began to get myself together. Fifteen minutes later I joined her on the sunny balcony.

After we had eaten - chicken, she said, not black pig - and she had poured two more rums, I felt better and gazed out towards the sun scorched plantation.

Barbarella walked in to take the tray. "How was the pig?"

"Fine," I said, not admitting to a certain trepidation as Cordelia burst into an unrestrained fit of laughter.

"How did you manage to get Mandy to do everything I told her to?" I asked.

"Easy," she said, "I just said you were considering her as your wife but you didn't think she was sexy enough... Listen, let's ride out onto the plantation and I'll choose a girl for you and I'll tell you what her fancies are and you can invite her back to the house on some pretence and then we'll have some fun with her."

"They all belong to me anyway," I said. "Why don't I just order her to do whatever I want?"

"I know you could," she said, "but it's more fun this way."

Which echoed my own feelings exactly, as I have said, so after a couple more drinks we set off, and after about two minutes of galloping we reached the plantation path and settled into a leisurely trot. We passed a few black girls, some of them naked or nearly so,. She looked at one girl and slowed down, but then seemed to change her mind. I began to suspect that if she did indeed have a sixth sense then she was looking for a girl with an unusual interest in order to prove to me that it was true.

After another couple of minutes she stopped and stared at a young white girl who looked to be about seventeen and had short blonde hair.

"That's the one!"

I rode up to the girl she had indicated and told her to go to the house.

We rode back ourselves, and as we sat down Cordelia asked me the girl's name. Fortunately I did know it. "Elizabeth Pendle," I replied.

She consulted my notes, then shouted out in glee. "Just look at her crime! Blackmailer of a Church Minister!"

"Before she gets here," I said, pouring out a rum, "tell me what your sixth sense revealed to you?"

"No, no, I'll write her peculiarity down and stick it under the carpet where you can get it. I'll hide behind the bedroom door and watch everything. We'll soon see if I'm right."

Looking over the balcony I saw the girl approaching, and went down to meet her.

"You wanted to see me, sir?"

"Yes, Elizabeth. Follow me upstairs."

"Oh, you can call me Lizzie sir."

When we reached the room I told her to sit on the sofa and asked if she wanted some rum to cool her down.

"That's very kind of you sir." She spoke in a working class twang which I shall not endeavour to reproduce here.

Her short blonde hair was swept back off her high forehead and softly grazed the nape of her neck. She had big innocent eyes, a freckled nose and small uneven teeth that displayed the tops of her gums every time she smiled. Her sleeveless light blue dress exposed her slim arms and shapely legs. The thin material did nothing to hide her fine figure, a figure made to turn a man on.

I handed her a full glass and sat opposite her.

"Oh!" She suddenly jumped up. "I've spilled it!"

She put the glass on the table, pulled her dress to the top of her curvy thigh and started to wipe her leg vigorously.

My John Thomas immediately stiffened further when she turned sideways and unnecessarily lifted her dress higher, exposing half of her naked bottom cheeks. Then she sat down and continued to sip her drink. She didn't bother to pull her dress down, just sat there displaying most of her shapely thighs and legs.

"I hope to meet most of my girls over the next few weeks and find out if they are happy and content," I said.

"That's really good of you sir. It's not many gentlemen would take the trouble."

"And what was your crime, Lizzie?"

"Well, sir, my Ma were very poor. She weren't my proper Ma, not really, sort of an aunty. Anyway, we didn't have anywhere special to wash you know, and one day I were washing myself in the room when she had a gentleman visitor. When he saw me all naked like he were about to go but

181

Ma said never mind and when he did go he give her a shilling.

"Next night she said to wash like before and another gentleman come, and he give her a shilling an' all. Then after that there was lots of 'em."

"Didn't you mind, my child?"

"Naaah!" She blushed. "I quite enjoyed it, see? I were younger then, remember."

I poured her another rum, which she gulped greedily whilst lying back on the sofa with her light blue dress dishevelled up around her hips.

"Anyways," she continued, "after a few days the regular gentleman, that first one, he came round and instead of allowing me to wash myself Ma took the cloth and started doing it, then she gave the cloth to the gentleman and told him to finish me off because she were off for a drink. He didn't bother with the cloth, though, he just used his hands and he washed me all over and then he rubbed me dry and then he give Ma two shilling when she come back.

"After that it happened every night with a different gentleman and I thought to myself why should Ma have all the money so after one had finished stroking an' rubbing me I stood facing him as he huffed and puffed and I began to stroke his thingy through his trousers, it were hard already. Well, he didn't tell me to stop, so I undid his buttons an' pulled it out 'an started to pull it up and down like an' rub it and he still didn't tell me to stop so I got to my knees and took it in my mouth and started to suck it...know what, sir, 'e didn't even last half a minute!"

"And did he pay you?"

"Damn right 'e did sir, 'e give me a penny!"

She blurted it out proudly, and I coughed and choked into my rum but didn't say a word.

"Anyway," she continued, "I'm not stupid, you know! Every time she went out after that, after I were washed, I

182

gave 'em a right good sucking! It were real good, sir. I'd have done it for nothing!"

"Why is that, Lizzie?"

"Well, sir, after they'd washed and stroked me all over it made me feel all funny... anyway, Ma brought a new gentleman one night. He wasn't all old and horrible like the others, he was dressed all smart and everything. You could tell he were a proper gentleman." She looked up at me slyly. "A bit like yourself, sir... anyways, after he'd washed and stroked me I got down to suck him but he lifted me up and turned me round and did something that the others had never done... he told me to bend over and he started to smack my bottom. I thought it were a bit strange when I'd done nothing wrong but I didn't mind, after five minutes or so I sort of got used to it."

She was now completely drunk and had obviously stopped caring what she said.

"Anyways sir, after another few more minutes, with all the smacking and everything, I found I was getting hotter and hotter. Then something happened that had never happened before. I started to shake and splutter, then I just... I don't know... it's never happened before... I wanted to suck his thingy and I did, as fast and as deep as I could...then I got this funny feeling an' I just exploded like!"

I saw she needed another rum and poured it quickly.

"Anyways sir, after he finished 'e gave me sixpence! But I wasn't bothered about the money, I'd found out what really get's me going. So next night when the regular gentleman came round I told him from now on I'd only suck him if he gives me a good spanking first. He looked at me a bit strange, so I told him forget the money, just do it. So 'e gives me a good belting an' it happens again, the explosion. After that I had a real hunger to suck his thingy so I did and the hot feeling came on again... after that, I made sure to get a good belting afore I sucked 'em!"

183

My head was close to exploding as I listened to the drunken wench. She rolled about laughing and giggling, not caring that she exposed half of her luscious naked body.

Suddenly she spilt a drop of rum onto her dress and quickly lifted it, exposing delightful breasts tipped with stiff nipples. She then started to rub her tight waist.

"Ooh look sir, I've done it again!"

She sat wiping a nonexistent stain and displaying the whole of her naked lusty body! I thought my head would burst at the alluring sight.

She looked up to see that I had noticed, then let the dress fall.

The scurrilous wench had me burning with fire and I was just about to jump on her when she said: "You know what, sir? Every time I walked on the beach back home and men looked at me I got these strange feelings."

"Do you get them when I look at you?" I asked.

She suddenly went quiet and began to blush again. "Yes. I suppose I do, sir." She was hitching her dress up. "I know it's not right sir, but I can't help it, I've always been this way. That's how I had the little misunderstanding with the church minister which got me deported."

When she was sure that my gaze was inextricably locked onto her wet open cunnie, she slowly, with the deftest of touches, raised the dress over her waist. Inch by minute inch she uncovered her full breasts, then slowly slid her other hand down her waist until eventually she stopped with a feather-light touch on her blonde-white curly hairs. She stared into my eyes, then slowly and softly began to glide her finger-tips in and out of the curly wisps. After a minute she speeded up and started to gasp and moan.

"Are you watching sir? Are you watching?"

Her moans became louder and louder and her heaving breasts shook higher as her fingers turned into a maddening blur.

"YAAAAAAH!"

She lay back gasping loudly as her jerking fingers gradually slowed down and her dress fell over her waist. Then she opened her eyes and blushed as she saw me looking at her. She grabbed eagerly at the rum I was pouring for her and gulped it down hungrily, staring at my swollen John Thomas.

"I'm sorry sir," she said. "I deserve to be punished for that!"

"You do indeed!" I said, taking off my belt and running it lovingly through my fingers.

The tip of her tongue ran over her lips, then without a word she knelt on the sofa with her bottom presented invitingly. Slowly I lifted the thin blue hem of her dress up her legs and over her round white bottom and pushed her buttocks into a comfortable position to receive the belting that we both knew was coming.

I cracked down on her with a sudden flurry, and soon had her gasping. Gasping for more! I started to strike both cheeks in turn with my full strength.

"Yeah, yeah, yeah, yeah, yeee!"

I gave her bottom a rest for a minute to allow her to recover her breath.

"Phew, phew, phew, ooh, ooh!" she panted.

After she had calmed down I looked at the quivering round cheeks just inches in front of my eyes, then grabbed both and began to squeeze and twist the flesh.

"Oh yeah, yeah, yeah, yeah!" she choked.

When I let go of the burning flesh, she answered by suddenly shaking and thrusting her bottom backwards and forwards, from left to right, in every way that her jumping knees would carry her. As she bounced up and down I responded with alternating lashes on each cheek.

"Yaoow, yaooh, yaooh!" she yelped. "Ya ya ya, whee whee whee!"

185

I belted her backwards and forwards, up and down, from side to side, across and back, and still she screamed for more.

When she had calmed slightly I eased her up into a standing position on the cushion and bent her compliant body forward so that her palms rested on the back of the sofa. Then I began to belt her reddening cheeks upwards from my sitting position.

"Yeeeeeeooooooow!"

I stopped hitting her and watched her bottom squirm and shudder whilst she moaned and groaned.

After a minute she jumped off the sofa, fell to her knees and started frantically to tear at my trouser buttons. When she finally released my aching cock, she threw her mouth onto it and instantly began to suck with an intensity I hadn't experienced for a long time. Her mouth plunged up and down, in and out, until after a minute her whole body started to shudder. She grasped my thighs in a tight grip and milked my fire into the back of her throat...

Percy, you old devil," Cordelia laughed as soon as the girl had gone, "What a splendid little wench!" She retrieved her piece of paper from under the carpet. "And now read this!"

I unfurled the paper and looked at the words.

'This one gets sexually excited by exposing her nakedness to men.'

"True," I said, "but that's only the half of it!"

12

Another night had come: Cordelia and I crossed the field to the right so as not to disturb any of the girls in the huts.

The night breeze whistled eerily, whilst the searching eyes of the moths and other insects danced and frolicked at the curtain of the jungle trees. A canopy of bats seemed to follow us, the occasional one swooping down screeching its almost inaudible omen of doom.

A rustling of undergrowth caused us to stop. It grew louder and louder, swishing and turning, then silence!

We stood frozen, listening and waiting.

Suddenly a flurry of screaming black pigs leaped out of the undergrowth and ran gulping and wheezing across the field.

"Did you see how many there were?" hissed Cordelia. "I counted nine."

We continued on past the plantation and finally reached the other side, then threaded our way through the pitch black jungle, treading as quietly as possible.

Then I saw a shadowy light. We stumbled towards it, pushing through more foliage until we could see the flickering tops of dancing flames. A few more steps and we stopped and peered into the clearing.

An amazing sight met our eyes. Three girls danced naked, turning and swaying their bodies in a circle round the fire. I instantly recognised all of them from the previous night.

Suddenly they stopped. One went over to a bag on the ground and withdrew two long black objects which she handed to her friends. Then she sat down and pulled a cloth off a large round drum.

Slowly at first, she pounded out a steady rhythm as the girls started to dance around the fire. As she increased the beat, the dancers lifted their Banga sticks into the air, then the drum stopped.

They stood frozen, looking up into the sky, pointing their sticks upward with outstretched arms. Then the drummer struck up again loudly with a quick resounding throb.

The two girls started to dance again, lifting their naked knees high into the air. First one, then the second, inserted her Banga stick into her mouth, pushing it lewdly in and out.

The sitting girl beat the drum faster as the others swopped their Banga sticks from mouth to bottoms, then to their cunnies.

I stood fascinated as Cordelia squeezed my arm and stared at the obscene ritual.

Then the drum fell silent and the two dancers stopped, withdrew their black instruments and lifted their arms skyward again. Slowly they thrust their hips backwards and forwards in the direction of the fire.

Cordelia gave me a quick nudge and as the drum started they resumed their dance once more. I looked down into her open bag - she had had the foresight to pack a coiled black whip. Underneath were pieces of pig meat. My little adventuress had taken care of my needs.

I attached the whip to my belt and picked up the bag. The sight of the naked display had awoken my appetite and I strode forward into the clearing.

"What is the meaning of this behaviour!" I shouted. "I have told you all that I will not tolerate voodoo!"

All three froze and stood open mouthed in horror. The girl who had been beating the drum broke out of her trance.

"Bwana, we's only practising for Manunga husbands. What you see is not voodoo."

I saw that all her teeth were missing. I went over to her and pulled her mouth open.

"And what is this girl? I know you had them pulled out because of Exu!"

She stood quaking in shock, not able to denounce her prince for fear he might find out.

"You will all be punished immediately!" I shouted. "Do

you understand? Over to that fallen tree and bend over. Move!"

They all scurried to the edge of the clearing and bent forward with their palms resting on the large trunk. The little toothless girl was quite tiny compared to her taller sisters, one of whom was well built and the same height as her slim friend. They all had short crinkly hair and typical negroid features, and an eye to the whip at my belt.

They waited patiently for the first searing cut of the whip's tongue, but I wasn't in any particular hurry and drank from the bottle that Cordelia had packed as the brown bodies glistened and shimmered before me.

The fire threw shadows and glints of light around the dark clearing as I studied the waiting bottom cheeks. Those of the toothless girl on the left were tight and round, almost boyish. In contrast, those of her larger friend in the centre were about a foot higher, plump and broad. The slim girl's were sinewy and shapely, rounded like an athlete's.

After a further swig of rum I unfurled the long whip and cracked it quickly through the night air. Immediately all three girls flinched, tensing their back muscles and wriggling their bottoms in anticipation.

I took a few steps forward, measured the distance, and cracked the whip across the toothless girl's quivering rump.

"Come here!" I barked, as she yelped in pain.

She quickly came to me and followed as I walked to the other side of the clearing, where Cordelia's bag rested on the ground.

I sat on a tree trunk, holding the whip, as she stood trembling before me. Her sharp coned breasts lifted in panic as I sat admiring her delicate waist, which gently filled out to boyish hips and slim sinewy legs.

Closer!"

She immediately shuffled forward and a brown thigh touched my knee accidentally, inflaming me further.

189

"Open your mouth!"

She opened wide and exposed pink gums devoid of any teeth. As she strained her lips wider, her eyes looked skyward, shifting nervously from side to side.

I pushed four fingers into her mouth and nudged her throat, making her almost gag. Then I lifted a piece of pig meat from Cordelia's bag.

"Do you know what this is?"

"Aaaaagh!" she screamed, and started to back away, holding her hands over her mouth.

"Come back!" She shuffled forward again, holding her trembling hands over her face. When she stood between my legs I twisted her sideways. I gave her tight round bottom a few sharp smacks, then roughly pushed my fingers deep into her bottom crack. As she struggled, swaying backwards and forwards, I picked up the pig meat again and began to rub it over her cringing bottom.

Her mouth opened wide in shock and her throat muscles gurgled, but no sound came out. She stood frozen to the spot looking down at me with wide open eyes that were full of terror.

"On your knees!"

Her eyes followed my fingers as I slowly undid my trouser buttons.

When my raging weapon sprang into view I asked, "Shall it be this or pig meat?"

Before I had finished the sentence she fell onto my cock with her open mouth and immediately began to swallow the whole length as if her whole life depended on it.

As the fire slowly started to consume my head I shook myself clear of her, then glanced across the clearing and was relieved to find that the other two girls remained bent over.

"Take the whip," I said, "and show me how you practise on each other."

I could see the relief on her face as she took the whip from me and almost ran to the other side of the clearing. When she reached her bent-over sisters, she stood back about six feet and began to flay them with vicious stinging cracks.

I watched the slip of a girl as she wielded the long black whip with more verve and ferocity than any taskmaster taking his final revenge, then, before the damage was too great, I walked over, took the whip from her tiny hand and bent her forward onto the tree trunk beside the others.

This time I swung the sharp tongue across the larger bottom of the middle girl and told her to follow me. She lifted her trembling arms off the wood and meekly followed me across the glade.

I sat down and lifted the bottle to my lips. As I drank, I looked at the tall girl's proud rounded face and then her shoulders and melon breasts, flat waist and outward curving hips that fell into strong legs.

As I took a final swig and put the bottle down, the girl burst into frantic entreaty.

"Bwana, no needs beat me, I's not like the others, I's better than your European women! I's can please a man better than any white woman!"

Listening to her was more than my raging John Thomas could bear. I pulled off my shirt, dropped my trousers and leant back on the tree trunk.

"Show me what you can do with your tongue!"

She immediately fell to her knees and in a maddening frenzy started to lick my thighs. Her head lunged back and forth, seeking out every nook and cranny. Then she dropped her head to my rigid cock and, with a single plunge, swallowed the whole length, nudging my pubic hair with her nose. She stayed embedded for a few seconds, squeezing the base with rapid jerks of her throat muscles, then began to lift her head up and down.

Amazingly, she took my hand into hers, placed it on the back of her head and encouraged me to force it down. I immediately grabbed her head with both hands and wrenched it up and down my shaft with brutal lunges.

After a few minutes she jerked her head away and picked up the whip. She turned round, bent over and eased the blunt end into her anal opening.

"Whack ma bottom!" she gasped, ramming the whip handle in and out of her sphincter muscle.

I started to belt the shuddering cheeks with stinging smacks as her hand prodded herself with faster thrusting movements.

The obscene spectacle slowly filled my head with a raging fire and I grabbed the black whip handle and pulled it out of her, then put my shirt on, buttoned my trousers, and bent the gasping girl over the tree trunk.

I stood back a few feet and swung the whip sharply back and forth across her bottom. Her halting gasps and squirms inflamed my head and I lifted the whip higher into the air.

Crack!

Crack!

Crack!

The noise reverberated around the clearing, melting into the sound of the burning wood.

"More!" she yelled out suddenly. "More! More! More!"

The whore was determined to show me the extent of her greedy perverse appetite and I was more than willing to test her to the extreme.

I stood back a couple of paces and flicked the tip of the whip through the air. Then with a fury and madness that threatened to burst my head, I began to thrash the writhing bottom.

"Aagh, aagh, aagh, whah, whah, whah!" she howled and yelped, pounding her clenched fists into the tree trunk.

I lifted the whip again, this time intent on making her scream and beg forgiveness in having dared to challenge me, when suddenly she turned her head round. Her panic stricken eyes caught sight of the raised whip and she jumped to her feet and ran off into the jungle.

I sat on the tree trunk and grabbed the rum bottle. A few long gulps jolted me back to some sanity and I looked across at the two arses still stuck up in the air awaiting the whip. They belonged to the toothless girl and the slim girl, and I remembered that when I first entered the clearing I had detected a streak of arrogance in the demeanour of the slim girl.

I would soon cure that!

I crossed the clearing and prodded the toothless girl.

"You can go."

Then I rested the whip on the slim girl's shoulder. She was very tense. "Not you!" I said. "You follow me!"

She walked slowly behind me, but her manner was haughty. When we reached the tree trunk, I sat down and studied her. She was the same height as her friend, but slimmer. Her small round face looked down at me with proud disdainful eyes. Her svelte frame held small firm breasts with button hard nipples and her tight waist flowed into womanly hips supported by slender but shapely legs.

"You have no right -" she started to say.

"Silence!" I was incensed at her brazen words. "I am your master and I own you, I do what I wish with you, whenever I wish. Do you understand?"

She looked at me with a smug expression and the corners of her lips slowly curled into a condescending scowl.

"I have only one master," she sneered, "and never a white man!"

"And who is your master?" I enquired sternly.

"I am not afraid to say the name of my prince. Exu! Exu! EXU! You cannot punish me for your pleasure! He

193

will protect me and watch over me!"

I reached down for the rum bottle and saw a piece of rope in Cordelia's bag. Quickly I grabbed the girl's wrists and tied them together tightly.

"What are you doing?" she cried out, struggling helplessly as I tied the loose end of the rope firmly around a sturdy branch sticking out of the tree trunk. The effect was to bend her forward with her bare rump thrust out into the air.

She turned to look up at me. "You better be careful, white man!" She looked up at the bright stars. "My prince is watching!" she declared, and spat insolently at my feet.

I stood up and picked up the whip.

Crack!

Crack!

Crack!

The noise resounded from her tight cheeks. She writhed about, but laughed. "You are wasting your time, white man. I've had many weeks training, waiting for my prince."

I stood back and began to deliver a frightening crescendo of blows. I scourged her with a flood of brutal blows she could not evade. Then suddenly I heard a faint trickle of laughter from her slanderous lips and stopped to listen.

"I told you, you white piece of shit, you can't do nothing with me!"

Those diabolical words stabbed my mind as surely as if it had been a newly sharpened dagger. I threw down the whip and grabbed a portion of pig meat and lifted it to her nose.

"Whaa, whaa?" she gulped, straining at the rope. Then she screamed at the top of her voice. "AAAAAGH!" She shrunk from the meat in revulsion and her wrists twisted and wrenched against the tight grip of the rope.

"EXU SAVE MEEEE!"

It was a loud wail. I quickly stepped over the tree trunk

194

and stopped her noise by grabbing her roughly by the chin and squeezing her cheeks together. I dropped the pig meat to the ground and started to undo my trouser buttons. She glared in disgust as I loosened the last button and pulled out my bloated cock.

Immediately she began to claw and rip against the rope, whilst her bloodshot eyes threatened to jump out of their sockets.

I picked up the pig meat and held it to her face again.

"Which one is it to be?"

She gagged and choked for a second as her eyes danced wildly, alternating from the meat to my engorged weapon, then with a suffocating yelp she took half of me into her mouth. With a quick nudge onto the back of her head, she started to move up and down my cock, swallowing more and more.

I picked up the whip and cracked it across the top of her tight cheeks.

Crack!

Crack!

Crack!

The next three blows forced her mouth completely into my pubic hair. "Ugh!" she gagged again. Every time she withdrew I hit her sharply at an angle. "Ugh!" she choked, as every searing tear propelled her protesting mouth back down onto her tormentor.

As the fire slowly enveloped my mind, I began to thrash her like a lunatic, not caring where the fiery tip landed, until finally, with a last lunge, I exploded into her mouth.

When the last spasm ended I withdrew and untied her. She kept sucking my cock, then, after a minute, she seemed to awake and quickly ran away.

13

It was the night of Exu's coming!

I had spent the two previous days preparing my disguise, and now I was ready to become that evil creature - the horned mask in particular was really fearsome! Cordelia had pestered me to rehearse with the red powder, but I managed to put her off.

As to my safety, it was arranged that she would take a rifle and hide in a tree - just in case!

After she had gone I put the powder and the mask into a bag and covered my naked painted body with a long coat.

As I left the house I noticed how deathly quiet everything seemed to be. Even the demonic frogs cast their voices in a subdued manner, and the moon winked silently from behind black clouds, teasing and hiding its yellow face.

As I walked in the pitch blackness, a sudden distant drumming spurred me on. Eventually I saw the circle of fires, and picked my way to a spot where I could see them clearly, and also the mound of earth in the centre.

Susie sat next to one of the fires, beating out a quick regular rhythm on a drum. I hardly recognised her, because her cheeks bore gashes of red and yellow paint, whilst the remainder of her naked body was streaked with thin white lines. Her hair was adorned with flashes of long black feathers, fixed behind her ears and falling onto her shoulders. She sat apparently mesmerised at the sound of her own drum and stared wildly at the dark earth mound. The light of the small fires cast unearthly shadows around the clearing, giving it an eerie mystical appearance.

Now she abruptly stopped beating the drum and approached the nearest fire. She threw a pinch of grey substance into its heart and it instantly gave out a faint smoky plume. She went to each fire in turn and did the same. An aroma of the sweet heavy scent of decaying rose petals filled the air. As I watched her return to her drum, my head began to swim from the pungent smell and my body seemed to develop a strange weightlessness.

Susie started a soft but more urgent thumping on the drum and suddenly a faint chorus of chants wafted out from behind her. I peered to where the moaning sounds came from and detected a number of sitting figures amongst the foliage - Susie's friends, sitting in a row.

Slowly the chants grew louder and louder until I recognised the urgent lament: Exu! Exu! Exu!

Susie's drumming slowly increased in volume and intensity to match the rising chorus. The time for my appearance was at hand. I was just opening the little box of red powder when the little hairs at the back of my head stood up.

There was a feeling of evil in the air!

I froze as a faint rustle seemed to come from among the trees on the opposite side of the clearing. I looked up in dread. Something seemed to move. Through the smoke that hung over everything, I was almost sure I detected a faint shadow.

The drum beats grew louder and louder and then I saw a dark shape slowly come into view.

I stared in disbelief at the unearthly sight!

A seemingly floating figure with horns on his head inched closer and closer through the trees towards the edge of the clearing.

I rubbed my eyes and pinched myself to make sure I wasn't having some infernal dream as I stared at the approaching demonic figure from hell.

Exu!

Now I finally saw the figure emerge and stand proudly beside the illuminating fire.

He must have stood some seven feet in height and with

the extra elevation of his horns he looked a truly frightening monstrosity. His horrible snoutish mouth turned from side to side and his red demonic eyes glinted hungrily from the black face that was part of the black half of his body. Below the waist he was white and his penis was a true monster.

To the incessant pounding beat of the drum and the background chants, he lumbered forward to the earth mound and sat spread-legged upon it, waiting.

Aenga appeared from behind Susie's beating drum and entered the circle, kneeling with her head to the ground. Her body was painted in long vertical yellow and red stripes that matched the colours of the leaping flames.

She lifted her head, stood up and slowly approached the growling demon. Without warning she fell on the mighty phallus and instantly began to milk it, swallowing nearly the whole length into her mouth. She quickly increased her speed whilst the creature lifted its horned head and shook it from side to side.

After a minute he grew weary of her and pushed her away and she ran off crying bitterly into the jungle.

Danda emerged from behind Susie. They must have drawn lots to establish the order of their chance with this appalling monster, I supposed. Danda was also painted in bright vertical colours from her face to her ankles. She immediately turned her back on Exu and started to thrust her large bottom backwards and forwards.

The demonic beast snarled and growled, staring red eyes devouring the thrusting flesh.

Suddenly he leant forward, grabbed the girl's head and twisted her round, jamming her open mouth onto his huge cock. He mercilessly forced her head up and down, then in a minute threw her off and instead impaled her upon his organ. She screamed in pain as he lifted her bodily up and down, then, after a few minutes, he tired of her also and flung her away to run howling into the jungle.

Susie in the meantime continued her loud pounding on the drum, swaying from side to side as she did so.

Now another girl emerged, smaller than the previous one but also painted from head to toe, apart from her shaking bottom. She carried a long black whip and placed it at the beast's feet. When he saw it, he stood and picked it up, and threw his unfortunate to the ground.

He looked a terrifying sight as he swung the whip round and round his head, turned to the poor girl spread-eagle on the mound and began to flay her bottom. He swung the whip with such ferocity that I doubted if she would survive.

If I had brought my pistol I would have felled the demon with a single shot. Why did not Cordelia shoot? I supposed that she thought it was me!

He continued with no respite, no mercy, slowly moving around his prey as he lashed the poor girl to what must surely be oblivion.

Finally he threw down the whip and fell upon the girl, took her into his mighty arms and speared her with his enormous member. Despite her heart-rending screams he continued to pound into her remorselessly, each new powerful thrust seeming to propel her further over the mound.

The incessant drum beat blended inescapably with the screams of the girl and the obscene chants of her waiting sisters.

Suddenly, with a last humiliating lunge, he dismounted and sent her too scurrying for the safety of the jungle as he waited for his next suitor.

It was the toothless girl. She was painted with blue and white diagonal stripes and had thick coloured plumage decorating her hair.

She instantly fell to her knees before him and began one of the most obscene acts I have ever seen in my life!

She started to lick and suck the toes of his feet. She moved quickly up to his ankles, scraping her maddening tongue all over his calves, then up to his knees. Then she pushed her body forwards and began to lick the whole of his thighs from top to bottom.

When she reached the top I assumed that she would swallow his huge cock, but instead she gently lifted one of his legs and slowly persuaded him to bend his body backwards, until the round orbs of his buttocks were exposed to her searching eyes.

She stared lewdly at his exposed cheeks, then yanked them apart and threw her face into the horrible flesh. She began again her vile licking and sucking. As I stared at the obscene unspeakable act that the little whore was performing with her hot searching tongue, the monster put his mighty hand behind her head and pulled her further in. When he let her go, she increased the speed of her actions, shaking her head back and forth and moaning in ecstasy.

Then he finally tired of her and kicked her away, but instead of running off into the jungle, she stood up before him and swayed her hips from side to side.

The beast lifted his body upright and snarled, then he slowly lifted his huge frame down from his throne and stood close to her. Her diminutive height meant that his monstrous penis was just inches from her lips. She quickly took it in with one suck and immediately began to swallow as much as her size would allow.

As she plunged on the fearsome weapon, he lifted his snout into the sky and howled in glee as his whole body shook from the effects of her teasing mouth. Then, after a few minutes, he condescended to look down at the small creature who was trying her eager best to satisfy him - and failing.

He suddenly pulled out of her mouth, bent down and lifted her to his shoulders. He looked into her terrified face with his red demonic glinting eyes, then simply dropped her onto his huge penis. The poor girl screamed as he fell with her to the ground and rolled round and round upon her. Past the fires they rolled as he propelled himself and his speared prey round his throne, shaking the earth with their revolting coupling.

Then the obscene exhibition stopped and the beast stood up and kicked the girl out of the clearing, then sat back on his throne, snarling for his next victim.

He didn't have long to wait. It was the well-built girl who had boasted to me of her sexual prowess. She walked confidently towards her intended mate. She wore no decoration or paint whatsoever! Her belief in herself was shown in the haughty way in which she approached the sitting demon and instantly bent forward to do homage to him - the whole of his penis instantly vanished into her mouth!

Exu seemed to be taken aback and looked down quietly at the proud girl as she demonstrated her lewd ability, confidently moving her mouth up and down his shaft.

She continued the uninhibited display, speeding up then slowing down, and from time to time she freed her mouth and slid her hungry lips up and down the sides of his cock and back.

After a further few minutes of this, she withdrew and bent down to pick up the whip. She made sure Exu was watching her, then turned her back and started flaying her own bottom to the sound of the heavy drum beat. She curled and twisted the whip in order to inflict the cruelest blows. It flicked from side to side, coiling round her hungry flesh with stinging impacts. She used every possible method in cracking it over her shoulder, round her belly and even up between her outstretched legs.

Eventually the growling beast rose and pulled the whip from her hand and threw it to the ground. Then with a mighty swipe of his hand he sent her reeling away into the undergrowth and proudly returned to his throne.

As he sat there, master of all he surveyed and lusting for more victims, a small girl fell into the clearing. She must have been pushed in, and she was terrified, too terrified even to run.

Exu seemed to sense the girl's reluctance and feasted his red eyes of the slight trembling figure. She was easily the smallest of the lot and I suspected she might have been persuaded to this against her wishes.

The snarling black demon probably sensed the same as he slowly dismounted his throne and approached the shivering girl. She yelped when he grabbed her by the hand and with a sudden pull yanked her to his throne. Then he threw her face forward over the mound and stood looking down, his growling silenced for the first time.

Suddenly he lifted his snout to the moonlit sky and let out a second earth shattering howl. Then he pulled the small bottom cheeks apart. The miserable girl gave a scream at the very thought of the abomination that was about to fall upon her, and the screams as he entered her and broke her to his will, plunging mercilessly in and out of her, were heart-rending indeed.

Thankfully, the horrible act only lasted a few minutes more, then he allowed the whimpering girl to crawl pathetically out of the clearing.

Next came the proud arrogant girl I had punished in the clearing, the one who had called upon her prince for succour. Well, here he was! She had painted the word Exu in different colours all over her naked body.

She ran to him and started to kiss him all over. For the second time that night he fell silent at the unexpected worshipful homage.

Susie momentarily skipped a beat, but when the demon flashed his red piercing stare in her direction she lowered her head and continued her pounding with a vengeance.

Exu allowed this girl to kiss him for a while, leaving out none of his sensitive areas, then suddenly she bent down and picked up the whip. She slowly turned her back to him, first making sure he was watching her, then bent forward with the handle of the whip in her fist. She pushed her bottom cheeks apart and gently inserted the blunt end into her tight anus, then, satisfied it was positioned at the required angle, pushed it fully in. Then she wriggled her bottom from side to side, allowing the long sinewy whip to wriggle and fly through the air, following her sideway movements.

She stopped abruptly and screamed out the name of the beast. Then she took hold of the handle and began to force the whip in and out of her quivering bottom. She pushed and jabbed with such force that once again Exu fell silent. Then, unable to control the lust raging in his satanic mind, he stood up, roughly pulled the whip out of the shaking girl and, grabbing her small bottom cheeks, impaled her flesh with his huge weapon.

Instantly she started a thrusting backward movement, so that both their bodies clashed savagely. He skewered and pumped her pulsating eager rump with all the bestiality and sadism that he could muster. In the end he lifted her by the undersides of her thighs, placed his hands under her knees, and drove her up and down on his fiery weapon.

After a few minutes he dropped her to the ground and she immediately stood up and began to lick and slobber at his gruesome chest, whilst he stood snarling as he watched her grovel and humiliate herself.

Then he knocked her to the ground.

When he saw that she was kissing and worshipping his feet, he quickly lunged at her with a massive kick that caused even her to scurry away

At a gesture from Susie she went to the drums and took her turn there. Susie stood up and stretched, then took two steps forward. She was the next smallest of all the girls and barely reached to the waist of the beast.

She listened to the rising beat of the drum, biding her time as Exu stood in front of his throne, growling and snarling. She advanced another few steps, until she stood looking down at the beast's huge projecting weapon, then suddenly lunged forward and instantly impaled her mouth onto the massive cock.

As Exu looked down at her, Susie stood frozen to the spot as if waiting for his reaction. Then she placed her hands behind her back and started to slowly withdraw, then gradually swallow again. As if motivated by the drum beat, she began a sudden spearing action, sucking as hard and fast as her little head would go.

Exu seemed captivated for a few minutes, then yanked his weapon out and lifted Susie bodily into the air and dropped her onto his phallus. He easily lifted her up and down and she seemed to encourage him by holding his shoulders tightly as she bounced up and down in rhythm to his lifting movements.

But he tired of her after a while, and dropped her onto the earth mound. She instantly recovered, knelt on her hands and knees and offered her tight little arse as a sacrifice.

He looked at the offering as Susie obscenely thrust her bottom backwards and forwards, snarling and growling at the crude exhibition. Then he slowly advanced. When Susie felt his huge weapon touch her bottom, she grabbed it from behind and began to smear his helmet up and down her wet orifices. He allowed her to tease for a minute, then suddenly pushed her arm away. He grabbed her tight bottom cheeks and abruptly entered her anus. Susie began to shout encouragement, urging him on as he started to thrust in and out with the utmost brutality.

The power of his thrust lifted her off her knees at every lunge as her friend pounded the drum louder and louder, totally mesmerised by what was happening.

Then, once again, the beast lost interest. He dropped Susie on the ground, and his snout turned from side to side, sniffing the breeze.

Then he got to his feet and moved over to where the proud girl pounded on the drums. He threw her over his shoulder and was gone.

She had found her prince!

EPILOGUE

Cordelia says she saw nothing of Exu's coming.

She even insinuated that I had fallen asleep on account of the rum which I had taken to fortify myself against danger, and all that I have recounted was the product of nightmarish dreams. Ridiculous, of course! It was all so real. I may enjoy an occasional glass of rum, but I am no drunkard. My theory is that Cordelia had been too frightened to take her place in the tree, and had left me totally unprotected.

It was somewhat of a surprise, however, to see the girl I had thought to be Exu's bride working as normal the following morning.

Perhaps it is time to clear my mind of this diabolical plantation and come to writing about what happened at the first one. I have hesitated to do so, because it was all rather dreadful, but maybe writing of it will purge it from me.

If I do drink a trifle too much at times, it is due brooding over that first plantation and the slave girls I abused there... was I over the top with them, I sometimes wonder...

BONUS PAGES

First, here is the opening of next month's title:-
NAKED PLUNDER by J.T.Pearce

The house Abu took me was at the very edge of the city, past all the poor people's barrios with the bright-eyed nubile women hanging around outside. Waiting in the streets for somebody to come and buy their bodies. That's how they made enough money to survive at the edge of Sao Paolo. In the midst of glitter and wealth beyond belief, they sold their flesh, not always necessarily to the highest bidder, for pretty as these girls were, they were also mostly uneducated, and easy to take advantage of in their desperate state.

Abu had dressed me in off-white loose cotton trousers and a loose shirt. He'd insisted I wear a frayed straw hat on my head.

"No good if they see you're rich then master," he winked at me as he said it.

In truth I am no more the master of Abu than I am fabulously wealthy. What I am is a journalist out to do a dirty job and Abu, my childhood friend, was my ticket into the slave trade world I wished to bare to my readers.

"Whatever you see in there," Abu admonished me, "for God's sake say nothing."

Mentally I'd prepared myself for the worst, but nothing could have prepared me for what we encountered when we reached the house.

It was perched high on a hill choked with vegetation, and the outside of it looked flimsy enough. It gave the appearance of having been constructed of dark wood and cheap brick. The truth however became more apparent the closer we approached.

"Good evening master Sahim," Abu yelled into the shadows by the gate.

A fierce looking black man emerged. A large machine gun hung from his shoulder. "Who's that with you Abu?" he asked eyeing me with great suspicion.

"Ask no impertinent questions and you shall receive no falsehood," Abu said cheerfully. "The master with me is not for naming. Has the show began inside?"

The guard hesitated for a moment, obviously weighing the options available to him, then he consulted his watch. "You're right on time, it's starting any minute now."

"Be on your guard then master Sahim." Abu waved a benevolent hand towards the brute. "There's no telling what unwanted elements may want to grace us inside if you let them." And with that we slipped past the big metal gates and found ourselves on the grounds of a big villa.

I could now see that the impression of a little house upon a hill was a cleverly constructed fake, much like a purpose-built movie set, and could admire the ingenuity of the builder.

"Not a word now, mind you. Or both our lives will hang in the balance," Abu hissed, and taking me firmly by the elbow he led me inside.

I followed Abu to a huge semi-darkened room. The windows were shut, the blinds drawn to keep out prying eyes, and a quiet air-conditioner piped out the Brazilian heat.

When my eyes became accustomed to the gloom I noticed that the edges of the room were strewn with chairs. Men dressed much as myself occupied these chairs, and scantily clad mulatto girls circulated freely between them, passing the men drinks and thick cigars in the manner of usherettes.

One of these girls passed right in front of me, her short tunic bobbing merrily at the front, evidence, if I needed any, of the fact that her nubile breasts rode unfettered.

I smelt her scent, a mixture of juniper and jasmine, and then she was past, her round dark eyes downcast, her long black hair drawn back to show off her slender neck and fine chocolate coloured features.

The sleeveless tunics these girls wore were short. Barely preserving their modesty. As I followed the girl with my eyes I saw her stop and curtsy quickly before a bald, corpulent looking man, and offer him a thick cigar from the tray she held in her hands.

The man nodded imperceptibly and as the girl bent to light the cigar for him his thick-fingered white hands crawled up the backs of the girl's shapely thighs and hefted a plump, round buttock.

The girl's short tunic had ridden high enough as she bent forward to reveal her complete lack of underwear.

I watched fascinated as the fat man's roving hand squeezed and kneaded the girl's pliant buttocks and then, before my very eyes, moved to the tender lips of her open sex, and inserted a thick index finger inside her vulva.

In all this time the girl didn't so much as flinch. She finished lighting the fat man's cigar, waited patiently for him to extract his finger from her vulva, and the minute this was done, with a suggestive swing of her hips, eyes still downcast, she went on her way, to ask the next man if he would like a cigar.

I counted eight of these girls, making the rounds, willowy, exotic usherettes. Offering both cigars and drink.

"Drink nothing from here," Abu hissed by my side. "Half the time the drinks are drugged, and the cigars are so strong they'll make you sick."

A young girl stopped before us. She too wore a short tunic and judging by the fine lithe lines of her young figure, I judged she couldn't have been more than nineteen.

"Cigar young masters?" she asked, and I could see she meant it. The language of masters and slaves, which Abu

208

sometimes playfully employed, was here spoken for real.

"Not for us,.." Abu waved her away. But before she could depart, a devil possessed me. It was not often I was given the chance to see close up such fine girls being so easily available. Mesmerised with temptation, I reached out and put my hand on her left knee. Instantly the girl froze.

Intrigued how far I could push it, unable to believe that I could have such power to make a girl stop and submit just by a simple touch, I let my hand travel up her left thigh. I caressed the smooth silk of her inner thigh, going up, under her tunic to the junction between her legs.

Her sex, I felt, was depilated, its smooth round lips slightly raised. Entranced by the girl's young beauty, her inability to raise her eyes, I stroked her between her legs, gently pushed open her nether lips, parted them with my fingers. My crotch in response was tight with arousal. The front of the loose white trousers I wore ballooned in a way that was impossible to hide.

The girl bit her bottom lip. Small, white, even teeth left tiny indentations in the dark cherry coloured flesh and it is only then that I noticed that Abu, even as I invaded with a finger the moist coral depths of the girl's sex, had parted the tight, round, cheeks of her ass and had inserted his own calloused digit into the tight bud of her anus.

"Let her be," he said with a wicked glint in his eye when he noticed I'd discovered him. "There'll be better sport to be had later if you have a mind to, and besides the show's about to begin."

Indeed, even as he spoke a gong sounded from the depths of the house somewhere. Instantly an air of transformation came over all the men seated in the room. On cue, the young girls withdrew to their assigned positions by the walls and a spotlight lit the centre of that cavernous hall.

From a doorway I had not noticed, a dark haired man, about my age, impeccably dressed and carrying a wireless microphone, took centre stage.

"Gentlemen!" He addressed the gathering with a fine flourish.

"That's Mr Soames," Abu whispered urgently by my side.

I straightened up immediately. So this was the legendary Edward Soames, a native of England reputed to be on the run for some heinous crime no one had discovered. I watched him turn to take in the men, his eyes quickly surveying the positions the girls had taken up. I noticed then more figures, strategically placed in the shadows. Figures more reminiscent of the Neanderthal guarding the gate downstairs than of the willowy girls who served cigars and alcohol.

"Good to see so many of you tonight," Soames continued. "It is good to take such active interest in the welfare of our less fortunate citizens. Rescuing them from poverty and starvation. Offering them the chance to enjoy a different life. A more gracious one, perhaps." He stopped here and surveyed us all, read the fever pitch of excitement in our eyes, smelled perhaps the animal smell of our primitive lust.

I was not fooled by his words, aroused though I was. I knew them for the justification these wealthy magnates used for the depravities they practised upon the nubile flesh of the unwilling barrio girls they so illegally bought here.

"There are some of you here tonight I have never seen before. Perhaps afterwards, if you could be so kind as to indulge me I would like a very brief word." His eyes were directed at me when he spoke, and I suddenly felt chills run down my spine.

Although officially nothing had ever been found against Soames, he had a reputation for being ruthless, and I already knew of one case of a journalist who had been inconsiderate enough to pry too deeply into this man's affairs.

"And now, let tonight's show begin!" and with that he clapped his hands.

Immediately the lights fell even lower. Artificial smoke was piped in from somewhere and as if by magic a beautiful cluster of young girls appeared in the very middle of the room.

They were all of mixed blood, their fine features and smooth limbs the colour of burnished sandalwood, tinged with the barest hint of chocolate.

Ethereal music piped in from somewhere and the girls started slowly to undulate their bodies to its oriental rhythms.

Whereas the usherettes had been dressed in short sleeveless tunics, each with a different motif adorned on it, the girls I saw now were dressed in scraps of clothing, like they'd just been picked up from the street.

The glowing sheen of their finely washed long hair, the healthy appearance of their long limbs, lent as much a lie to this fact as the strategically placed rips in their clothing.

They were all barefoot and dressed in full ankle length skirts and a cropped top that left their midriff bare.

Rips and tears in their skirts and tops gave tantalising glimpses of their bodies as they danced. There would be the flare of a young thigh glimpsed through a long rent in a wide peasant skirt, the suggestive curve of tight young buttocks, the darkened thrust of a nippled mound of flesh.

In the midst of them all a bull-headed man moved like a primitive animal. His body was square and squat, his head shaved completely. In one hand he carried a riding crop, and as the girls danced and swirled about him, he would use it to flick a long skirt up, revealing a slim leg to the very top of its thigh. Or he would take hold of a girl, her willowy body looking suddenly very fragile in his meaty grip, and to the onlooker's expressed delight he would slip a rough hand under her top, begin to heft and squeeze her firm breasts.

The girl would stoically bear this, unresisting, though an expression of terror and distaste would creep into her face, and this would drive the white-clad gentlemen wild.

I noticed then the subtle hand-signals. The slight nods. And saw how clear across the room stood Soames, by a gigantic black board, chalk in hand, and as the nods and hand-signals came in, a young assistant would whisper them to him, and up would go some numbers. Numerical values assigned beside each name. The names being those of the dancing girls. The numbers being the prices different masters were thus bidding for them.

I kept my hands on my lap, unwilling to participate in this debasement of young girls, even to maintain my cover. My eyes were firmly riveted on the brute amidst the dancing girls, and I saw now how artful was his act, for as the prices mounted, the bidding frenzy took hold, so was he emboldened and by design descended into new levels of lewdness.

His riding crop cut the air, the girls around him, quickened their step in response, cavorted and gyrated more frantically, but this was all part of the design. Their increased alacrity would not save them.

With a cobra-like motion the brute grabbed a girl. She was an exceptional beauty. The exertion of the dance had made her cheeks flash and had brought the sheen of vitality to her young face, and as the brute caught her the erotic effect was accentuated by the undisguised terror in her eyes.

The rest of the girls kept on twisting, throwing their skirts up as they span, showing everybody the long, sexy lines of their legs, throwing their hair forward and then flicking it back, making their breasts jiggle beneath their cropped tops. But it was to the caught girl that every man's eyes in that room now centred.

The brute sensed this and judged his moment finely,

212

waiting for the oriental tune and the girls' dance to reach a crescendo, and as this happened he turned the girl, a firm hand round her slim waist, to face the circle of onlookers.

"Please," the girl's lips silently whispered, but the brute was inured to such pleadings.

With his free hand he raked her skirt up, bunched it around her slender waist, and forced her to kneel on hands and knees, facing away from him.

The round cheeks of the girl's full backside were revealed to us all.

"Watch this," Abu said to me from my side. The excitement evident on his face made me think that he'd seen what was to come before, and more, he even approved of it.

With her backside exposed, her sex vulnerably open, the girl tried to take sudden flight, to crawl away from the man who held her. But the brute had expected this. With one firm hand he grabbed her hair. Pulled her head back. Displayed to us all her fine, young features. The full lips. The languid, liquid eyes, now so full of terror. With his other he tore at her flimsy dress ripped the skirt off her body. Pulled at the cropped top she had on her back.

The girl's naked body was now displayed in all its glorious beauty. Already I could see Soames, in the background, scribbling furiously against a name, MELLISA, and almost astronomical numbers being written next to it.

Melissa, if that was her real name, tried vainly to hide the fulsome bounty of her exposed breasts with one hand across her chest. In vain. The instant she did that, the brute behind her whipped her across the full round buttocks with his riding crop. The impact was audible even above the tunes of the oriental music and the effect was obvious.

The cheeks of Melissa's buttocks shook. Her head shot back, eyes now awash in pain as well as terror. The hand she held across her chest, fell away and her round, full breasts fell free, their dark nippled tips, engorged with pain,

213

stood out tightly against the burnished background of her flesh.

The display made those around me go wild. They half rose out of their seats, ignoring the rest of the dancing girls, their voices hoarse with excitement.

"Again, again, hit her again."

"Plough those sweet rear mounds for us."

"Give it to her."

And the brute complied. He raised his hand to full swing, the riding crop held high, and then brought it swinging down, raising a red welt across the girl's full buttocks, less than an inch above the one his previous stroke had marked.

He could have gone like that for some time, for he obviously enjoyed this part of his work, but a quick glance at his master was enough to let the brute know that the girl was fast approaching the maximum of her potential value.

Something extra was required to raise the bidding the final distance.

Grabbing the girl by the back of the head the brute pushed her face down towards the plush carpet. Grateful not to be hit again, she lay with her head held low, cradled in her arms, the round cheeks of her ass on show, the tight bud of her anus and the open depilated lips of her cunt clearly visible to the onlookers.

With a quick chopping motion of his left hand the brute made the dancing girls stop. At his bidding they each sat on the floor, forming a rough circle around the naked Melissa, prostate now on the floor, her ass raised vulnerably to the brute standing behind her.

The music stopped.

We all watched with bated breath as the brute changed his grip upon the riding crop, not one of us not secretly wishing to change places with him. He held the riding crop now so that the long slender handle of it pointed threateningly towards the vulnerable orifices the girl's posture so openly displayed.

"Gentlemen, what am I bid for her?" Soames called out from the far end of the room. "Place your final bids now!" And at a nod from him, the brute behind Melissa pushed the handle of the riding crop between her legs, smoothly parted the raised lips of her sex and gave us all a brief glimpse of succulent pink folds before the handle of the riding crop was engulfed within them.

Melissa, head down, let out a moan, and her hips rolled a little. Apart from that she made no other reaction.

"A magnificent animal gentlemen, an asset to any man's life," Soames said as the bidders went frantic.

The brute left the riding crop where it was, but, of his own accord now, slid his hands over the smooth round globes of the girl's ass. He caressed them with unexpected gentleness, then suddenly slapped her ass. First with one hand, then with the other, making her cheeks tremble, the reddening imprint of his thick hand visible to most buyers.

Melissa cried out in response. A muffled, pained cry at this new assault, and to my shame I found myself aroused by this display. Her beautiful ripe body, submissive, available to any use a man could dream to put it to.

The punters beside me and all around went near hysterical. They rose out of their chairs, waved straw hats, handkerchiefs, even shoes at Soames.

Sensing the success of his actions, the brute now withdrew the riding crop, making Melissa's hips roll again. Its end, as it came out her body, was glistening with her fluids, and I can swear that every man in that room was imagining what it would be like to stick their cocks inside her and make her cry out with passion.

The brute wasn't yet finished. He played the glistening end of the riding crop upon the girl's flesh, first moving it down the length of one inside thigh, almost to the floor, then sliding it up the other, and then suddenly as he slid it

215

past her open sex, he stopped, arrested its movement.

Poised above her bottom.

There was instant silence. We could all read his intent and waited. The brute looked around teasingly, and then with a grin that bared all his teeth he drove the poised end of the riding crop against the tightly closed button of the girl's anus.

Melissa's head flew up, her mouth opened to cry out in direct response to the pain that was being inflicted upon her flesh, but at the last possible moment, Soames cried: "Enough! We have a buyer."

The brute stopped, disappointment at not having been able to ram his riding crop deep enough up Melissa's ass evident on his blunt face.

A couple of effeminate looking men, dressed in orange, suddenly appeared and, wrapping a red robe around Melissa's body, helped lift her to her feet and quickly whisked her away.

The rest of the girls followed the two men, heads down, shuffling their feet, ashamed at having failed to arouse enough interest in their prospective masters.

The usherettes once more started circulating amongst us. Their charms, however, now looked very tame compared to what we had just witnessed, and not many men seemed interested.

"Time to go?" Abu asked. I detected a note of anxiety in his voice. "It would not do to overstay. Soames can be a nasty bastard if he suspects he's being set up and -"

At that exact minute a door opened just behind us. Mr Soames stood momentarily silhouetted in its frame, the massive bulk of the brute who'd just used Melissa, stood just behind him.

"Mr Sinhail!" he addressed Abu first. "Mr Lewis!" he called me by my real name. "Feel yourselves my guests. Malakai here will show you your quarters."

216

And now for the first instalment of the expanded version
of ERICA: PROPERTY OF REX by Rex Saviour (1997)
Episode 2 will be included with NAKED PLUNDER

PRELUDE

Balik, the capital of Your Majesty's Sahdist Kingdom
of Balikpan, would pass for a normal Oriental city if one
could ignore the constant molestation of the nubile young
street cleaners, who wear nothing but short smocks and
broad-brimmed coolie hats, and the street vendors who
pester passing tourists to finger some beautiful young creature standing on tiptoe with her feet astride a couple of
orange boxes.

Tourists here are not the normal family group, but the
rich, the discreet and above all the cruel of this world, come
to practise your diabolical religion. I know that they are
gathered by subtle promotion and word of mouth and very
carefully screened before they receive the impressive visa
without which they cannot pass the soldiers who protect
the unobtrusive departure lounge of Balikpan Airways at
Don Muang Airport, Bangkok. There is no other way in or
out of Balikpan, since there is no deep water harbour and
fast patrol vessels guard the fishing fleet - and that suits
you, does it not, Your Majesty?

There are many casual tourists at present, attracted by
the annual Festival of Obedience just concluded, though
not many will have done as I did and entered a competitor.
Some, the more knowledgeable or maybe richer, come and
go frequently and maintain establishments here, and would
not deal with street vendors when the auction rooms offer
better bargains.

Your ornate palace is a magnificent gilded structure
within massive walls: one has to admire it from the outside
even if one detests the perversities that are practised within.

A rather fine miniature of itself, standing on stilts between two ancient rain trees at the front gates, provides the customary spirit-house. The palace is a many-storied building and the royal quarters are, of course, at the greatest height: no structure in the city may rise higher than the lowest spires of your palace, Great Lord.

My balcony, as Your Majesty knows, looks out on a paved way bordered on one side with colourful bushes cloaked in lazy butterflies and on the other with flowering reeds that sway in the gentle breeze. It divides the outer bastions of the palace from the muddy banks of the broad slow-flowing river Baliknahm, beside which sacred white peacocks strut up and down: the area is an enclave of the past in the midst of the modern city.

And here, along the river bank, comes a ceremonial procession, its stately progress flanked by two lines of marching soldiers in full regalia.

First come seven tall naked black women, magnificent specimens, matched for height, with plumes and strings of pearls in their long black hair and perspiration sheening their ebony skins. They are chained together ankle to ankle and wrist to wrist so that they step forward together and the palm leaves they are carrying rise and fall in perfect unison as they sweep the dust from the dirt road, baked hard by the heat of the blazing sun.

They are followed by a man magnificently dressed and wearing a conical hat, who sits cross-legged upon a sacred white elephant that is richly comparisoned with rugs and jewels. Diamonds and rubies sparkle in the bright sunlight.

Behind are lesser elephants bearing lesser mandarins, and on foot come the trumpeters, the courtiers and a long retinue of slaves.

More slaves run out from the heavy golden palace gates, swinging them apart, striking gongs, then prostrating themselves on the steps as the Barcalon is helped down from his great beast. A naked woman walks gracefully before him as he mounts the palace steps, this one blonde and white. His insignia, a silver betel box and golden parasol, are balanced upon her head, which is held high by a wide jewel-encrusted leather collar. She is very erect because her arms are bound behind her straight back with golden cord so tightly drawn that the elbows are pressed together, and each knot is sealed with the Imperial dragon seal that may not be broken.

Now he passes from my sight - he will be entering the first courtyard, where fifty of the elite guard, holding swords of gold, squat on fine Persian carpets.

Thus, Your Infinite Majesty, comes your Chief Minister. He is here to collect the few poor pages I have written so far. Soon he will bear my words upstairs on a golden platter so that his hands may not defile what his master is to touch.

As I scribbled away for you in my cell at the palace, at least one armed soldier always in sight, I have had reason enough to sweat even if the climate were different. Cell? How could I call this magnificent apartment a cell? The gorgeous view of the brightly painted high-prowed boats that come and go from the palace quay, the huge iridescent dragonflies that hover over the slow stir of muddy water, the fine verdant mountains defiled by the sleeping volcano which dribbles ominous traces of dark black smoke, these form a spectacular backdrop but are no comfort.

I find it hard to write because of the way you use women as decoration throughout the palace, specially the one who has a strap secured around the knees and balances upon a slim pedestal in this very room, her elbows tied up to a rod which passes behind her shoulders, making sport for the soldiers whenever she loses her balance and falls. It is a constant reminder of the cruelty that is worshipped in this evil island paradise of yours, unique, surely, in the world of today.

Here, Radiance of the World, you are the ultimate authority and in you cruelty knows no curb: you do great credit to the Marquis de Sade whom you worship so ardently.

So - I hope Erica's history will please you, Oh Mightiest of Kings. Do with me as you will for the Lord is my shepherd, but I humbly beg of you, in the name of the Marquis whom you hold sacred, release my girl Erica when you tire of her. She might yet recover even from so traumatic a beginning and find happiness in a life without me: in my foolishness I brought her here for your accursed festival and doubtless I shall die for that, but she is innocent.

I have done as you ordered - I have twisted the facts to suit your perversities, and embroidered my tale a little. As you wished, I have made Erica seem much younger than she really was when I first met her, so there is falsehood here. And of course Erica is actually the supreme masochist - the worst thing you can do to her is to withhold her daily beating or humiliation. You know this and I know it, but you instructed me to conceal the fact and I have done my best to obey. I suppose it will titillate you more that way, and it would be her wish too, no doubt, for it is pretending to hate what secretly turns her on that gives her the biggest 'buzz' - her word not mine. But not here, no, not in your Court, Great Lord, not with a cruel tyrant who abuses for amusement - no no, it should be with someone who loves her dearly, as I do.

In falsifying my writing in these ways I seek to please you not for myself, but for Erica. My mission to save her crippled soul was genuine, it came from the true Lord, and He will support me in my present peril. If I do not mention my God again, do not forget that He is there: with His help lesser Monarchs may be toppled from their thrones, however permanent those thrones may seem, however many jewels may be woven into them.

BOOK ONE: ERICA ACQUIRED

1

Paint was peeling from the woodwork of the dingy inner-city terrace house at the end of the pathetic strip of unkempt garden. The family might well have gone away after all that publicity: neighbours get very militant when youngsters are abused, even in this foulest of London slums.

The front door was ajar. I thought I heard crying from inside, or perhaps this was an abandoned kitten. Nobody answered my knock. The noise that had disturbed me stopped abruptly, that was all.

I pushed open the creaking door. It led to a bare narrow uncarpeted passage. In front I could see into a cheerless kitchen with unwashed dishes piled high in a sink with a dripping tap. A door was half open on my left. I went in, and there she was, lying naked on her stomach on a shabby green couch, her slim body shaking with inner sobs, her face turned away from the door into a mass of gorgeous long red hair, her legs apart and bent up at the knees by the shortness of the couch, ankles crossed over a luscious little bottom.

Her arms were held high up behind her back, bound in such a way that each hand held the opposite elbow!

She drew up her legs as she turned over and sat up in alarm, an extremely pretty girl, extremely frightened. For a moment big bewildered blue eyes peeped through glorious long red hair, now falling over her face in a haze, then she jumped to her feet and scampered to a corner as far away from me as she could get, turning to face me shyly, shaking her head so that the hair swung behind her.

221

She had a perfect little figure, slim but nicely rounded. With her arms secured behind her so tightly she stood unnaturally erect, which drew attention to those budding breasts, so high and firm.

There was no heating or comfort in that bare room, apparently no one else in the house.

"Are you Erica?" I asked.

"Yes." It was almost a whisper. She was shrinking into the corner as if she would like to vanish into the woodwork, and she was shaking all over. She had the wide sort of mouth that so easily shows the upper teeth, and hers were good, regular and very white.

A very kissable mouth!

"Where's your step-Mother?"

"G-gone to the pub."

"Does she always leave you like this, no clothes?"

"That's so I don't run away."

"Why would you run away?"

"Because -"

"Because what?"

"Oh God!"

It was the first time I heard her blaspheme, but I decided to overlook it. This was no time to upbraid her, even for so serious a fault.

"Because what?" I asked again, gently, easing my trousers where they had tightened very inconveniently at the crotch.

"Uncle Willie -"

"Yes?"

"He's - he's coming to punish me -"

I stood up, and as she cowered away from me, caught in the corner, my eyes dwelt on her skin, so very smooth, a beautiful light brown, maybe olive, verging on golden, inviting the fingers to slide over it, all over it, to explore its shyness and secret recesses slowly and at leisure...

I licked my lips. "I think I'll wait for your step-mother," I said. After all, there are limits. "Will she be long?"

"What - what time is it?"

I looked at my watch, the one I had won at Sunday school. The thought of that should have made me turn round and walk out of that evil house, because the sight of her nakedness was doing bad things to my mind. "It's just after three," I said.

"Oh God!" she said again. Her delicate face - elfin, perhaps, one might call it - her face screwed up. She had stopped crying, but now she began to whimper: she was still pretty when she did that, it was cute, somehow appealing, and I didn't want her to stop.

"They - they'll be back any minute!" she said despairingly. This was in the days when pubs had to close at 3 o'clock.

"And your Uncle Willie is coming to punish you?" It seemed incredible. "What do you mean, punish?"

She hesitated, quiet for a moment, biting her full lower lip, as I waited for her to go on. "He - he'll beat me first, I think, and then - yes, he'll beat me with the belt I expect, he usually does."

"THE belt?" I repeated, for that was the way it had sounded.

"Yes," she said, as if it was obvious, "the leather one, the one that hangs by my bed."

I tried to suppress the illicit excitement that the image of her being beaten aroused in me: my feelings were totally unworthy, not at all Godly, yet not easy to brush aside. She was whimpering even more now, in between speaking, and I was edging closer to her despite myself.

"What did you do?" I asked. I fear my voice was not totally under control.

"I - I s-stole some money."

"How much money?"

223

"A lot of money." She glanced up at me timidly: I seemed to have got within touching distance without realising it, and I am quite tall, so she had to turn her face upwards towards me. Her eyes were brimming with more tears, but bright and blue and appealing. They kind of sparkled in a sexy way, though I am sure she didn't mean to be sexy. And they were very frightened. "Ten pounds," she whispered.

I could not condone that. "'Thou shalt not steal,'" I said sternly. "Exodus, 20, 15."

"Yes, well, but I need some - well - knickers and nightie and things."

"Did you say your Uncle is coming to beat you?" I asked. Probably disbelief was battling with shock and horror all over my face: the excitement I hope I hid. Somehow I was very close beside her now. She went on tiptoe and I felt hot breath on my ear as she leant against me and whispered.

"Oh yes, he's awful! Oh God, he - he's just too awful!"

"That is blasphemy again!" I said sternly.

"Sorry, I didn't know!" She was peeping out at me from behind her long red mane. "I don't think you're anything like him, whoever you are," she whispered, "you could teach me about God and things without being unkind, you look so nice, so devastated!"

That is what I was - devastated. She was reaching up, armless, her toes almost off the floor, her rich red lips seeking mine, no lip stick, just - well, moist, nice.

"You're the first person I've been alone with for ages," she said. "I have to get away from here but I can't by myself, I don't have any money and they lock up my clothes and I don't have anywhere to go and the police would bring me back..."

The nuzzling turned to kissing, frantic, embarrassing, her warm naked body wriggling against me.

Erotic!

I thought I ought to untie her arms.

But I didn't. I took her by the shoulders instead, and felt her trembling, so that I drew back abruptly.

"Turn round," I said.

She was reluctant, but she did so. I examined the binding of her arms.

"That's very elaborate for a short time," I said.

"Willie was a sailor," she said. "He's proud of his knots and -"

"Yes?"

"He likes me to be like this all the time." She turned to face me again. "So you see why I have to escape!" she said urgently. "I just have to - and oh God! we don't have long!"

"Are you asking me, a complete stranger, to help you to run away from home?" I exclaimed.

"Oh God - I mean, well, yes, I'm getting so desperate - oh please, please -"

"Just because you are to be punished for stealing, which is a sin?"

I hadn't intended to sound unfriendly, but perhaps my expression seemed so. I am told I look a little Biblical. Anyway, she seemed to be on the point of tears. "If I have to be beaten, you could do it," she whispered, wriggling further into my arms, her face wet with tears as she started to kiss my hand.

Then she dropped to her knees and light lips were working on my flies...

The gate creaking! Voices! Sounds of someone arriving at the door!

I hastily pulled away from what had become almost a seduction and stood well back as a substantial blousy woman occupied the doorway, smelling of beer and tobacco and shouting.

"Shut up you snivelling little bitch and come 'ere." Erica ran to her step-mother, who slapped her on the cheek, too incensed to notice me. The girl fell to the floor, unbalanced without the use of her arms, and the woman actually kicked her as she struggled to her feet. "Upstairs with you! Uncle Willie's in the hall!"

She pushed the girl roughly so that she stumbled out of the room, and almost at once I heard her being dragged up the stairs, presumably by this unseen Uncle Willie. I stepped forward and coughed, and the big woman's hand went to her mouth.

"Oh my Gawd the bleeding welfare!"

"No," I said. "Oh no."

"She's difficult, that one, bin stealing she has."

"That's wrong, stealing, sinful. You get small thanks for raising her to be Godly, I dare say."

"She's in bad with the fuzz already. Can't have 'er thieving and such." She was listening uneasily to the distressing sounds that came from upstairs. "She has to be taught a lesson sometimes, don't she?"

"Yes indeed," I agreed. I am of course strongly against stealing, though I did not fully condone their treatment of the girl: that did seem a little severe. "Does she go to Church?"

"Nah! A right little heathen, she is, stealing and lying and such!"

That was the moment I was granted the revelation. Yes, a sacred task was laid upon my humble shoulders and I was inspired to act, then and there, without hesitation. I had come for an interview, hoping for a story on which to base an uplifting article that elaborated on what the newspapers had said, but I understood immediately that I could do better: with the Lord's help I could rescue a lost lamb from abuse and at the same time become her Saviour in a Christian as well as a physical sense.

A little heathen, was she? That could not be permitted.

"I was told you had a room to let?" I asked.

"Where'd you hear that?"

"Oh," I said vaguely, "down the street. I want to live round here, I've been trying a few places. I listen to God."

"What?"

"God speaks to me. I am respectable."

"Respectable is it?" She sniffed, evidently not fully appreciating the point. "Know who I am? I'm Mrs Rita Fernandez, the one whose wicked step daughter knocked off 'er Dad. You must have read about it all?"

I had recognised her at once from the tabloid and TV photographs. Oh yes, the girl being beaten upstairs was my quarry, the one mentioned in those titillating press reports I had brooded over for so long before plucking up the courage to seek her out.

I have changed all names, for obvious reasons, as there was an effort to keep them secret. But I, of course, have my sources. As to myself, I shall adopt the name of 'Saviour' because her saviour is how I came to see myself, may God forgive me.

'Erica' had been born, if one believes her birth certificate, to an Argentinian pimp and one of his women, in the red-light district of Buenos Aires. If he really was her natural father it would explain her skin colour, though her mother must have been white, and even so her red hair and big blue eyes always puzzle me.

The man, Julio Fernandez, had brought her to England a few years before. He claimed to be a refugee from the military junta that had overthrown Maria Estela Peron. He was, so he said, one of the desaparecidos, disappearers, an opponent of the new regime, more fortunate than others in that he had escaped with his life. This was probably a fabrication: it is more likely that he merely hoped to exploit the child more successfully in England. He eventually obtained British citizenship, due to his marriage to an English woman, this Rita I was talking to.

The cellar of the house had steep dark steps and there

227

had been quite a scandal when Fernandez fell down them, cracking his skull pretty comprehensively in the process. He died on the way to hospital, having muttered what was taken to be an accusation against Erica, that she had hit him with a hammer. No hammer was found and his head could have struck the wall or a step during his fall.

A newspaper bought an obscene video of Erica from the widow and the police confiscated others. They provided a strong enough motive for murder. Due to her youth and to lack of evidence, Erica was not put on trial, but the media had a field day.

"Poor bleeding Rita Fernandez," the woman ran on, "that's me, Rita Fernandez what is a one parent family to a step daughter what done in 'er loving 'usband."

"It wasn't proved, was it?"

She put her finger to her nose and winked. "That's as may be. He'd 'ave made me rich if she hadn't done him in."

She was grinning at me. "She deserves everything she gets."

Following her eyes, I glanced down and became aware of a large damp patch over a bulge in my trousers, spreading even as I gazed at it.

"Everything she gets," the woman repeated. "I think you'll hagree?"

I could no longer deny it to myself: the sounds of the girl being thrashed were disturbing me unduly, tugging irresistibly at those dark parts of my mind I dreaded so much, stirring up a perverted lust I had repressed for a long time.

Let me admit it: I should love to have been up there spanking her bare bottom myself.

"She's a saucy little bitch," the woman continued. "Needs a firm hand she does, and that comes best from a man, someone strong and severe looking, such as your good self!"

I wished I was wearing an overcoat, for I was an inno-

228

cent at that time and had not anticipated anything like this. I pulled out my wallet and began to count the notes in it - it was well filled that afternoon as I had expected to pay for a story, maybe the basis of another novel. A gleam came into the woman's eyes as she assessed the value of me and my damp patch.

"There's only the back room. You'd have to share it with the girl."

"What! Share?"

"Well, why not? She can 'ave a mattress on the floor. She 'as to sleep somewheres for Gawd sake. Besides, she can look out for herself, she ain't exactly a child no more."

I needed an excuse to accept the lewd proposition. I can see myself now, fishing for it. I tried to look as if I was considering the matter calmly.

"Well," I said, pretending to be dubious, "couldn't you put her somewhere else? Nobody round here seems to have a room, and I do want to be in this neighbourhood. It's the underground station you see, I need to be near the underground. I could afford a bit over the odds."

"Could you hindeed!" I think she had just realised that the Rolls I had left a few doors away was mine. She might be on to a very good thing. All sorts of calculations were going on behind those hard greedy eyes, and compassion would not come into it.

"I could do with the money," she said, "but there's no way she comes in with me, the snivelling little brat. Anyway, Willie stays sometimes. There's her old bed in the cellar if she wants it."

"Oh, so she does have somewhere else to go?"

"'Course she does, if she wants ... how long would it be for, like?"

"Several weeks," I said. "Several weeks, at least." I appeared to think hard: if we were playing a game I would keep my end up. "Well, I don't think I'd mind the girl having a mattress in my room, so long as she has a place somewhere else if she wants. I don't suppose she's much bother?"

"She best bloody not be!" The woman peered at me with cunning as well as avarice in those hard piggy little eyes, no trace of mercy. I began to realise what bad hands Erica had fallen into. "She does as she's told, that one. If not she gets what for." She glanced at the ceiling. "I just sends for Willie. As you can 'ear."

"I see."

"Sometimes he drops round anyway, just to keep 'er in line -" She licked her lips. "So you reckon it's right to be a bit strict, for her own good like?"

"Spare the rod and spoil the child," I said. It was still necessary to go along with this horrible woman, and of course there is much truth in the saying. I tried to ease the swelling in my crotch as unobtrusively as possible, but it didn't escape her eagle eye.

"Right!" she said. "You'd know what to do if she sauced you then?"

"Wouldn't you mind a little discipline?"

"You does as you please so long as you pays for your room generous and regular." I took out my wallet, and her eyes followed it as I played with it. "Willie ain't always around - maybe she'll not get out of hand if I have a man about the house to see to her."

"Maybe not."

"Well then - shall us have a cup of tea?"

It came in chipped china, not too clean. She looked at me over her cup. "You did say fifty?"

I hadn't said anything of the sort. The room would be worth about fifteen pounds a week, I suppose, on a regular basis, with meals, but money was no problem to me, my investigative journalism does pretty well and I still had a very substantial nest egg from my days as a top research chemist, not to mention the country mansion I had inherited with no mortgage on it. But I didn't want to seem too eager.

"Erica sharing won't be no bother. If she cheeks you, you can always knock a bit of sense into 'er. Only thing, that makes it a bit noisy like, little bugger carries on so."

"Don't the neighbours complain?"

"Not now, we only got one neighbour now." I had already noticed that the corner shop next door was boarded up.

"Shop's empty and him upstairs right now, Big Willie what she calls Uncle, he's on the other side, and he ain't likely to complain, being a friend of the family, like."

"Quite."

"Mind you, there has been complaints. Ho yes! Them Patels at the corner shop, nosey devils they was, they rang the welfare once or twice, which didn't come to much, Erica was too scared of Willie to say anything bad. Then they tried 999. The cops come right round but Erica, well she's in their bad books already, or thinks she is. Anyway, she didn't want them getting her, said to go away, explained as how she was treated real good, she just was a bad person who needed to be punished sometimes."

"Is that true? She really wants to be punished?"

"I sometimes wonder, though you wouldn't think it when Willie gets after her. Her Dad had this thing going, you see, making her have the snake in her bed to keep it warm, the snake not the bed, but the days he beat her for the videos - you read about them videos? - well, those days he left it in its tank, turned its heater on, see, and she didn't have to sleep in the cellar. She really hates that snake, and the cellar too, so maybe she did used to be naughty just to be beaten instead of having the snake in the cellar."

"He was trying to make a masochist of her?"

"Never heard tell of that." The woman chuckled, quite an evil sound. "Well, she wouldn't run off, I reckon, even if

231

she had clothes and money. She's dead scared of uniforms and such. She reckons I might tell as how she done in 'er Dad, then she'd be locked up for sure."

"She did kill her father, then?"

Those harpy eyes looked at me slyly, wondering how much to say.

"Oh, I could tell a thing or two! The girl's daft, thinks prison would be like her Dad locking her in the cellar except it'd be for ever. She reckons there's this snake monster she goes on and on about, what looks for people what are bad enough to be locked up by the police."

"Why would she think that?"

"Well, who knows, but don't you be saying no different 'cos it's bloody useful, her thinking that. Anyway, Big Willie went round and had a few words with the Patels in the shop. Windows got broke see, and maybe a leg or two, before they cleared off. Willie don't like wogs anyway, and he don't like nobody interfering, Willie don't. Folks round here mind their own business mostly. Anyway, they don't tangle with Willie after what happened to the Patels, specially when he's had a few pints! Once when he'd had a beer or two Erica ran out into the garden in her nightie and he went on thrashing her there, harder I dare say. Got 'er over the dust-bin he did, twisted up her nightie to get at her bare bottom with his belt, oh yes he give it her good and strong that time."

She licked her lips, relishing her nasty little story. It was really shocking, what she said and the way she said it: there was not a trace of love in her for her step-daughter.

"Kept it up a good ten minutes, Willie did, little cow didn't half yell! Twisted around so much she tore 'er nightie to bits in the end, 'er only one it were, stupid little bitch, and all the good it did 'e got a hold of her hair instead! May as well have plenty noise, see what happens, says Willie, and that's why he went at it so hard. Nothing ever did happen, not a dickie bird was ever said, so now I don't bother too much if she yells a bit."

There was a small garden at the front of the house, or rather a strip of dispirited weeds and a dust-bin surrounded by a little wall set the house back from the street. I knew there was no road at the back just a canal.

"Now," said Rita, "about you staying, Mr -"

"Saviour, Rex Saviour."

"Well now, Mr Saviour, there'd be a lot of extra work for me, cleaning and cooking and such."

"You said the girl did the cooking? Surely she can do the rest of it? Maybe you can go out more if I'm here."

"Well, I don't usually bother about that. Friends drop in, like as not, or Big Willie from next door. They usually brings a bottle for me." She paused and winked, glancing at the ceiling. "And go up to say good-night to Erica."

The screaming was louder now. The woman waddled to the door. "Put a sock in 'er bleeding mouth for Gawd sake, can't hear myself speak."

The screams became muffled.

That was the second time this evil woman had invoked the name of the Lord in a lewd fashion. His help was sorely needed and I had clearly been sent to be His chosen vehicle.

"Sixty then," she said. "With meals."

"Fifty. Less because of sharing." May the Lord forgive me! "That should see you on the right side."

"Do you need a rent book?"

"Oh no, cash in hand."

Her eyes were round with greed. "Fifty-five?"

"OK," I said. "I'll be back with my things tomorrow, then."

Thus was the die cast, with the Devil at my shoulder: I was experiencing another surge of lust at the thought of sharing a bedroom with the sinner who's self-appointed saviour I was about to become.

She had almost certainly killed her father.

She was a self-confessed thief.

I had heard her blaspheme and she had blatantly sought to seduce me into a conspiracy to abscond.

Although I must save her from ungodly people who exploited her for their selfish reasons, I also must discipline her to the full extent necessary for her own good.

Such chastisement would only be sinful if I went beyond what was necessary.

If she was over my lap and a slipper to hand...

I must suppress these strange illicit lusts of mine.

She had no knickers, she had said ... and no nightie ...

As I walked to the Rolls, my pulse quickened.

Over my lap ... there was so much to punish her for ...

I must not yield to temptation!

She was virtually a prisoner in that house and it didn't matter if she screamed ...

Her bare bottom would be smooth and quivering, that lovely olive brown colour ... I would bring the slipper down with a thwack ... again and again ... how she would wriggle, how she would squirm, but I must hold her tight, press her against me ... again the slipper, again, again ...

I came in my trousers, not the sort of thing I am accustomed to, other than in perverted dreams sent by the Devil.

2

I nearly didn't go back there. Would I have done so if I could have seen the future?

I think I would have done. The Lord had laid a mission upon me, a mission to save this youngster who had fallen amongst evil people, and also to train her to better things, to stop her thieving and pagan ways. That was a sacred

234

duty not lightly to be set aside.

Besides, however grim the consequences, I surely would not have foregone the strangest and deepest love of my life, my strange love for Erica.

Due to prayer and doubt it was already half-past two the next afternoon when I arrived. The seedy place where I was to stay was very different to my isolated manor house, centrally heated and lavishly carpeted but deep in the green countryside, where I lived alone miles from the nearest neighbours. However, I was resigned to a little discomfort in the service of the Lord. My doubts were not about my physical state, but my mental one. I dreaded the pit of lust into which proximity to this young person, so very attractive to the eye and disturbing to the mind, might lead me. Warped desires concerning the discipline I might have to administer had already surfaced like evil bubbles that festered in my skull and threatened to explode it: I had hardly slept at all that night.

As I took my bags from the Rolls a small group of unruly boys ran from the house, laughing and waving a cushion in the air like a trophy.

They had left the front door open. I went in and found Erica lying on the sofa, naked and bound just as before, and this time she didn't stop crying. I saw again how shy she was about her nakedness. She looked round for something to hide behind, a flush upon her cheeks, but there was nothing.

"Some boys took the cushion," I said.

"Yes, and guess who gets the blame when they take things!"

I licked my lips. "You will be beaten because of that?"

She nodded.

"Not friends of yours, then?

"God no, I hate them!" I don't think she really understood about blasphemy: I would take that up another time, and punish her only after a warning. Her speech may sound somewhat refined for that locality, but I am reporting it faithfully. It did sound strange, until I found out about her extra education: she lacked religious teaching but excellent tutors in several other subjects had paid for private sessions with her. Fernandez had known exactly the right undercover magazines in which to advertise this expensive facility.

"Did they hurt you?"

"They're only kids but they're so, so rough, dirty fingers, they come in sometimes to amuse themselves. Those boys are nasty, I hate being tickled and pinched and stuff."

"You should lock the front door when you're alone."

I aren't allowed to, even if I could." She shuddered, trying to move her arms. "In case some friend of Rita's comes, and I have to - to look after him.

"I'll talk to your step-mother," I said. "I'll say my things might be stolen."

"Oh yes, they might be, then you'd punish me too - but anyway, I can't stand being locked in, I truly truly can't,I'd rather have the boys."

"You suffer from claustrophobia?"

"I suppose so, it really bugs me if that's what it is - oh God, what time is it?

"Nearly three. What did you do this time?"

"Nothing. A punishment is every day for a week."

"Is that why you're still tied up?"

"They say I'm less trouble like this anyway."

"Well," I said, "suppose I do the punishment." It was a notion that really appealed to me. "Then we'll tell them you've had it for today."

"What if they don't agree?"

"Well, that wouldn't be very fair, would it?"

"Uncle Willie will do it all over again, his way, I just know he will!"

She seemed really apprehensive, but that only made me feel closer to her. I tried to think of something to cheer her up. "Would you like a ride in my car?"

"Are you going to take me away like I said?"

"No, I can't do that. Just for a ride."

"Well then, can we go to see the sea? I never have."

"Alright. I'll give you your spanking in the country."

"I can't go without you asking. Besides, she locks up my clothes.

"We'll get the punishment over here, then." I took a fistful of hair - I'd been longing to do that! - and pulled her towards the stairs: I really thought I was doing the right thing, saving her from a beating from this Willie, who she clearly hated. I didn't intend to hit her hard, of course, but then again stealing is a sin, is it not?

She tried to pull her hair free, and started to cry when she couldn't stop me pulling her up the steep stairs. "He'll do it all over again, truly he will!"

"Nonsense," I said. I was quite excited, I didn't want to miss this opportunity of having her over my lap, naked as she was. "I'll see that he doesn't. Shut up, or I really will hurt you."

We were upstairs by then, in her room.

My room!

As soon as I released her she scampered into a corner. She stood there with her back to me, spine arched, legs apart. It was a very erotic pose. Trying to compose myself, I walked over to the window: outside was the unused canal, defiled by all manner of unsightly debris. A cat, bloated by death, empty beer cans, over ripe tomatoes. At that moment I heard the faint rumble of a train on the underground - the line must pass beneath the house. Erica shrank further into her corner.

"What's the matter?" I asked. "Are you frightened of that noise? Turn round and tell me."

She turned reluctantly.

"Not up here. It can't get me up here."

I was staring at her, and she flushed again. "You acted as if you were. Scared."

"It - it thinks I'm in the cellar. I'm safe up here. Fairly safe."

"Oh?"

"It's the snake monster. He's looking for me. In the cellar you can feel him shaking the walls, trying to get in - one night he will, and then - oh God!"

"Calm down," I said. "There isn't really a monster, there aren't any monsters."

"Oh but there are, he's an enormous slimy snake that's after me, a purple one. Willie told me. She says so too. It can't find me in prison, so it looks in the cellar next."

I didn't fully understand, of course, not then. I assumed she knew all about the underground trains, and thought it best to distract her from her obvious fear of this monster she had created in her mind.

"Why are you standing in the corner?"

"Uncle Willie says to. I have to wait like this till he's ready."

I had to put off the moment I would touch her, my desire was making me tremble. "Uncle Willie? Is he a real Uncle?"

"Oh no. Anyway, that isn't his real name, it's sort of a joke, I think, Big Willie. And I must have my back to you until you clap your hands."

She turned to face the corner again: her toes were turned slightly in, feet wide apart, as she went on tiptoe. She was talking in a small trembling voice, into the corner. "You clap your hands and then I come -"

I walked up to her and her buttocks flinched as she sensed my closeness behind her, so I went back and sat on the bed, up against the headboard, and clapped my hands.

She jumped at the sound and turned round, her eyes wide when she saw me. "You aren't ready at all. You haven't even got your trousers off."

"Why should I take my trousers off?"

"I can't do it."

"No, but why take them off?"

"So I can - be nice to you -"

"What do you mean, be nice to me?"

"He - he likes to be kissed -"

"You can kiss me with my trousers on, if you want to."

"Not properly, not like Willie wants!" She came over slowly, reluctantly, and sat beside me. "Not where Uncle Willie likes, where it makes your snake grow."

"My snake?"

But I knew what she wanted, and, God help me, I had undone my flies. Her tongue was on my penis, delicately, making it rock hard. "It's quite big," she said, "but not nearly as big as Uncle Willie's, not ready to spit. It has to be kissed first, doesn't it?"

I was very shocked. Tempted too, I admit, terribly tempted, but somehow I fought the Devil down. "We won't do any of that sort of stuff. Just come over my lap for your spanking."

She considered. "Shall I fetch the slipper, then, or would you rather the belt?"

"Just the slipper," I said.

I can't describe my feelings when she acted so meekly, as if it was the most natural thing in the world to fetch in her teeth the slipper she was to be beaten with. I stayed there with my back propped against the head of the bed, and she walked away very gracefully, someone had taught her to walk with a seductive sway. Then she came back with a towel and slipper in her mouth.

I saw tears in her eyes as I took the slipper from her - it was a pretty solid one with a good leather sole. She

TITLES IN PRINT

Silver Moon

ISBN 1-897809-03-4 Barbary Slavegirl *Allan Aldiss*
ISBN 1-897809-08-5 Barbary Pasha *Allan Aldiss*
ISBN 1-897809-11-5 The Hunted Aristocrat *Lia Anderssen*
ISBN 1-897809-14-X Barbary Enslavement *Allan Aldiss*
ISBN 1-897809-16-6 Rorigs Dawn *Ray Arneson*
ISBN 1-897809-17-4 Bikers Girl on the Run *Lia Anderssen*
ISBN 1-897809-20-4 Caravan of Slaves *Janey Jones*
ISBN 1-897809-23-9 Slave to the System *Rosetta Stone*
ISBN 1-897809-25-5 Barbary Revenge *Allan Aldiss*
ISBN 1-897809-27-1 White Slavers *Jack Norman*
ISBN 1-897809-29-8 The Drivers *Henry Morgan*
ISBN 1-897809-31-X Slave to the State *Rosetta Stone*
ISBN 1-897809-35-2 Jane and her Master *Stephen Rawlings*
ISBN 1-897809-36-0 Island of Slavegirls *Mark Slade*
ISBN 1-897809-37-9 Bush Slave *Lia Anderssen*
ISBN 1-897809-38-7 Desert Discipline *Mark Stewart*

Silver Mink

ISBN 1-897809-09-3 When the Master Speaks *Josephine Scott*
ISBN 1-897809-13-1 Amelia *Josephine Oliver*
ISBN 1-897809-15-8 The Darker Side *Larry Stern*
ISBN 1-897809-19-0 Training of Annie Corran *Terry Smith*
ISBN 1-897809-21-2 Sonia *RD Hall*
ISBN 1-897809-22-0 The Captive *Amber Jameson*
ISBN 1-897809-24-7 Dear Master *Terry Smith*
ISBN 1-897809-26-3 Sisters in Servitude *Nicole Dere*
ISBN 1-897809-28-X Cradle of Pain *Krys Antarakis*
ISBN 1-897809-30-1 Owning Sarah *Nicole Dere*
ISBN 1-897809-32-8 The Contract *Sarah Fisher*
ISBN 1-897809-33-6 Virgin for Sale *Nicole Dere*
ISBN 1-897809-34-4 The Story of Caroline *As told to Barbie*
ISBN 1-897809-39-5 Training Jenny *Rosetta Stone*

All our titles can be ordered from any bookshop in the UK and an
increasing number in the USA and Australia by quoting the title and
ISBN Or they are available from us direct for £5.60 each (UK) or $9.95
(USA) postage included. Credit Cards accepted as EBS (Electronic
Book Services - £ converted to $ and back!)